THE PREACHER

To: Hunter

Thank you for your support.

Chris Snider

CHRIS SNIDER

THE PREACHER

Cover Art: Melinda S Reynolds
Book Design: The Author's Mentor,
www.LittleRoniPublishers.com
Cover Design: Elizabeth E. Little, http://hyliian.deviantart.com
Contact the Author on Facebook:
chris.snider.104@facebook.com

ISBN-13: 978-1484809563
ISBN-10: 1484809564
Also available in eBook

PRINTED IN THE UNITED STATES OF AMERICA

DEDICATION

Joanne Sloan, David Sloan, Christopher Sloan, and Cheryl Sloan Wray whom without I would not have gotten this far.

Also in memory of Teresa Sanders.

A NEW DARK AGE

In the early 2000s, chaos bloomed. Violence lurked in every corner and people were easily offended and provoked to retaliation. School shootings and random acts of cruelty of every kind rose exponentially.

Liberals warred with conservatives. Gay marriage supporters bickered with the ones who thought it an unholy act. Prolife supporters warred with those who believed a woman's body was her own and she had the right to do whatever she wanted with it.

Republicans battled with Democrats over all of these issues. Atheism became more and more common. "No proof" equaled "nonexistence." Even religions disagreed with each other, each claiming superiority. God's name became a curse word and was rarely publicly uttered.

Alcohol, drugs, and sex were the most popular religions around the world. People sold their very souls for a taste of the poison that enslaved them. Teen pregnancy was more than commonplace, and the Christian home had all but disappeared.

All of the issues argued over continued for years until by the year 2100, the war of words became wars of bloodshed. Society began to fall apart. If you stated your opinion and someone disagreed with it, you were likely to be gunned down in the streets.

Countless murders happened every day until even the ones who once followed God were swept up in the chaos and began taking matters into their own hands. This terror did not contain itself to the

United States. Every neighboring country around the world began killing each other until the very population of the world itself was cut by a quarter.

Then one day, the gunfire ceased and complete silence settled across the world. Something was about to happen.

God revealed himself to the world for the first time in over a millennium. All cowered before him and begged forgiveness, even those who had never once believed in him.

His message to the world was a simple one. He was fed up with the world. He loved his children, but he could not watch one day longer as they turned the world he created into a mockery of what he had envisioned. The world was to be punished.

The punishment was our technology. He took it away, wiped the knowledge of it from our minds so that the world was as it once was. Soon after that, natural disasters cropped up. God promised never to flood the world again, so he sent earthquakes, tornados, volcanic eruptions, and hurricanes. By the time this was over, the world was no longer recognizable.

Everyone who survived had been sent into a new Dark Age. The people that survived built new lives and began repopulating the world. The only remnants of the past were books. The most important book of all was the Holy Bible. This book had been spared so that the people of the world might once again live by it. Here in the darkest hour, the world's survivors clung to God's holy word in hopes that one day they might earn back the right to the technology God had granted them before.

As time went by, things slowly advanced. Simple things such as the wheel were put into use as men built carriages for transportation and to build crude tools to help them live off the land. People could no longer rely on advanced medicine and science, therefore they were forced to turn back to the land for herbs and other plants to help heal sickness and injuries.

Inspired by stories of the past from various books that still remained, many began writing their own stories and began painting pictures. It was somewhat of a new Renaissance period.

It seemed that the world was once again becoming a place that God could be proud of. Of course as always, Satan was there to temp mankind. Then for a third time, humanity failed its creator.

Alcohol was reinvented and once again people began to abuse it. People began giving into their lustful instincts and fulfilling their carnal desires without concern of right or wrong.

New kingdoms began and new wars were fought. Religions who had found peace with one another once again became discordant. The world soon became the living hell it once was.

Over nine hundred years after the new world began it was back to the way it once was. This time it didn't even take half as long to be poisoned. People didn't have guns, but the human nature to kill prevailed anyway. Swords, staffs, bows and arrows, and crossbows were the killing instruments now.

Still, God would not give up on us. In the place once called Europe, though no history of what it once was remained, God decided to test mankind one more time. His tool in this endeavor is a Preacher named Jacob Cross...

THE PREACHER

CHAPTER 1

The thick, musty air tickled Jacob Cross's nose as he walked slowly down the dirt road. Wherever he was, he was fairly certain that it had recently rained. Where was he? Was he really in this place? Was he dreaming? At one point, he was absolutely *sure* he was dreaming, but then the eerie feeling that you might very well be awake kicked in.

Everything in sight emanated an odd glow. His senses had heightened dramatically and he could actually *see* the aura of every tree, leaf, and rock in his vicinity. The trees on either side of the road did not branch off into a forest; rather they grew close together. So close that you could not fit a piece of paper between their trunks. Their configuration formed an endless wall that threatened to trap Jacob on his current path with nowhere to run. The only place he could possibly go was forward.

Being only twenty-three, Jacob was very young to be the pastor of a small hamlet and overall, it was a difficult situation. Even though he consistently preached to a moderate number of people on Sunday, how far his messages actually went he didn't know. He wasn't too young and he wasn't too old, nevertheless, the older people considered him too young to take seriously. If they were going to be told how to live for God it was going to be by someone on a cane and with hair as grey as theirs. As for the young people, who were gradually going to hell in a hand basket, all they ever did was tell him to stop acting like an old fogey and accept their drunkenness and fornication. The only people who took him remotely seriously were those between the ages of thirty and forty.

Getting back to his present time and place (whatever it might be), Jacob had the sense of being followed. Once he thought he heard a step behind him on the gravel, but when he jerked around he saw nothing. In his mind, some sort of deformed, mutilated, and possibly demon-possessed human being pursued him, howling and clutching a sharp object. Escaping into the woods was not an option; he would have no choice but to run down the seemingly endless path where he'd most likely be chased down, stabbed fifty times, and suffer an untimely and horrible death.

At that thought, Jacob reached behind him to find that he was without his sword and crossbow. Consumed with dread, Jacob slowed his progress. With every step, the sharp pain in his heart grew deeper and deeper. The path had seemed never ending, but out of nowhere in the distance, the arrow-straight path veered off to the right. Had he come to the end? To *his* end?

As he stepped closer, his respirations reached an uncomfortable race in his chest, as if his heart knew something, but wasn't letting his mind in on it. His hand squeezed around a firm object; he was carrying his Bible all along. Of all the time he was conscious of being in this strange place, he hadn't realized that he had brought his best weapon.

Looking down, he realized his wooden crucifix rested in the left side of his belt and he clutched it with his free hand. If this was a dream, he was ready for Sunday. Jacob wore his preaching attire: round brimmed hat, a long coat that hung to his knees, tight-fitting pants, with black boots and gloves. Dressed as such, many people had joked that he looked more like an undertaker than a minister. Some had actually gone as far as saying he looked scary, though he was kind and gentle, and mostly kept to himself.

Continuing on, Jacob noticed that he heard no sound whatsoever. No wind blew through the trees and no birds chirped in their still branches. The only sound that reached his ears was that of the gravel crunching beneath his feet.

Jacob reached the curve in the road and stopped dead. He glanced behind him, but still had no memory of from where he had come. After thinking twice, he stepped onto the gloomy path. There he saw what he had been so deathly afraid of.

How stupid. Up ahead sat a small house with an "over the river and through the woods to Grandmother's house we go" look about it. Jacob smiled and almost laughed out loud. Everything about the house seemed safe and secure, and he imagined a kindly old woman walking out smiling. But his first impression quickly faded. After blinking a couple of times, he began to notice a few imperfections. Whether they were there before and he somehow didn't notice them, the house didn't seem as warm and fuzzy as it had before.

Chipped paint marred the exterior and huge blotches of unpainted wood stood out like the bones of a skeleton. The wood of the tiny porch seemed to be rotting by the second. The aforementioned door was full of holes and mildewed a putrid yellow. Decaying like a corpse, it was obvious that no one had cared for or even inhabited the home in twenty years.

Jacob stood staring with one foot propped up on the steps leading up to the porch. He jumped back nearly three feet back into the yard as he looked up to see a small community of black spiders half the size of a human fist crawling in thick webbing.

Even the grass that stood two feet high was discolored and yellow. At that moment the safe little cottage turned into one of the most frightening sights he had ever seen. If Grandma *did* live here, she was inhabited by the devil. By impulse, Jacob raised his crucifix to the empty shell with a trembling hand. All at once, an array of new sounds and scents filled the air. Around the door, green blowflies buzzed around in a frenzied dance.

At first the aroma was simply musty, like that of an old basement that hadn't been entered in a month or two. Then it evolved into the most sickening, putrid smell he could possibly imagine. Jacob gagged and balled his hand into a fist and covered his mouth as bile rose in his throat. Going to one knee, he breathed carefully and waited for his stomach to quit turning somersaults.

The smell took him back to three years ago when he had first come to the village. The previous minister had just died by what he assumed was natural causes and had been looked to as the leader of the community. So naturally Jacob had taken over the former pastor's responsibilities.

One day, a few concerned citizens came to ask him about an old man that had been missing for three days. Jacob asked if any of them had checked his house and all of them had seemed to overlook the simplest solution. So he and the three men went to the old man's house. The second they entered, there was no doubt what had happened. The horrifying smell hit them before they walked in the door. One man ran to vomit in the bushes while the other two managed to hang on and go with Jacob deeper into the house, cupping their hands into masks. When they reached the small living room, they found the old man laid back into his resting chair.

He was a gruesome sight, solid white with his mouth hanging open. He had already began to decompose in the heat of the hot summer day. When the second man noticed that the dead man's eyes were wide open and staring at them, he too decided that this was too much to handle.

"Oh God!" he yelped and ran to the exit, presumably to join the first.

The last man who obviously had more stomach than his counterparts followed Jacob into the room.

"Don't you think you should bless the body?" he asked.

Jacob nodded in agreement and offered a muffled version of the Lord's prayer.

Back in the yard of the ramshackle house, a frightening thought then crossed his mind and his stomach turned anew. How was able to remember all of these things? If this were indeed a dream, he had never had one in which he had conscious thoughts of his own memories. What if this were all real and he was only in a trance-like state that had erased the memory of where he had come from or where he was going?

He then began to come to many realizations. The flies weren't trying to burst into the house to feed on a week-old body; they were hovering around the house itself, as if the entire foundation was a giant piece of rotting flesh going through rigor mortis right before his eyes. The urge to run and leave the entire morbid scene behind filled his mind. Unfortunately his body was doing the exact opposite of what his mind wanted. Without being able to control himself, he began to walk under the spiders and cobwebs and onto the rickety old porch.

Overhead clouds covered the already bleak sky, and it looked as if it would be flooding rain momentarily. He couldn't imagine a more frightening thought than being trapped in this place during a thunderstorm. As he pushed the door, it opened with a creak. Walking in, the door slammed shut behind him causing him to jump.

It was a good thing that he wasn't hoping for an improvement from the outside to the inside. Besides no flies buzzing, bad smells, or knee high grass, it still left much to be desired. Cobwebs decorated every corner of the room. He could see many more eight-legged friends crawling about, including on his boot which he instinctively kicked off and stomped hoping its relatives didn't wish to avenge its death.

A thick coat of dust filled the air like a thin film over his pupils. Looking on, he saw a small staircase ahead of him that led straight up. The rickety structure didn't look as if it could hold the weight of a moderately-sized housecat, much less a human being.

The old floor creaked with every step and Jacob wondered if it would bear his weight. The house was a lot smaller than it appeared to be on the outside. Besides the small corridor behind him and the stairs in front of him, there was only one small room beside the steps and a single room on either side of the house.

He glanced into the small room on the right and noted a small nightstand and a single bed. He didn't feel that this room or the one in front of him held any significance as to why he was here. Whatever he was meant to see was upstairs. Jacob stepped towards them, but was then drawn to the room on his left. He entered the room to find what he assumed he was meant to see.

What he saw wasn't torn, dead bodies or a psychotic old woman with an axe. He saw only a den of sin. Candles circled the room as if some demonic ritual were taking place. In all corners of the room, everything he had ever preached against was being performed before his very eyes.

The one room had now become the size of the entire house. In one corner, a man was being murdered and his money stolen. They stabbed him in the back and left him for dead. The man reached a bloody hand toward Jacob and mouthed the words "Help me". Before Jacob could take a step the man disappeared in a cloud of smoke.

In another corner, young teens he recognized from his village drank and fornicated with a look in their eyes that said their very lives revolved around it. Their manic giggling and lustful smiles brought the sick feeling back to his stomach. One of the girls he recognized and had always thought to be a good Christian girl was only thirteen. At this sight he tilted his hat over his eyes to keep from beholding the pitiful sight.

In the center of the room, a group of middle-aged men gambled with a pile of gold pieces in the middle. The only image that went through his mind was that of the Roman soldiers beneath the body of Christ on the cross. Finally he had to look away from this evil room that Satan had inhabited.

Suddenly, his right hand jerked uncontrollably. An invisible force tugged at his bible and after holding on a few seconds, he let go and the book hit the floor. Instantly, the pages began flipping back and forth and stopped on the fifth chapter of Isaiah. Blood then came up from the pages to underline Isaiah 5:20. *Woe unto those who call evil good and good evil; that put darkness for light and light for darkness; that put bitter for sweet and sweet for bitter.*

Is this what he was supposed to see? No, there was more to it Jacob took a deep breath as he was once again drawn toward the old stairs. The answer lied at the top. One of the center steps had already collapsed and he continued with caution.

In a moment of distraction, Jacob took a heavy step and the board collapsed underneath him. He caught himself and hanged onto the railing. Looking down, he expected to see a basement, but saw only darkness. Without wanting to take the risk of falling into a deep, endless abyss he pulled himself up and continued his climb with lighter steps.

When he reached the top, there was a single slender door. He had no idea what was behind the door, but in his heart he knew he wasn't going to like what he found. Taking a deep breath, he turned the knob and walked in. His intuition had been right. What he saw was something he didn't want to see.

Here in the dust-filled attic was the body of every person he had just seen in the other room, each hanging from his or her own separate noose. Their faces were blue and lifeless and their eyes were opened wide toward him. Now he felt it. This is what he was meant to see. This was why he was drawn down the old dirt road. This was why he was being called to by the house. This was why the house itself was rotting. It all made perfect sense.

Jacob turned to exit the room, but before he could move an inch the door slammed itself shut. He grabbed the knob and jerked, but it wouldn't budge. Propping one foot on the wall, he pulled as hard as he could. It was no use. Whatever forced held the door shut was much stronger than he was. Jacob then heard small creaks behind him and froze.

He turned to see each body swinging slightly back and forth as if a gust of wind had entered the room.

"This can't be good," he mumbled.

Out of nowhere, one of the bodies burst into flames. Then one by one, they all ignited until the room became a blazing inferno.

Jacob stepped backward until he was cornered against the jammed door. Now was the point where he knew he was either going to wake up or die.

Then the flames began to do something strange. They didn't move forward, but flowed into the center of the room where they formed a flaming wall. At that moment the most demonic, frightening, nightmarish face he had ever seen in his life materialized from the flames and rushed toward him. Jacob jerked awake instantly.

Sitting up in bed, wide-eyed and drenched in sweat, Jacob glanced out his window. It was raining heavily and coming a pretty bad storm. He glanced around the room, cautiously blind until his eyes adjusted to the darkness. Every few seconds, a flash of lightning would enter the room, and for a second, he could swear he saw the shadow of something in the room with him. He finally shook his head, rationalizing that it was post nightmare jitters.

His breath came in ragged pulls, on the verge of hyperventilating. What he had awoken from wasn't merely a disturbing dream that he would forget about by the day's end. It was a terrifying and realistic vision that would make any grown man afraid of the dark.

He felt like a child, sitting in bed, wishing he could hide under the covers and everything would be all right. Jacob's eyes began to adjust and he started to calm down. Each new flash proved to him that he was alone, allowing his breathing and heart rate to slow to normal.

At last, he decided that he wasn't going to lie wide awake in bed until dawn. He would get an early start on planning his sermon.

Standing up, he had that dull, achy feeling he had whenever he slept until noon. The thought of eating made him nauseous, but he was dying for water.

As he walked into the kitchen, he noticed light pouring in from the house across from his. Listening, he heard music and laughing coming from the house. For a moment, he wondered if he were truly awake. Then he remembered who his not-so-pleasant neighbor was.

A rebellious fifteen-year-old girl named Ashley Arcane inhabited the home. Young Ashley was the ring leader for every disobedient child in the hamlet. If it was right to the world it was wrong to her, and vice versa. Jacob would have hated to count the number of times she had broken the commandment, “Honor thy Father and Mother” or any of the other nine for that matter. Ashley’s road to delinquency had started at the tender age of twelve. It was at this time that she began sassing, back talking, and cursing her parents. A firm believer in the verse, “Take the rod to thy child so that they might walk in the way of the Lord,” Jacob wondered why Mother and Father Arcane had never beaten her backside blue. They apparently figured it was a phase that she would grow out of. Unfortunately, they were dead wrong. Things only got worse. Soon she was drinking every alcoholic beverage she could get hands on and switching sexual partners like changes of clothes. As for her apparel, Jacob had seen prostitutes that didn’t show off as much as she did.

He was returning home from a trip one day when he witnessed the boiling point between mother and daughter. Ashley was going out half-drunk in one of her over-revealing outfits. He thought he heard her yelling something about meeting her boyfriend in the woods. If he heard the name correctly, the guy was twenty years old.

Her mother had decided, albeit too late, to put her foot down. She told her to get back inside and put on some decent clothes. She also told her that there would be no more drinking or back-talk of any kind. Jacob was shocked and disgusted by her response: “Back off and shut the hell up, you stupid bitch!” At this point, her mother proceeded to slap the taste out of her mouth. Jacob hoped this long overdue discipline would prove beneficial, but what happened next proved him wrong.

A demonic flash hit the girl's eyes and she tackled her mother while beating her with every ounce of strength she had. Jacob usually never got involved in other people's affairs, but felt compelled to now. He ran over and pulled the teen off her mother and Ashley fought him with everything she had.

When he finally he flung her to the ground, she bounced back up and tried to attack her mother again. Jacob caught her and sat her back on the ground. It was right then and there that she stared into his very soul and he became her enemy for life.

Jacob helped Mrs. Arcane to her feet, and she clung to him terrified of her own daughter. Her nose was bloodied and she was covered in dirt.

"It's okay," he had said. "She's not going to hurt you anymore." A small crowd of teenagers had gathered around.

"Why don't you mind your own business, you creepy freak!" Ashley shouted.

He ignored her.

"Look! Ashley beat the hell out of her mom!" a young boy from the crowd yelled.

"Way to go Ashley!" a girl said.

Jacob snapped. "Hold your tongues, you little brats! You like this? You like seeing a child terrorize her parent? Is it because you want to do the same thing? How selfish can you children be? They clothe you and feed you. They held you as a baby while you cried and kept you warm. You think all they want to do is keep you from having fun, but all they want is for you to be decent citizens and not heathens in the eyes of God. Now get back to your homes all of you!"

Soon after that incident, Ashley's parents moved away. They feared her and gave up on her. They left her the house and from that day forward it was her versus Jacob in a battle for the young souls.

Later that day, in full attire, Jacob stood before the gathered villagers holding his bible under his hat to prevent it from becoming drenched. Half the town had come to hear him despite the pouring rain. Surprisingly, the front row was peopled mostly with the town's raucous youth. Jacob hoped the hand of God was pressing down on them, making them feel guilty for what they had done the night before. Amongst them, with her customary sneer of repulsion, Ashley stood with crossed arms.

"What happened to innocence?" Jacob began. "Tell me, when did it die? When did childhood cease to be? Look around you. Look at all of the young people. Do you see them? I don't because they aren't here anymore. Now in their place is a bunch of underage adults who know the sins of this world. Do you see how the world has deteriorated? Think back. Think a long way back through the years. A long time ago it was unheard of for a couple to have sex out of wedlock, but today it is commonplace. It was once unheard of for a girl of sixteen to lose her virginity, but among us, innocence has perished. They became younger: fifteen, fourteen, thirteen... and below. Oh, if only it stopped with fornication. Alas, it has been elevated to drunkenness, disobedience, and God only knows what else. I ask you, where does it end?!

"I look at thirteen-year-old boys and girls and I see alcohol in their hands where I should see a toy or a doll. At that tender age, they should be frolicking around, enjoying the innocence of childhood. Instead, they know the evils and remorse of adulthood before they reach twenty."

"I've had elderly people come up to me and reminisce, longing for their lost childhood; they remember the joy of that age. When the children of this town look back at seventy or eighty years old, they will wonder, 'did I have a childhood at all?'

"But, it isn't entirely their fault. You the parents are also to blame. Let me tell you a little story from the book of Samuel. When Samuel was just a child, the voice of God called him awake three times. Each time, he thought Eli, the head priest of the temple, called him. The third time, Eli said to him, 'I believe the Lord is calling you. Go speak with him and don't be afraid.' So, Samuel went and spoke with God who told him some distressing news. When Eli asked Samuel to tell him what God had told him he didn't want to because it would upset Eli. But Eli insisted he tell him anyway.

"The message to Samuel concerned Eli's two sons who did not walk in God's way. Each and every day they broke God's commandments and turned their backs on him. God's message was that they would be severely punished, and so would Eli.

"God was mad at Eli because he saw how his sons were and never once did he try to correct them. He, like many of you, turned a blind eye as his children sinned against him. All it would have taken was an effort, but Eli never put forth that effort."

"Finally, the day came when the Israelites were to battle the Philistines. God brought his punishment onto Israel. The Holy Ark was stolen and both of Eli's sons were killed in battle. When news came to Eli that his sons were dead and the Ark had been stolen, he fell backward in his chair and broke his neck."

"If you parents don't change your ways, not only will your children pay, but you will, too. All of you are headed down Eli's path. Stop now before it's too late."

Jacob paused and in the silence that followed, a man in the center of the crowd took his son by the arm.

"Jacob's right! We may not want to hear it, but he's right. Devin, this ends now! You are not going to disrespect me anymore. I'm the parent and you are the child. There will be no more drinking and partying. You're going to be an upstanding Christian boy again."

"Y…yes dad."

One by one, each parent became braver and at least made an attempt to take back control of their children. Ashley's contemptuous glare deepened as she watched her followers slipping away.

"Jacob?" said a voice from the crowd. It was Austin, a young boy of around sixteen. He was tall with blond hair and blue eyes with light facial hair.

"Yes?"

"I… I did some really bad things last night that I'm really ashamed of. Is…is it too late for me to ask forgiveness?"

Jacob game him a warm smile. "No, it's never too late to be forgiven. All you have to do is ask."

A glimmer of hope came into the boy's eyes and he smiled. "Can you help me?"

"Of course, I'm always here to help. Come, pray with me."

"Do I need to tell you everything I've done?"

"No, God already knows what is in your heart. All you have to do is tell him you're sorry for everything you have done." Then

Jacob prayed, "Heavenly Father, this young boy has come to you today because he wants to be forgiven of his sins and filled with your mercy. He has seen the error of his ways and wishes to enter your kingdom. Father, I pray you lead him and guide him in your way and be with him in times of happiness and despair. He realizes you sent your only Son to die on a cross at Cavalry for him. I just ask that you walk by his side for the rest of his days. These things we ask in your loving name and the name of your son, Jesus Christ. Amen."

"Is that all?" he asked.

"That's all." Jacob turned back to the crowd. "Did all of you children see how easy that was? Do you see the look of absolute peace in his eyes? You, too, can have that peace if you only ask. I'm willing to stay here all day and night if people keep coming. If not, go back to your homes with my words in your heart and remember that if you ever need me, my door is always open."

At that, the people slowly left the square, until only Ashley remained. The angry teen stood facing away with her arms crossed, pouting like a toddler. Jacob walked up behind her and stared at her a moment before speaking. Finally, he said softly, "Ashley, when I said my door is always open, I meant to anyone."

He expected her to turn and scream something disrespectful. Instead, she merely looked at him. Then, she nodded and walked away. Jacob wondered if the rain on her cheeks hid tears of repentance. He held no ill will toward her and only hoped that one day she would find her way home as young Austin did.

Later that evening, as Jacob read his Bible in his favorite chair, the sound of the rain hitting his roof gently hypnotized him. With every scripture, he grew drowsier and drowsier. Since childhood, the gentle patter of rain relaxed him and he remembered many such times when he fell asleep and woke up in bed where his mother had laid him.

Ironically, he'd been reading of the time when Daniel interpreted King Nebuchadnezzar's dream. Jacob's eyelids became so heavy he couldn't keep them open.

This is so peaceful. I always have the nicest dreams when I fall asleep like this.

Dream?

At that thought, Jacob jerked upright in his chair. Somehow, he had forgotten the strange and disturbing vision of the night before. Fully awake, Jacob remembered every vivid detail of the previous dream. The dirt road, the rotting house, the burning corpses, not one image slipped his mind. The one thing that stuck with him the most was that face; the face that had come from the flames.

Jacob shuddered and a chill ran through him. No lights burned in the house and the shadows of the rain pouring down the windows dredged up feelings of terror he could not easily squelch. His mature side scolded him for being so childish. He wasn't afraid of the dark. He tried to convince himself that it was only a simple nightmare, but in his heart, he knew differently.

Looking to his left, Jacob caught the dim outline of his crossbow within arm's reach. Perhaps he had placed it there subconsciously because he had never before felt threatened enough to do so.

What's happening to me?

Jacob ran both hands through his hair and sank into his seat. He was afraid to be alone in his own house. "I have to get out of here," he said out loud, even if only for a leisurely walk in the rain.

He hoped the townspeople wouldn't be ready to commit him. Hopefully they would come to the conclusion that he needed something in the next town bad enough to risk the inclement weather. On the other hand, the way he felt right now, he really didn't care if anyone thought he was crazy or not.

Jacob grabbed his hat, equipped his sword and crossbow, and headed for the door. As he reached for the knob, the room was washed in total silence. Not a drop of rain fell, and even though it was not yet five in the evening, the town had fallen into complete darkness.

Am I asleep again?

Jacob was hesitant to turn the knob. Deep inside, he heard, *Don't do it. Don't do it,* and he wasn't going to argue with his instinct. Jacob tip-toed over to the window and peered out. His life was forever changed by what he saw.

Jacob was hesitant to turn the knob. Deep inside, he heard, "*Don't do it. Don't do it,*" and he wasn't going to argue with his instinct. Jacob peered out the window and his life was forever changed.

"Whoa!"

Jacob fell backward in surprise. Looking back at him, a hellish creature with burning red eyes, the nose and mouth of an alligator, and stringy black hair that dripped from a gruesome scalp. Startled and wide-eyed, Jacob steeled his nerve and burst through the door. Outside, three of hideous creatures surrounded him, hunched down and moving their hands in circles. Their claws looked as if they could rip through tree bark, and an eerie phlegmy hiss issued from their lips.

Jacob discerned a smile on their grotesque mouths and their groans in unison uttered, "Gotcha!"

In one quick action, the nearest creature raised an arm and slashed at him. Quick on the draw, Jacob unsheathed his sword and decapitated the monster before it could carry out its attack. The head spun and dropped to the ground, spurting blue blood.

The two remaining hung their heads and backed away, no longer smiling. This weak little human protected itself.

Jacob froze in his fighting stance ready to fend off any more quick attacks. Only his gaze went past the two creatures and into the distance behind them. He couldn't believe his eyes. Countless numbers of these things had surrounded the town and the whole place was on fire.

"Mother of God," Jacob whispered, his eyes beholding horrible sights.

A little blonde-haired girl was hidden under her doorsteps screaming for her mother. The creatures slowly stalked their prey before going in for the kill.

A woman—he didn't know if it was the mother on or not—struggled in one's clutches while screaming for dear life. With animalistic ferocity, the creature clamped its jaws to her neck. There was a spray of blood and she fell dead in its arms.

A man laid dead on the ground a short distance away, though he wasn't a man anymore. He had become a dead piece of cattle and the creatures fed on him like hungry wolves.

I've got to do something!

In his distraction, he took his eyes off his attackers and let his guard down. One of them took notice and leapt into action. At the movement, Jacob extended his arm and the monster impaled itself on his sword. With satisfaction, he sliced upward to finish it off as it squealed like a dying pig.

Then the third one jumped forward as the last one had, claws drawn to tear off Jacob's face. With one quick strike, he dismembered its right arm before removing its head as well.

Jacob stared in rage at all of the destruction and suffering around him. He let out an angry cry that made half the creatures look his way. Bodies decorated half the town, but maybe he wasn't too late to save somebody.

One by one, the things charged toward him in an ape-like stride, using their fists to run. He showed no mercy and left a blue blooded path in his wake, slicing anything in reach of his blade.

One of them made a hissing charge at him with both claw-filled hands raised. Without flinching he cut it perfectly in half at the waist. He showed no fear. They began to get smart though as three of them came in three different directions. One was directly in front of him and one to the right and left.

The one in front attacked first in hopes of making an opening for the other two. Jacob buried his sword up through its jaw clamping its mouth together, and like a gunslinger brought out his crossbow. He was a decent swordsman, but had eyes like a hawk and was a deadly shot. By barely aiming, he took the other two out with perfect heart-shots. Ripping back his sword he took yet another head as a trophy. The others scampered away in fear and he finally had a chance to breathe. Before he could so much as inhale he heard a desperate voice call to him from behind.

"Jacob! Help me please!"

It was Ashley; somehow, she had managed to survive. He ran to her as quickly as he could and checked her for injury. Her thigh was ripped down to the knee.

It was bad; Jacob could see the muscle tissue and a flash of white tendon. The girl sat in a puddle of her own blood, tears streaming down her face. For once, she didn't seem like an underage adult, but rather a scared little girl.

"Owwww! It hurts so bad."

Her voice was weak; she was bleeding to death fast. Off to the side, he saw the monster that must have attacked her; it lay dead with a knife through its eye.

Jacob had to stop the bleeding. He tore off a piece of his coat and tied it around her small leg above the gaping wound.

"Ahhh!"

"Calm down, honey, this will help," he said as he tightened the tourniquet. A small stream of blood squirted onto his glove as he did so and he prayed there was no artery damage. "You need a doctor. Maybe I drove those things off so we can get out of here."

He picked her up in his arms and she weakly wrapped her arms around his neck.

"Hold on, sweetie."

"Jacob?" she said in a whisper.

"Yes?"

I'm sorry for everything I did. I…I was wrong. I *do* believe in God and I *do* believe in hell."

"Ashley, that's all I've wanted to hear you say since I met you."

"I've done so many bad things. The sex, the drinking, driving my parents away. Do you think God will forgive me?"

"I know he will, Ashley. You have only to ask."

"I don't want to go to hell and be tortured by those creatures, Jacob."

"You won't, Ashley, you won't."

He ran, carrying her toward the long wooded path that led to the next town. It was a long way, but he hoped the bleeding had slowed enough to save her life. All he could do now was pray.

Inwardly, Jacob dreaded going down the small wooded area. With all the trees those things could pop out from anywhere. And unfortunately, as he turned the corner at the town square, he was reunited with his new enemies. Jacob gasped and fell backward, dropping Ashley, as he saw the living barricade.

It wasn't the minions he had driven off that startled him so badly; it was what was standing in the middle of them. It was *him*. It was the demon whose face had erupted from the flames. He had been terrifying enough as only a face, yet here the rest of him stood.

It was over seven feet tall with burning red eyes and pointed ears. Its eye sockets were filled with red light, and below, the nose was two small holes in the skull.

The demon snarled at him as thick saliva dripped down its three-inch canines. It wore a brown, hooded robe making it look like an unholy monk. By its movements, it appeared to recognize him and Jacob stepped back. The thing's threatening gargle deepened as it stared Jacob down. Did it know he was a man of God? Had it discerned Jacob as the human's leader and thus a worse enemy? The other minions were crouched at the demon's feet as if they were saying, "Daddy! Daddy! He's the one that hurt us!"

Jacob wasn't afraid of the followers, but he had no idea what kind of power this newfound monstrosity possessed. By the looks of him, Satan had blessed him with plenty. Even though he was surrounded by fire, Jacob was in a cold sweat, paralyzed with fear. It was everything he could do to slowly back away.

"Nooo!" Ashley cried.

"It's okay; we'll get out of this," said Jacob, backing up. Then, to his horror, the demon spoke his name.

"Jacob Cross!"

Jacob froze instantly.

"A pitiful small town preacher like you has no power over me!"

Its voice was hoarse and it sounded as if it were out of breath. Looking closely, he saw that its mouth wasn't moving as the words came out. It was speaking into Jacob's mind using some kind of strange telepathy. As it spoke, it gave him a headache, making everything around him seem blurry and unrealistic.

"No! I may not, but the one I serve has total power over you!" Jacob cried.

"Is that so? Where is your God as I murder and destroy everything in my path? Where is he now that you're about to die?"

Jacob looked for an escape. He had no such luck as the hooded demon pointed one razor-clawed finger at him and hissed to the others. Jacob assumed it was something to the effect of, "Bring me his head."

Jacob pulled out his crossbow glad that he had managed to back fifty yards from the closest one. It was time for target practice. The handful of minions that were left began to charge full blast at him. It took him barely a second to aim and pull the trigger and just over a second to reload and do it again. First was the lead runner. With one careful shot he buried his arrow into its left eye socket. The next ran through one's throat. The next was in the dead center of one's heart. One of them managed to get close enough to attack, but Jacob fired into its open mouth.

Now there were four left, but they were too close to shoot. The closest one hissed and swung wildly. Dodging one of the blows, he took off its head. Another one managed to tackle him to the ground. It used one hand to balance over him and the other went for Jacob's throat. They were incredibly strong. He had to use both hands to stop its forward motion. Quickly, he brought up his feet and catapulted it away before killing it with a shot between the eyes. The remaining two came at him from each side. They were fond of jumping attacks even though it left them completely vulnerable. He ducked the closest one and it slashed its partner's eyes out. He turned and ran them both through at the same time.

The hooded demon made its angry gargling noise again; apparently it hadn't expected its entire army to be taken down by one man.

Now Jacob had no choice; he had to see what this thing could do. It wasn't going to be satisfied until Jacob was dead. It was him or it. Jacob took aim and pulled the trigger, the arrow flying towards the demon's heart. But it stopped in mid-air before it hit its target and the demon circled its hand and the arrow.

"Uh oh," Jacob muttered. There was no time to react. Before he knew it, the arrow had struck his shoulder and sent him flying through the porch of the house behind him. The whole thing collapsed, burying Jacob under a pile of rubble.

CHAPTER 2

"*Jacob?"* An echoing voice called to Jacob, pulling him slowly out of a deep sleep. *"Jacob? Wake up, Jacob."*

Jacob opened his eyes to the brightest light he had ever seen. In the center of the brilliance a human silhouette glowed with intensity. As his eyes adjusted, the being came into view. Somehow, he had overlooked the dove-white wings extending from each side. Jacob had always wondered what angels truly looked like and now he was beholding one firsthand.

The luminous being appeared to be a clean shaven male with short blonde hair. Though he had the similarities of a normal man, there was an obvious benevolence about him. The glow that surrounded him gave him a look of absolute peace. His eyes were a color of blue that Jacob had never seen before. It was like staring into mystic water. The angel smiled and Jacob was speechless. It took him a moment to realize he was sitting on the ground.

"Hello, Jacob. I've been waiting for you."

The angel extended his hand to help Jacob to his feet. As he rose, Jacob still could not utter a single word. Then an odd thought hit him.

"Am I dead?" he finally managed.

"No, you're only sleeping. I've come to you in a dream."

Jacob looked around. There was nothing but light. It was nowhere yet it was the most beautiful place he had ever seen. Suddenly, everything came together and Jacob knelt to his knees.

"Rise, Jacob. I'm not the one you should bow to. I am only a messenger of the living God."

Dumbfounded, Jacob didn't know what to say. "Are you my guardian angel?"

The angel's expression did not waver as he replied. *"No, I am merely a messenger angel. God sent me to you."*

"God has a message for me?"

"Yes. He wants you to know that he is so happy that you have led so many souls away from Satan. You have served him faithfully and he is well pleased with you."

Jacob had never felt so happy or unworthy in his entire life.

"Do you remember what happened?"

It all came flooding back.

"Yes. Those horrible creatures attacked the village. They killed everyone. Their leader was so powerful." Jacob hadn't known what to say, but now a thousand questions rushed through his mind. "Did God want this to happen?"

The angel's smile became a look of absolute seriousness. *"No, had God meant to pass judgment on your town, he wouldn't have used unholy creatures such as the ones you saw."*

"Then, they were demons?"

"Yes. Low class ones, but demons nonetheless."

"What about the other one?"

"The hooded demon has no name, but he holds high authority in hell. That is why Satan sent him."

"Satan sent them? I thought Satan's powers were limited to hell and he couldn't send demons to terrorize the earth."

"Normally that is true, but the sins of the world have made him even more hungry for power. Every time someone becomes lost in sin and serves him he becomes more determined to rule the world. The sinners of the world are the source of his power. Therefore it finally became so bad that he couldn't restrain himself. He sent his army beyond hell's boundaries and your village was their first destination. His goal is to kill every man woman and child that serves God as well as anyone that stands in his way."

"Why isn't God stopping him? Can't he wave his hand and send them all back where they came from?"

"Yes, but that isn't his plan. He has chosen you to fight the hooded demon."

Jacob's eyes widened. "Me? Why has he chosen a mortal to fight this being and why me of all people? I'm only a preacher. How can I fight him all by myself?"

"*You speak too lightly of yourself. God himself could have delivered his people from Egypt's bondage. Instead he chose a shepherd named Moses to deliver them. Why? Not even I know that, but it was his plan as it is now for you to fight the hooded demon. Moses asked the same questions you did. He asked why God had chosen him and what could one man do? But, you will not be by yourself. You will find three companions, three warriors from three villages. Together, nothing can stop you. Apart, you will surely die fighting the demon.*"

"Who are these warriors?"

"*Ask for guidance and you will know them when you see them.*"

"But… I'm afraid. I'm ashamed to say it, but I am."

"*Jacob, God doesn't expect his children to never be afraid. He knows your limits for he created you. That is why in situations you are afraid and don't think you can go any farther he asks that you put your faith in him.*"

"Okay. I'm ready. If God has chosen me to fight this thing, then I will. I'll follow him until the end of time and give every drop of my blood to send the demon back to the fiery depths of hell from whence he came."

"*Very good. Now you will awaken back in your village. Go to Bruton and find your first ally. And Jacob, remember, no matter what happens, you'll always have a place in heaven. Good-bye Jacob.*"

"Ohhhh… my head." Jacob opened his eyes to total darkness. He was face down on the ground underneath a huge pile of debris. Jacob pushed himself to his feet. The world was spinning so he closed his eyes momentarily to gain his composure.

Besides a dire headache, he was fine. He didn't have a scratch on him. Any blood on him wasn't his own. He felt the area where the arrow had struck him and nothing. God had started him off on a clean slate.

After looking himself over he took notice of the carnage that had once been his town. Not a house was left standing. Bodies not even recognizable as human littered the square.

The small girl who had been crying for her mother lay face down on the ground, covered with blood. Not even twenty-four hours earlier, she ran, playing and full of life. Jacob clenched his fists.

On the ground beside him was one of his deacons that took up the collection each Sunday. He had never known a better man. He was elderly, but had plenty of good years left in him, that is, before the current tragedy.

Finally, Jacob's gaze fell upon Ashley. He ran to her, limping slightly. Even though she had been alive when he left her, she, too, was dead. The gash in her leg had been uncovered and the truncate was nowhere to be seen. Jacob frowned. The sick bastard had taken it. The demon didn't slit her throat or break her neck to finish her. He took the one thing stemming the blood flow so she would die slowly knowing there was nothing she could do.

Jacob screamed until his throat was raw. The demon had slaughtered everyone in his town and now all he could think of was avenging their deaths.

"Spawn of hell! I'll have your head!" he screamed into the night. The clouds released the rain as Jacob walked through the gates of Bruton. Luckily, he had gotten there before the demon, but, he felt himself being watched at every corner. Jacob sniffed, the rain more like the tears of heaven as he contemplated the events to come.

Jacob walked down the street with shops and houses on each side, noticing the odd looks he received from every eye that met his own. The city was nice enough, but not big on religion. It was a den of prostitution, thievery, and if you weren't careful, murder. Jacob never worried about these things since he could handle himself pretty well.

He knew people probably recognized him from the many times he had been here to trade and shop. He supposed the strange looks were because people wondered what in the world could be so important that he had to travel in a storm. If they only knew.

Jacob was cautious to stay as far away from dark alleys as possible. At the same time he wondered how he was supposed to find this person. The town wasn't what you would call enormous, but big enough to get lost in if you didn't know your way around.

"God? Could you give me some help here?" he asked aloud.

No sooner had the words came out of his mouth than a chair came flying through the window of the building next to him. A few seconds later, a large man over six feet tall came to the door and threw two smaller men into the streets.

"Stay out!" he yelled. "I don't need trouble in here!"

The two men crawled around aimless, barely aware they had been thrown out, too drunk to even stand. The sign above the door alerted him that he had reached the local tavern.

"You have got to be kidding me," Jacob sighed as he walked through the door.

Just inside the door, the odor of alcohol nearly knocked him down. Jacob ignore the aroma and scanned the room for potential demon hunters. He didn't notice anyone right off, but he did see the large bartender behind the bar. Next to women in church, a bartender was the next best person to talk to if you needed to know something about the community.

Walking up, the large man gave him a friendly smile. He had long Sandy blonde hair and a goatee. Surely a bartender wasn't supposed to help him deliver the world from evil.

"Aren't you that preacher that comes round here from time to time?" the barkeep asked still smiling.

Jacob returned the gesture.

"I didn't think you guys were allowed to drink."

"No, I'm here for another reason, not drinking."

"Ah, so what brings a holy man like you to a dump like this?"

"Actually I was hoping you could help me."

"Well, I'll do my best. Can I get you anything?"

"Do you have water?

"Uhh, yeah, but you'll have to make it holy yourself." The bartender joked. "So, what is it you need to know?"

"Can you tell me if there are any fighters in this town?"

"Ummm, no offense buddy, but have you ever paid attention during your visits? This place is crawling with fighters. Hell, some of these guys get into a brawl every day."

"Well, that's not exactly what I meant. Is there any one fighter that stands up above the rest?"

"Oh, I think I know what you mean. You need someone that is good with a sword and doesn't back down?"

"Yes, I guess you could say that."

"I think I know just the guy you're looking for."

"Where can I find him?"

"Well, you don't have to look very far." He pointed to the end of the bar.

Jacob looked to see a man with his head bowed into one arm and a bottle in his free hand. "*I don't believe this.*"

The bartender noticed Jacob's disappointment and revealed more.

"That's Mark," he said gesturing to the drunk. "Now, I know he doesn't look like much, but he's one of the toughest bast….um, guys I've ever known. A while back he put up money against any swordsman, saying he could beat them in a fair fight. He did it every day for a month. People came from all around to take a shot at him. He only lost once."

Curious, Jacob awaited for more.

"The guy that took him out was a professional swordsman that had competed in a lot of tournaments all over the world. I was watching that day, and even though he lost, Mark gave him a run for his money. Earned his respect. I would say old Mark is about the best fighter you'll find around these parts."

"What kind of person is he?"

"Well, he's not in church every Sunday if that's what you mean. Besides his little drinking problem, he's one of the nicest guys you'll ever know. Everyone loves him, especially the kids. I don't know how much you'll get out of him, but you're welcome to go talk to him."

"Thank you for your help. How much do I owe you for the water?"

"It's on the house. I might go to hell if I charge you."

Jacob shook his hand and walked to the end of the bar. Was his first ally to be this drunk? Jacob shrugged; he'd learned long ago not to question God's will.

Jacob cleared his throat as he approached. He smelled as if he had been bathed in what he was drinking. The man finally raised his head to stare at the wall. Jacob had learned that most heavy drinkers were unhappy with their lives. They drank to forget everything that was wrong with it. It was understandable, but not justifiable. Because as it said in Isaiah 5:11, "Woe unto those who rise up early in the morning that they may follow strong drink; that continue until night till wine inflame them!" Jacob took a seat.

"Mark?" he asked finally after being ignored a few moments.

The man looked over at him glossy-eyed, appearing sick, sleepy, confused, and angry all at the same time. He was about Jacob's age with curly brown hair and a carefully shaped beard, wearing shabby unassuming garb.

"Don't tell me I wandered into church," he said with slurred speech. "I didn't think I had that much to drink."

"No, you're still in the bar."

"Huh? Aren't you a preacher man?"

"Yes, I am."

"Well, you guys sure have a lot of nerve preaching against drinking then walking into a bar. Heh, I've got a lot of jokes that begin with a preacher walking into a bar."

Jacob couldn't help but smile at the childish ramblings. "No, no, I'm not here to drink."

"Oh, well then, that's okay. Hey! You're not here to preach to me, are you? This isn't fair. Normally, I have a chance to run, but if I do that now I'll fall flat on my face….or was that your plan all along, Mr. Preachy?! Ugh! You guys are getting too smart for your own good. Get a guy when he's drunk. That's low."

Jacob shook his head slowly at the whole conversation. "No, I'm not here to preach to you either."

"You're not? Well then, what in the name of the virgin Mary could you be here for? It sure as heck couldn't be for the scenery, and the food isn't that good."

The bartender gave him an irritated look.

"No offense, Johnny!"

"No, the reason I came was to see you."

"Me? What's a guy like you want with someone like me?"

"I need your help."

"My help? It looks like with the big guy behind you, you wouldn't need much help. What kind of help are we talking about? Most of my connections don't exactly fall into the holy category, but what do I know? What do ya need?"

"They tell me you're a fighter."

The drunk's demeanor become more serious. "I'm not *a* fighter. I am *the* fighter. I'll take on any man alive. If I can't take them down, then I'll give them a serious limp before they take me down."

"That's what I'm looking for."

"Ah, I'm starting to understand where this is going. Let me guess, some smart-aleck tough guy is trying to push you and your church around. Since you guys aren't supposed to fight, you want me to rough them up? No problem, but it will cost you."

Jacob thought for a second about exactly what he was trying to say. "It isn't exactly a man I want you to fight."

"Really? Do you have a rat problem? I'm no exterminator."

"Tell me, are you a brave man?"

Mark responded with a sneer. "Well, I always thought I could stare the devil in the face and not flinch."

"That's good to hear."

"Uhhh, could you clear things up for me a little bit here? You have me just a little lost. What is it you're trying to tell me?"

Jacob looked down, afraid of what he would say when he told him the truth. Finally, he sighed.

"Okay, I'll level with you. You may think I'm crazy, but I'm going to tell you everything that has happened to me in the last twenty-four hours. Do you promise to let me finish before you declare me insane?"

Mark looked him over carefully. "Okay shoot."

"First off, my name is Jacob Cross."

"Nice to meet ya, Jacob," Mark said shaking his hand. "I'm Mark Raven."

"I'm a preacher, or at least I was in a small town to the north. Do you know of it?"

"Yeah, its full of traders who sell vegetables and raise chickens. Its quite a bit different from this place."

Jacob took a deep breath before he continued. "At this moment, every man woman and child is lying dead and the village is burned to the ground."

Mark's eyes grew wide. "What? You're kidding, right?"

"I wish I were, Mark. Do you see the blood on my coat and gloves? It's the blood of a young girl who had just turned her life around. I carried her in my arms, but she didn't make it. I was the only one that survived, and it's only by the grace of God that I did."

Mark looked aside. He was a tough guy, but for a second,

Jacob thought he was going to cry.

"What kind of sick bastard would do something like that?" Mark whispered. "Those people were peaceful farmers who never hurt anyone. What could they possibly have done to deserve that? Even if someone could be that cruel, how could they murder little kids? It would take a monster out of hell to do that."

Jacob looked deep into his eyes. "You don't know how right you are. Listen to me, Mark. What I'm about to tell you is the God-honest truth. I know it will be hard to believe, but try. It wasn't men who attacked the village. Something not of this world has come here, creatures like you have never seen before."

There was a momentary silence.

"Huh?"

"Demons, Mark. They are real and hell does exist. These things have come to take this world as their own. They are dangerous. They have razor sharp claws and teeth, but they are nothing compared to the one that leads them. He has the face of fear itself and powers beyond comprehension. He nearly killed me. I shot an arrow at him and he sent it straight back at me. When the arrow struck me I went flying through a house and was knocked out cold."

Mark looked at him in disbelief. Jacob couldn't blame him. He didn't know if he believed the story, but he ran his hand over his arm and felt chill bumps.

"While I was out, an angel came to me. He told me what these things were and that I have been chosen to fight them, but that I wouldn't be alone. He told me I would find three warriors in three towns. Mark, I'm hoping that you are the first."

Mark sat up straight and stared at Jacob. "You really are serious, aren't you?"

"Yes, I am."

"If anyone else had walked in here and told me this story, I would have thought they were drunker than I am, but I believe you. I don't know why, but I do."

He wasn't lying. There was something about this man shrouded in black clothing that he believed. He thought Jacob had the most sincere eyes he had ever seen. He generally liked this man, and that didn't happen very often.

"Let's say all of this is true. Why me? Why you, for that matter? If God is so powerful, why doesn't he wipe these things out himself?"

"I don't know, Mark. There were many times in the Bible where he could have done things himself, yet he chose people to work through him and put their faith in him.

"Why he did this we may never know, but what I do know is that he has chosen me to carry out this task and I will do everything in my power to accomplish it. You told me that you would take on any man alive and stare the devil straight in the face. If that isn't the description of someone chosen to be a warrior, I don't know what is."

Mark looked to the ground not knowing what to say.

"So, Mark, will you fight with me?"

"I… I…"

"NOOOOOO!" a voice screamed from outside.

"Huh?!" Mark jerked his head in the direction of the scream. Everyone present rushed to the door to see what was going on. One man's eyes grew wide and he staggered backward.

Every few seconds, Jacob felt the ground shake a little. With every small tremor, the place shook a little more. Whatever was out there was huge and getting closer.

"What in God's name is that thing?!" Johnny cried.

"It killed Todd!" another yelled.

"Isn't that John trying to fight it?"

All at once they made a sickened sound and turned their heads.

"That thing cut him in half!" a man shrieked on his knees.

Jacob started to the door, but before he could move a muscle there was another tremor and part of the roof collapsed on him.

"Jacob?! You okay?"

"Rrrr! I'm fine! Go on ahead! I'll catch up!"

"Got it!"

As Mark got to the door, Johnny held him back.

"Are you crazy, Mark?! You're good, but that thing isn't human!"

"Someone has to fight it, Johnny! If I don't, it will take us all out."

"Argh! Watch yourself, Mark."

As he ran out, Jacob tossed the wood off his back for the

second time of the night. *What is it with roofs falling on me tonight?*

When he reached the door, Johnny grabbed his arm. "You be careful, too, preacher."

Jacob nodded and exited.

Right away, he saw the cause of the commotion. A being at least twelve feet tall filled his vision, covered from head to toe in black armor. Not an inch of skin could be seen anywhere on it. The being's shoulders and chest were as wide as Jacob was tall. A helmet covered its head with only two holes for its trademark red eyes. Long curving bull horns extended from each side of its head and it held a gigantic sword dripped blood.

"God be with us," Jacob whispered.

Mark had already began attacking the beast. With every strike there was a loud *CLING* sound. He was giving it everything he had, but wasn't making so much as a dent. As he continued slashing and stabbing, the thing merely looked down at him as if he were a hovering bug. It finally let out an enraged cry and kicked Mark to the ground.

"Ahhh!" Mark muttered clutching his chest.

The creature let out another cry and raised its gigantic sword. Jacob knew what was happening next. Mark still had the wind knocked out of him and was completely helpless. The creature slashed down as Jacob jumped over Mark to block the attack.

It took everything he had not to fall to the ground as their swords clashed. He didn't know how with the size difference his sword didn't break in half. He had both hands on the hilt and his feet planted, but the armored terror seemed to be effortlessly pushing itself down on him.

"RRRRRGH! Are you okay Mark?"

"Ugh…yeah, I'm fine. My right ribs are broken, but I'm fine."

With one strong push Jacob rocked the creature and helped Mark to his feet. They took the opportunity to take cover in an alley.

"Man! That will sober a guy up quick!" Mark yelped as he peeked around the corner. "Is that thing a friend of yours?"

"No, I haven't seen it before. The things I fought were normal-sized and easy to kill."

"Well, I don't think we have that luxury now. What is this thing? I couldn't even scratch it. Unless you have a giant can opener I'm all out of ideas!"

Jacob peered out as it moved slowly down the street. "It has to have some kind of weakness. We have no choice, but to keep fighting it until we find something that hurts it. We just have to be careful. As far as I see, it's big, slow, and hopefully stupid. Since we're quick, maybe we can use that to our advantage."

"All right! Time for round two!" Mark cried.

They both charged, each taking a side and swinging away. Jacob worked unsuccessfully on the leg while Mark hacked uselessly at the arms.

"Hey, wasn't there something in that book of yours about a kid killing a giant?"

"Yes, but one, the giant was human, and two, I don't have a sling or a rock."

"Too bad. I guess we have to go to plan B."

A pattern was emerging. Every time the thing howled, it was also about to strike. As soon as they heard the cry they ducked for cover. The thing swung both arms sideways. Had it made contact they would have been unconscious or worse.

"What are we going to do, Jacob? There isn't an inch of this guy not covered in metal. The only offense we can put up is poking him in the eyes and I would have to stand on your shoulders to do that!"

Mark was joking, but that gave Jacob an idea. He pulled out his crossbow and took aim.

"Mark! Stand back.

Mark ducked behind as the creature eyeballed them both. Jacob took a deep breath and pulled the trigger. The arrow flew in what seemed like slow motion and landed square in the middle of the left eye socket. This time the armored beast let out a different kind of howl, one of chronic pain. It began shaking its head violently and cupped its hand around the arrow.

"Nice shot! That hurt the armored freak! Can you do it again?"

"I'm way ahead of you." Jacob was already taking aim, but this shot would be harder than the first one. The thing wasn't standing still, but was swinging its body back and forth in pain. Jacob took another deep breath and pulled the trigger. It hit just below the right eye hole and bounced to the ground.

"Curses! I can't hit it while it's moving like that."

"Don't worry about it, at least now it has a blind side."

Mark made a brave move and ran behind it. He then got on his hands and knees behind the thing's legs.

At first Jacob didn't know what he was doing, but he soon realized what he was thinking and took his signal. Jacob charged the beast head on with his shoulder. It was like running into a brick wall, but he wobbled it enough for it to trip over Mark.

"Bingo!" Mark cried triumphantly. "Now lets kick the man while he's down!" Mark leaped onto the monster's chest and wailed away with punches to the head. There was an ugly thud as each blow made contact. It made Jacob's hand hurt to watch him. Mark was giving it everything he had and soon, blood dripped from his fists. "This will teach you to come to villages uninvited and chop up the people!"

Suddenly, the thing let out an enraged howl.

"Mark! Watch out!" Jacob cried, but he was too late. The thing raised its fist and sent Mark flying.

"I think we pissed it off. Do we go with plan C now, Jacob?"

"What's plan C?"

"I'll tell you when I think of it."

"We don't have a choice, Mark, we have to fight it head on."

"I was afraid you would say that."

"When I tackled it, it staggered, so if we both do it, it should go down."

"Okay, but how do we get it to stay down?"

"We'll cross that bridge when we get there."

As they charged, the beast clothes-lined them. They went to the ground, out of breath.

The thing's single eye burned redder and it grabbed Jacob by the throat. It raised him high in the air and clasped his windpipe. Jacob gagged and gasped, his throat in a monstrous vise. He thought he heard Mark's voice, but it was only a whisper.

"I tried God," he thought and soon, he saw white before everything went black.

Meanwhile on the ground, Mark picked up his sword.

"Okay, this ends here!" With every ounce of strength he could muster, he plunged his sword forward. This time it penetrated as if he were stabbing sheet metal. The creature let out an agonized cry and it released Jacob, dropping him to the ground. In the heat of the moment neither of them saw the small river of blood flowing from the wound.

"Jacob? Are you okay, buddy?"

"Cough! Y-yeah. Ahh! I think my leg is cut."

He looked down to see his leg soaking in red. Huh? He felt over it and found no cut. He looked at Mark, but he was clean. Finally he looked back at the armored beast and saw the open wound flowing crimson.

"Mark! You hurt it!"

"Huh?"

"Look at the place where you stabbed through its armor."

"Whoa! It's bleeding all over the place!"

They watched as every step it took, a bloody trail followed.

"No wonder that thing is so protected. If it gets hurt, it bleeds like there is no tomorrow," Mark said.

"Right, if it lives on blood, eventually it's going to bleed to death. All we have to do is keep it busy until it weakens."

"Now *that* I can do." Mark ran in front of the thing and began taunting it. "Come on big, tall, and gruesome! Give me your best shot!"

The beast let out an angry cry that was noticeably weaker than before. It slashed down slowly at Mark, but he easily dodged it the blow.

"Come on! Is that all you've got?"

Another cry, shorter and weaker than the last. As it raised its sword as high as it would go, the beast's strength gave out and it fell to the ground. Jacob snuck slowly behind it hoping to grab the weapon.

"What's the matter, big guy? Blood loss making you dizzy? How about a fist fight? I'm not too shabby in that category either."

The beast scraped up what energy it had and punched down at Mark, but it was nowhere near fast enough to catch him.

"You punch like a girl!"

Jacob had managed to come up behind it without being

noticed. He took the hilt of the gigantic sword with both hands and lifted. It was the heaviest weapon he had ever held. The blade itself weighed at least fifty pounds. Mark caught his eye and gave him a thumbs up.

"All right, big guy, you have one more shot left in you?"

The creature made one last gurgling sound and balled both of its hands in the air. It practically collapsed down toward Mark, missing once again. It landed on its knees, and lacked the strength to regain its feet.

Jacob hovered over it with the giant sword in hand. He could see a thin area between the head and shoulders and took aim. After raising the blade as high as he could, he cut off its head.

"It's over," Mark said in relief and sat on the ground.

There the two of them stood victorious in their first battle together. However, their victory celebration would be short-lived. Suddenly they heard women and children screaming. Everyone, whether they were crying in fear or staring in disbelief, looked to the entrance gate of the town.

"It's the devil!" a man shouted.

"What is it?!" a woman cried.

Jacob knew what it was before he even looked. Mark joined at his side and they looked toward the gate. In a cloud of fog with the moon shining down on it stood the hooded demon. This time when Jacob looked at him it wasn't with fear, but with anger and a longing to cut it in half. Even with its natural snarled-up look, Jacob could tell it was seething with Anger.

"Is that the hooded guy you were talking about?" Mark whispered not taking his eyes off the demon.

"Yes." Jacob grasped the head of the recently-dispatched minion and lifted it toward its master.

"Servant of Satan! Like your minion that fell by our hands, I'll have your head and lift it to the one living God! Just keep sending your followers against us and they will fall one by one! Then, when it is only you left to face us, you will suffer an agonizing death and be sent back to the fiery pits of hell from whence you came, with the Mark of God scarring you for all eternity!"

The demon glared at them. Then, as it had before, it spoke telepathically into their minds. "*Foolish Minister! You will live to regret speaking to me in that manner! Do you honestly think that just because you and a drunk defeated one obstacle, that you have a chance of even scratching me?! You are weak pitiful creatures. I swear that in the end you will bow at my feet begging for mercy before I drink your blood and feed on your organs! You and your God have no power over me! To even speak of you having my head is enough to howl with laughter. Never will a creature as weak as a human ever spill one drop of my blood. I'll allow you to live for now. Remember though, that what you just faced is a grain of sand compared to what I could unleash on you."*

Then as quick as it had appeared the demon was gone. Its words had no effect on Jacob, but Mark was visibly shaken.

"This…is too much. I can't handle this, Jacob. Find someone else, I'm not your man."

"Mark!" he called as he walked away.

He raised his hand. "Find someone else, Jacob!"

Jacob hung his head. They had fought so well together. Had he made a mistake? He had earlier thought that surely God would not choose an alcoholic to fight for him. Had he been right? Still he couldn't help but feel a chemistry with him.

At that moment he had no idea what he was going to do. All he felt like doing after this night was finding a nice warm bed and praying for guidance. He felt a hand on his shoulder. He looked back to see Johnny giving him a look of comfort.

"Maybe he'll come around. I know Mark is a brave man, but you have to admit that seeing a thing like that is enough to make any man want to cower in a corner. This isn't just some guy you're talking about fighting. This is something other-worldly. I thought I was going to wet my pants when I saw that thing. That's a lot for someone to handle all at once."

Jacob thought about it for a second then nodded in agreement. It wasn't but mere hours earlier that he had been terrified and shaking at his own shadow because of this thing.

"You're right. I guess I am expecting too much too fast."

"Well, I guess you'll need somewhere to rest after going through all of that. Come on, there is a nice little inn just down the street."

"I….I don't have much money."

"Forget about it. If you can save the whole town from being crushed, than the least we can do is give you a place to sleep."

"Thank you, Johnny."

⋊⋉⋊

Mark sat on his bed wide-eyed and awake. Every sound he heard made his heart skip a beat. This was unlike any feeling he had ever had in his life. For the first time since he could remember he was paralyzed in fear. Even as a kid he was never afraid of monsters under the bed. But, this fear he had witnessed with his own eyes. Looking into that thing's face was like staring into hell itself.

He could still hear the demon's voice running through his head. He could picture it feeding on his dead body. He could feel so much power radiating from it even from a distance. Jacob was planning on fighting this thing? Mark couldn't help but feel guilty for refusing to help him, but he couldn't imagine anyone putting up a fight against that thing without ending up a smoking pile of flesh.

"I don't know what to do!" he said out loud while running his fingers through his hair.

He had never been a praying man, but he did keep a bottle of hard liquor in a drawer beside his bed. Some people used divine intervention to find peace; he used a bottle of the local bar's finest.

He raised the bottle to his lips, but before he could so much as take a sip, there came a loud knock at the door. Startled, Mark dropped the bottle to the floor.

"Man, I'm jumpier than a drunken jack rabbit!"

The knocking continued.

"Jacob, its nearly midnight. Can't this wait until morning?" He was surprised as he opened the door. It wasn't Jacob, but a woman carrying a hysterical little girl in her arms.

"Oh. Tara, what is it?"

"Mark, I hate to trouble you, but can we stay here tonight? Our house was completely destroyed and I can't calm Lily down. I didn't want to take her to the Inn. She's scared enough without being in a strange place."

"Of course you can stay here. My home is your home."

Her husband and Lily's father had been the man named John, who was cut in half by the armored monster.

"Come here, honey," he said with his arms outstretched. "Come to Uncle Mark."

He and John had been pretty good friends, but he saw Tara and Lily more than he had him. She wrapped her arms around his neck, still sobbing. Tears ran down her face and she buried her head into Mark's chest.

"It's okay, baby."

"That thing killed my daddy!" Her voice was muffled into Mark's shirt.

"I know, baby, but we killed it."

"That doesn't bring daddy back!"

"Good point," he thought. "I know sweetie, but everything will be okay."

"Our house is gone," she pouted finally raising her head.

"Yeah, but you can stay here as long as you want."

"You promise?"

"Yeah, I promise."

Tara smiled at the way he was connecting with her. "That's the calmest she's been since it happened."

"I miss daddy," she said softly as she laid her head on Mark's shoulder.

"I know. I know. He's in a better place now."

Mark hoped he was in a better place. He had always been on the fence about the whole heaven and hell thing. Though after everything he had seen tonight, there wasn't much doubt they existed.

"You'll see him again one day," he said running his fingers through his hair. There wasn't much more he could say to comfort her. He wished Jacob was here to do that. All was quiet until Lily asked a question that caught him totally off guard.

"Are you going to help the preacher man fight the bad man?"

Mark jerked his head up in surprise. "W-What honey?"

"Are you going to help fight the bad man?"

"We killed the bad man."

"Not him, the really scary one."

"Oh, so you saw him?"

"Everyone saw him," Tara cut in. "I've never seen anything

like it in my life."

"You're not afraid of him are you?" Lily asked with a look of pure innocence on her face.

"Afraid?" Mark cleared his throat. "No, of course I'm not afraid," he said lying through his teeth.

"So, does that mean you're going to help the preacher man?"

Mark thought for a second. "We'll talk about it in the morning. Right now you need some rest. You two can have the bed. I sleep on the floor half the time anyway."

Since she had calmed down, Lily had begun to get sleepy. As she yawned, he took her to the bed and tucked her in.

"Ah, it doesn't matter what age you girls are, I'm a sucker for all of you," he said walking back toward Tara. "Are you okay?" he asked.

"I've been crying for two straight hours. All I can do is accept that he's dead and move on."

"You always have been strong and independent, but don't overdo it."

She smiled. "Mark?"

"Yeah?"

"You never did answer her question. Are you going to help that preacher?"

"Ahh! Not you, too. Ugh. I don't know what I'm going to do."

"But, Mark, you can't just turn your back on him."

"You think I don't feel bad enough as it is? I can't help being such a coward. Oh, I'm going straight to hell for this. Did you see that thing? How can anyone fight it? It looked like it could only snap its fingers and rip me in half."

"Look, I know you've never been a religious person. Neither have I, but watching you and that guy…"

"Jacob," Mark said for her.

"Yeah, Jacob. It was incredible. It looked like nothing could stop the two of you. Jacob is a man of God and if he really is up there, then he looks out for him. If you're fighting with him then surely he'll protect you too."

Mark thought about it for a second.

"We were pretty good together weren't we? Maybe if we team up, we could give this thing a run for its money." Mark glimpsed into the room where Lily lay sleeping. Suddenly all of his fear was replaced with anger. "Do you know that small town to the north with all of the farmers and traders?"

"Yeah."

"Jacob said that it's burned to the ground and everyone is dead."

"Oh, my God. Those people never bothered anyone."

"I know. Then one day, this hooded freak get bored playing cards in hell and decides it might be fun to take over the world. Not on my watch! We're going to send this thing back to where it belongs!"

ꓘꓘ

The next morning, Jacob awoke surprised to be so refreshed. After what had happened last night, he figured he would toss and turn in a strange bed and what little sleep he did get would be filled with horrible dreams. It turned out to be the opposite; the bed was remarkably comfortable and he slept through the night.

As far as dreams went, he didn't recall any. And although he was still sore, he was ready for a new day. When he sat up, he noticed an outfit of clothes lying on a table beside the bed. There was a note:

Hey, preacher. Thought you might need a new outfit of clothes since yours got covered in blood. Hope you slept well. Thanks for saving us. From Johnny and the town.

Appreciating the gift as well as the gesture, Jacob dressed and went downstairs. He was greeted by the Innkeeper and his wife who led him to a table, where she had prepared a feast fit for a king. Stacked high with meat from at least three animals, plus eggs and bread, it took Jacob half an hour to eat everything. When he was stuffed, he thanked the two for their hospitality and wobbled to the door.

Outside, the street was full of activity. People were trading, playing cards and generally socializing. Jacob tried to plan his next move. Should he drop in on Mark? No; if the man had changed his mind he would have found him already. Jacob was back at square one.

Standing in the street, he saw Johnny sweeping out the bar door, preparing to open.

"Hey, preacher! Leaving already?"

Jacob smiled at the way he always called him preacher.

"Yes, I'm afraid I should be on my way. I have a long road ahead of me and I want to get an early start."

"Well, hold on a minute. I've got something for you." He disappeared back into the bar.

Jacob looked puzzled. This man had done so much for him, what else could he give him? He came back holding a small money bag.

"Everyone pitched in last night to show their appreciation for what you did. It's not a lot, but we want you to have it."

"Johnny, I can't accept this. You've given me a place to sleep, these clothes, and a good meal already. That's payment enough to me and then some."

"We insist. Besides, if you're going to be going from town to town you're going to need money, if anything for food."

He had a point. Jacob smiled and took the money.

"The Lord does provide. God bless you, Johnny. Take care."

"You, too, preacher," he said extending his hand. "I'm sorry things didn't go quite the way you planned."

Jacob nodded and shook his hand before turning to leave.

"Leaving without me, Jacob?" a voice said behind him.

He was glad to turn and see Mark wearing a mischievous grin.

"I'm glad to see you, Mark."

"Yeah, I decided you wouldn't stand a chance without me to back you up, so here I am."

"Thank you."

"Okay, I'm coming with you on one condition."

"Yes?"

"You keep your sermons about my drinking limited to one a day."

"Deal."

CHAPTER 3

With last night's events circling Jacob's mind, an awkward silence permeated the atmosphere as Mark and Jacob walked down the bright forest path.

Finally, Mark spoke up. "So...is it true you guys can't have sex?"

Confused and amused at the same time, Jacob considered his answer carefully saying, "Well, we can make love, but it should be with someone we love and are married to."

"You have to be married?"

"Yes, otherwise it's fornication."

"Oh, well I guess I've broken that commandment a few times."

Jacob smiled. "It's not exactly a commandment. You see, there are a lot more things we can do wrong besides what the Ten Commandments say. Those are mainly the really important ones."

"Oh, well I guess I've done a lot of stuff that book of yours says not to. I'm probably on a road to hell."

Jacob's smile faded. "You don't have to be."

Mark grunted. "I've done so many things that there is no going back."

"Mark, have you ever been taught the Bible?"

"Nah, not really. My mom used to tell me some stories when she was alive."

"Oh, so she's….."

"Yeah. She died when I was ten. After that I never bought into the whole Jesus, heaven, or hell thing. That is until last night."

"Mark, there's nothing you can do to assure yourself a place in hell, except not believing in God. He doesn't judge you for how many sins you commit. It doesn't matter what you've done in the past, his grace can always save you."

"Why would he want to forgive me? I don't even know why he wants me to fight for him. I'm no religious man. You're a better man than I'll ever be."

"I'm no saint, Mark. I make mistakes and fall along the way, too."

"Really?"

"Yes, no man or woman alive has never sinned. That's why we're human." Jacob turned his bible to John 3:16 and read it aloud. "For God so loved the world that he gave his only begotten son and whosoever believeth in him should not perish, but have everlasting life." Mark did not respond so Jacob continued. "That's the most important verse in the bible. It tells us that when Jesus died on the Cross we were all saved. All we must do is believe in him. God isn't up there holding a grudge against you for everything you do. If you only ask, it will be as if it never happened."

Mark stopped for a moment. "We've been walking nearly an hour. Mind if we take a break under a tree?"

Jacob agreed and they settled under a full oak.

Mark opened his pack and pulled out a bottle, in Jacob's mind, the wall that stood between Mark and God. Mark could give up swearing, fornication, and disbelief if he really tried, but the biggest battle would be putting down the bottle.

Mark took off the lid and without thinking said, "Want a drink?"

Jacob stared at him blankly.

"Okay, dumb question."

Jacob watched as he took a sip, his expression one of ultimate pleasure and rejuvenation. Mark closed his eyes and relaxed his head back against the tree and Jacob took the opportunity to play minister.

"Tell me, why do you drink, Mark?"

"What was our agreement?" Mark asked with his eyes still closed.

"Hey, you said I was allowed one sermon a day," Mark laughed.

"Me and my big mouth. Go ahead."

"Well, I've learned that most people who are alcoh…"

Mark opened one eye.

"Um, have drinking problems, usually use their drinking to escape the pressures in their lives. But, from what Johnny said about you, I would think that you have a happy life full of friends and family. You're a skilled fighter, so why didn't you ever compete on a professional level?"

"Ha! Those tournament fighters have their noses so high in the air that if it rained they would drown. I didn't want to end up like that. As far as what you said about my life… Happy? So-so. Friends? Yes. Family? No."

"So, is it that you want, a family, and you use alcohol as a means of filling that void?"

"Whoa! You analyze things too much, buddy. There isn't some deep dark meaning behind everything in life." Mark paused and then sighed. "You said that people sometimes use drinking as an excuse to escape from their life. People also use it to escape from their past."

"Something bad happened to you?"

"Yeah."

"You don't have to talk about it if you don't want to."

"Nah, I trust you enough to talk about it. Besides, maybe getting it off my chest will give me some peace. I've never told anyone about it. The only ones who know are the people from the town I grew up in. Remember how I told you my Mother died when I was ten?"

"Yes."

"Well, when she died, you might as well say my Dad died, too. He went nuts when he found out. He loved her more than anything in the world. I don't remember a day or night when he didn't kiss her and tell her he loved her. He had good reason, too. Even though I was young, I still remember her beautiful singing voice. On nights I couldn't sleep, she would sing to me until I fell off. She was a gentle God-fearing woman. She never said a harsh word about anyone." Mark smiled as he continued to remember.

"She spoiled me like I was royalty. Not once did she ever lay a hand on me. If I ever did anything bad and she knew I should be punished, she couldn't bring herself to do it. She always made my Dad spank me so she wouldn't have to be the bad guy. She was just an all-around good woman. It's bad, but I've started to forget what she looked like. I remember she had long, blonde, curly hair down her back. She was a tall woman, in fact she was taller than my Dad. But, as far as her face, its blurry."

"Anyway, she loved horses. She had a black one named Night. She went out riding one day and nobody really knows what happened, but for some reason she fell off the horse and hit her head on a sharp rock. She was dead when our neighbors found her. Everyone said that something must have scared the horse because she had it so well trained. They declared it a horrible accident. Unfortunately, my Dad didn't see it that way. In his rage he blamed the horse and massacred it with a butcher's knife. Everyone in town tried to calm him down, but nothing worked.

"Before they finally wrestled him to the ground he stabbed two men and beat the crap out of another. Luckily nobody was seriously hurt. He wasn't a violent man, so they all knew it was temporary insanity from losing Mother.

"I cried for a week over her. He cried for a month. He loved her so much it was unhealthy. Sometimes I would hear him talking to her and it freaked me out. Then after the nightly conversations, came the drinking. One night I saw him bring in a bottle and I didn't know what it was. He didn't say a word when he walked in. He just sat down in his chair and started drinking. I went to bed. Later on in the middle of the night he jerked me out of bed. He was furious about something. At first I thought I had done something wrong. Then he just started beating me repeatedly with his belt. He hit me like fifty times and I don't mean my backside either. It was my back, my arms, my legs, even my face a couple of times. I remember screaming 'What did I do?' But, all he could do was hit me.

"The next morning when I woke up, he asked me what the devil had happened to me. I told him and he begged me to forgive him, but he never stopped drinking. The whole song and dance continued for three years. I still have the scars."

Jacob furrowed his brow. “In all of that time, didn’t anyone notice your cuts and bruises?”

“Yeah, they saw.”

“Then why in the world didn’t anyone do anything?”

“The people in town were nice enough I guess, but they had a strict rule about not getting involved in other people’s business. I’ll never forgive them for that. All they did was say ‘Poor Mark. He doesn’t deserve that.’ If they didn’t think I deserved it, then why the hell didn’t they do anything?! I swear, if I ever see anyone beating their kid, I’ll beat the piss out of them, let them recover, then do it again!”

Jacob thought for a second. “But Mark, if your Father drank so much and hurt you so bad, then by drinking yourself, aren’t you being just like him?”

“I am nothing like him! Don’t ever compare me to that man! When I drink, I’m still aware of what I’m doing and If I do say so myself, drunk Mark is a pretty nice guy.”

“I’m sorry, Mark.”

“No, I’m sorry I bit your head off. I just swore that I would never be like him, even when I’m drunk.”

Jacob nodded. “So, what finally happened?”

“One day, I just snapped. He walked in one night loaded and I was sitting in front of the fireplace. He took off his belt and said. ‘Come on boy, you know what time it is.’ I said no. He screamed, ‘what boy?!’ and started towards me. I had the fire poker in my hand. I wanted to hurt him with it. My God! You don’t know how badly I wanted to hurt him. I used every bit of strength I had and knocked him in the head. I must have hit him just right because he went to the ground, jerking and drooling. I thought I had killed him, so I ran next door for help.

“When the doctor looked Dad over, he said there was permanent brain damage. He was never the same. He was like a three year old. I finally couldn’t stand watching him anymore. All he could do was mutter half-words and stumble. He couldn’t even feed himself.”

“Of course, nobody blamed me for what I did. But even though he drank and beat me, day after day, I still feel guilt for turning him into a fifty-year-old kid who couldn’t do anything without help. I live with that every day of my life.”

Mark finally broke down. Jacob put his hand on his shoulders to comfort him. "Mark, you can still make peace with him. Its not too late."

"Unfortunately, it is," Mark said wiping his eyes. "He died last year."

"I'm sorry."

"Yeah, added to the fact that I made him suffer so much I practically killed him. Now do you understand why I drink?"

Jacob looked to the ground. "Mark, I know you have had your tragedies in the past and its hard to forget, but drinking it away isn't the answer. You can't live your life relying on that bottle. I swear that as your friend and a minister I am going to do everything I can to help you to put down the bottle and replace it with the living water of Jesus Christ."

Mark stared in awe for a moment. There was power in Jacob's words. After their fight he had the feeling they might end up being best friends. He was finding his feeling to be true. This man cared about him and genuinely wanted to help. Mark had never had a friend like that. For the moment, he put the bottle back in his bag.

"Thanks, buddy."

"Here," Jacob said handing his Bible to Mark. "Try reading a little. I know a lot of it is hard to understand; even I don't get all of it, but just try. I recommend the book of Daniel. It was the first book of the Bible I ever read. You'll find a lot of good things in it. If you have any questions just ask me."

"Well, I'll give it a shot."

Jacob looked forward down the path.

How far away are we from the next town?"

"Takkar? Not too far. We should be there in half an hour. Have you ever been there before?"

"No, I've never gone that far east."

"Let me warn you ahead of time, it's not a pretty place. You know that place Sodom and Gomorrah?"

"Yeah."

"It's that place made over. There are drunks and prostitutes at every corner. Watch your back, too. These people won't think twice about cutting your throat and taking your money."

Jacob felt the need to pray for the strength to get out of this place alive.

"Come on, Jacob, let's go find our next partner."

XX

Jacob could tell before he walked through the gates that this wasn't going to be a pleasant trip. He never questioned God's methods, but could he really find someone to fight for God here?

"I guess asking if there is a church here would be a stupid question."

"Ha! You've got that right. I don't think the word Church is in this place's vocabulary."

"How did this place get so bad?"

"Well, you might say this is a reject town. Anyone who has ever been a troublemaker, a thief or even a murderer, you'll most likely find them here. Most of the people were once citizens of other towns, but they were banned because they were so dangerous."

"So, it's one big party huh?"

"Yeah, one big DANGEROUS party."

"You said you have been here a couple of times. What could possibly be here that you need?"

"Well, Jacob, as we determined before, I'm not an in-church-every-Sunday kind of guy. This is a good place to meet women."

"But aren't most of the women here prostitutes and ummm…."

"I'll say it for you. Cheap sluts?"

"Well…Yeah."

"Of course, why do you think I wanted to meet them. When I left home I was a fourteen year old with raging hormones, do the math."

"Haven't you ever wanted a meaningful relationship?"

"I've never been the kind of guy to be tied down by one woman. I tried it once. It lasted three months and the tramp broke my heart. I prefer to be the one doing the heart-breaking. Besides, even if I did have someone I wanted to marry, you don't get many girls looking for a raging alcoholic husband. How about you? Have you had any sweethearts?"

"Once. At one time I was engaged."

"Whoa, what happened?"

"It, like your relationship, ended in heartbreak."

"Man! Even you guys have trouble with women and you've got the big guy in your corner."

"I assure you, Mark. We don't get special attention."

"Anyway, it's not just the women. This place is also a black market of sorts. Sometimes you can find hard to find items at reasonable prices."

"Stolen?"

"Jacob! You make it sound so ugly. Tell me one line in the Bible that speaks against stealing."

"Thou shalt not steal."

"Oh? Is that one of them? Darn, that blows my argument out of the water."

"Mark, do you have any non-sinful reasons for coming to this place?"

"Does coming here with you count?"

"No."

"Then I've got nothing."

"That's what I thought."

Jacob looked around in every direction. "How are we going to get started trying to find a fighter?"

"Well, finding a fighter isn't hard. Finding the right fighter is the challenge. But don't worry; I know a guy who keeps tabs on everything that goes on in this place. Maybe he'll know something. It's a start anyway."

"Where does he live?"

"Oh, down this deep dark alley where anyone or anything could be hiding. After you."

"Why after me?"

"Because you're the one with the crucifix."

The alley wasn't quite as bad as he thought it would be, but it still left much to be desired. There weren't large knife wielding maniacs trying to rob them, but along the way they saw plenty of unhappiness. There was a man asleep beside the garbage cans clutching a bottle like a teddy bear, a small community of rats, and a woman kissing a man pressed against the wall, which he assumed was leading to much more.

This was more than Jacob was accustomed to. He had seen some pretty bad stuff, but for the most part he had always been in good Christian surroundings and rarely heard a foul word.

"Well, here we are," Mark said with his hands on his hips. "This is where my buddy stays."

"Its…charming."

"Go ahead and say it, it's a dump. Kain has never been much of a housekeeper. Wait until you see the inside." Mark knocked on the door.

"Come in," a voice lazily called out.

Mark pushed the door open. It wouldn't give at first for boxes blocking the entrance. There was paper strewn everywhere and with every step, a cloud of dust arose. In the far corner of the room, sat a man with his feet propped up on a desk. He was bald with a black goatee.

"Mark! Long time no see."

"How's it going, Kain?"

"Oh, same as always. The town is a living hell, this place is still a dump, and I still know every time someone sneezes. What about you? Still breaking the heart of every girl in town and hitting the hard stuff?"

"Uhhh, well…"

"Ah! What am I saying? Of course you are! You're Mark Raven, lady killer slash drunk man!"

Mark looked uneasily over at Jacob who only stared blankly ahead. Kain wasn't exactly helping his reputation.

"So, what's kept you away for so long? Its been close to a year since I saw you. Have you lost interest in our quaint little town."

"No, I just haven't had much business here."

"But you're here now and I know exactly why."

"You do?"

"You bet I do."

"There is this great bootlegged liquor this guy has in front of the inn."

"Kain?"

"This stuff will get you drunk in one sip, of course it might take two with you."

"Kain?"

"No, wait, that's not it. The old dog is lonely. Your old friend Travis just hired two new girls and good lord their bodies are…"

"Kain!" Mark shouted massaging his temples.

"Is that not it either? Well, I give up. Why are you here?"

"Kain, I would like you to meet my friend Jacob."

"A pleasure to meet you, Jacob. What are you hanging around with this bum for?"

"Well, that's a complicated story," Jacob replied.

"You see, Jacob here is a minister and…"

"Oh, my God, Mark! You kidnapped a preacher?! Now, I knew you weren't perfect, but this is low for you."

"I didn't kidnap him, you idiot! RRRR! Kain, I am this close to hitting you in the head with a blunt object, so can you shut up and listen for five minutes?"

"So, what's his story?"

"Kain, what I'm about to tell you is going to sound weird, but it's the God honest truth. The devil is taking over the world."

Kain looked at him wide-eyed and blinking.

"Mark, I could have sworn you were sober."

"I'm afraid I am, Kain. I know this sounds crazy and I wouldn't believe it myself if I hadn't fought a walking piece of scrap metal last night."

He stared at Mark a little longer, squinting his eyes. "Are you serious?"

"Yes, but it's a long story, so I'll let Jacob tell you."

"Jacob, are you sure this guy hasn't been to the bar?"

"I wish it were only a story, but it's not. I'm formerly from a town to the northwest. The town no longer exists because of a creature called the hooded demon. God has chosen me to fight this thing. I don't know if you're a religious man, but the world is in serious trouble."

Kain looked on intently as Jacob continued.

"Have you seen the sinful acts being done all around?"

"Only every time I leave my house."

"Well, it's gotten so bad that Satan wants it all for himself. He wants a world where religion doesn't exist and there is sin as far as the eye can see. In other words he wants the world to be just like this town."

"Man, that is a disturbing thought."

"Yes, it is, and it's up to us to stop it."

"So, what can I do to help?"

"We need your gift of gossip," Mark cut in. "Jacob was told he would find three fighters in three towns to help him. He can't do it alone. So, do you know any good fighters in the area? Preferably one that doesn't drink, swear, have sex, and who says their prayers every day?"

"Do they need wings and a halo, too?"

"Can you get someone like that?"

"Let me think for a second. I might know someone for you."

"Who is he?"

"We call him Rock. He has a face carved out of stone. I don't think I've ever seen the guy smile. He's the strong and silent type. Frankly he scares me. Now, I don't know about his personal life, but I hear he's a deadly fighter. If you can get a hold of him, then he might be who you're looking for."

"Where can we find him?" Jacob asked.

"You can usually find him somewhere near the town gates staring at God knows what."

"Well, Jacob, do you think we should recruit him?"

"It's a better lead than we had."

"Well, there is one other person," Kain said as it came to mind. "She may be more down your alley."

"Huh?"

"A little lady by the name of Marci."

"A girl?" Mark asked.

"Don't let her gender fool you. You see when she was young she watched some bandits kill her father and rape her mother before killing her, too. It messed her up pretty bad. She learned how to use a sword and hunted those same bandits down. She caught them in a bar in some town and from what I've heard, it got ugly. Her shoulder got cut, but none of the five were left in one piece when it was over."

"Wow, she must be good."

"Yeah, and from that day on she swore that no criminal would go unpunished."

This sounded good to Jacob. “I think we should see her Mark.”

“It’s your call, buddy. She does seem a little more of the demon-hunting kind doesn’t she?”

“Do you know where we can find her?” Jacob asked.

“She doesn’t get out too much, so you might want to try the inn.”

“Thank you. You have been a lot of help.”

“You’re welcome.”

“We’ll go straight to the inn, I know right where it is,” Mark said.

“I’m still not sure I believe your story, but good luck anyway. Ha. I never saw you as the type to be fighting for God. It must be hard for him to find good help these days.”

“Shut up!”

“So, do you think this girl is who we’re looking for, Jacob?”

“Let’s hope so. From the way Kain described her she seems like a decent girl willing to fight for a good cause.”

“Yeah, and I can’t think of a better cause than saving the world.”

“Well, in any case we have to find her first. How far are we from the inn? Haven’t we been through this alley three times already?”

“No, they all just look this crappy. We’re not far now, It should just be around the corner from the bar up here.” As they walked on, they saw two men with a woman down on the ground.

“Ugh!” Mark grunted. “Can’t these people get a room? Just close your eyes as we go by.”

“No, wait, Mark. That girl isn’t even conscious.”

“Those creeps! Even I don’t take advantage of drunk women.”

Jacob was half-right. The girl was barely conscious and moaning under her breath. With what little strength she had she tried to push them away. One of them held her down while the other one reached up her skirt.

Jacob rarely got enraged, but this sight was enough to do it. Taking aim he sent an arrow flying at the one reaching his hands where they didn't belong and missed his ear by only a hair.

"Whoa. Were you aiming at him?"

"If I had been aiming for him he would be dead."

"What the hell?!" the man shouted jumping to his feet.

He looked to Mark and Jacob giving him the devil's eyes.

"Are you two looking for a beating?! Mind your own business and walk away."

They looked at each other and stayed planted.

"Are you two hard of hearing?" the second one chimed in. "He said walk away or get your ass beat. Bottom line."

"Shut your mouth," Mark snapped. "Leave the girl alone or you're the one getting beat down."

"That's cute," number two giggled. "Boy, do you have any clue how many men we've killed for less than what you're doing? Last chance," he said pulling out a dagger. "Or I cut you open like a feed sack."

Mark pulled out his sword. "Well, look at that. Mine's bigger."

The two goons gave each other an uneasy look.

"Why are you trying to save her, anyway?" number one asked trying to plead his case. "Don't you know who she is? She's a local whore. Everyone has had a night with her."

"It was Jesus who said 'Let he who is without sin cast the first stone,' and from the looks of you, you would be struck down if you made that claim."

"I don't care what Jesus said! We play by our own rules and nobody tells us otherwise."

Mark chuckled. "A local whore, huh? You guys are pretty pathetic. You have to get a whore drunk to sleep with her. Ha! That's bad."

"You've got a smart mouth!" number two snapped. "But, you're right. She did turn us down and if the biggest slut around turns you down, what does that do for our reputation?"

"Well, bless your poor little perverted heart. I know about reputations and even some of the scummiest guys have no respect for rapists."

"Who says we raped her? As far as anyone will know she had too much to drink and did something naughty."

"You jackass! Well, since we're obviously better equipped

than you are, why don't you just walk away?" he said mocking them.

"Tell ya what. Let's settle this like men," number one proposed. "Why don't we drop all of our weapons and settle this with our fists."

"I don't fight unless it's necessary," Jacob answered.

"What? He doesn't fight and he's quoting Jesus? I think we have ourselves a holy man Colt!"

"You mean a wussy man, don't ya, Nick?"

"He's a better man than you two could be if you bathed in Holy water. He may not fight, but I will. Bring it on, big man."

They both began advancing on Mark.

"Two against one hardly seems like a fair fight," Jacob added.

"Hey, if you don't wanna fight that's his problem."

Jacob decided that whether they liked it or not, this was going to be fair. He shot Nick in the foot.

"ARRRRGH! Oh you stupid…"

"Hey!" Colt cried. "I thought you guys never hurt anyone!"

"I'll ask forgiveness in my prayers tonight."

"Ha! That's showing them Jacob."

"Proceed."

That uneasy look came back over Colt's face.

"What? Afraid of even odds?" Mark asked.

"I think it's time I shut your mouth for good. After this, you'll think twice before sticking your nose where it doesn't belong again. Then after I get done with you I'm going to cut your sermon spouting tongue out, holy man!"

Mark took his fighting stance. Colt walked toward him cockily without a fist raised. He left himself wide open for Mark to jab him in the nose. He went to the ground clutching it with both hands.

"Come on, Colt! What are you doing?" Nick yelled still clutching his foot.

"Oh, please have mercy on me. You are hurting me so bad. I regret ever crossing your path of greatness," Mark said mocking him.

It was an ugly sight as Colt took his hands away from his face. Mark apparently had a mean right jab. His nose was bloody, swollen and obviously broken.

"Grrrr! You're dead pig!" He jumped up and tackled Mark to

the ground. He began punching him in the side of his head repeatedly. He managed to create a small gash above his left eye.

"Get off me!"

Using his feet he catapulted him back and to the ground. He landed with a thud created a cloud of dust. He was stubborn and not opposed to fighting dirty. He clung to Mark's leg and began biting away.

"Gaaaah! You dog!"

With his free leg he began kneeing him in the face. With each blow his eye swelled up more and more. He finally let go and fell to the ground again. He was down, but not quite out.

"Give it up." Mark said.

Colt stood back up finally taking a fighting pose.

"I underestimated you." Colt said out of breath.

"What was your first clue? Mark asked.

"No more Mr. Nice guy. You're going down."

He picked up a hand full of dirt and threw it in Mark's eyes. While Mark was blinded he got three right hooks in and Mark went to the ground.

Jacob couldn't stand watching this creep fight dirty. He was tempted to disable him as he had his partner, but he restrained himself and watched on. Mark rolled on the ground rubbing dirt out of his eyes. Every second he was down was an opportunity for Colt to strike. He kicked him in the face busting his lip.

"Little boy! I told you to walk away, but you had to mess with the big dogs didn't you? Now, was it worth defending the honor of some stupid whore?"

Picking Mark up by the hair he began straight punching him in the jaw with everything he had. More streams of blood came from his mouth.

"Now little boy, let this be a lesson to you."

He drew back hoping to end it with one last blow. Unfortunately for him Mark took that moment to throw the rulebook away as well. It even pained Jacob to watch as Mark uppercut him in the groin.

He froze and didn't make a sound. Wheezing, he went to his knees. It was Mark who then finished *him* off in one punch straight to the jaw sending him down for the count.

"Looks like I win, Jackass!"

"Are you okay, Mark? Do you need a doctor?"

"Nah, I've been worse off than this. Thanks for the thought, though. Anyway, let's get the girl somewhere safe."

"I agree."

Behind him, Colt grabbed a spare blade from the side of his boot. "Die you bastard!"

He charged Mark before he could turn and the next few seconds happened in slow motion. Jacob had one chance to save Mark. Without thinking he pulled his crossbow and shot Colt in the wrist. It didn't kill him, but it stopped him.

"AHHHHHGH!" he screamed clutching his arm in shock. He fell to the ground and kicked like a child having a tantrum.

"Jacob! Look out!"

Jacob had forgotten about the other goon who had brought out his own weapon and limped over to Jacob. Jacob unsheathed his sword and swung blindly behind him. He heard a *cling* followed by a scream. Afraid of what he had done, he turned to see the man on the ground clutching his hand. Jacob had knocked the knife away and taken off the tips of his fingers. Both men were now crying and whimpering.

"Neither one of you had to get hurt!" Jacob yelled.

"Don't bother, Jacob. They knew what they were doing."

They turned their attention back to the girl.

"Can you pick her up, Jacob? I don't think she's going to be walking."

"Yeah, I'll carry her." As he kneeled down, he stopped and stared at her face. This was the first time he had actually seen it. From the way the two goons described her, he expected some trashy-looking girl. What he saw was the exact opposite. This young woman wasn't just mildly attractive, she was the definition of beauty. He wondered if she was actually this beautiful, or if it was just him. Mark noticed him looking hard at her.

"What are ya staring at, buddy?" He kneeled down with him. "Whoa. She's a looker. Hey, I know what's going on. You put those naughty thoughts out of your head."

Apparently Mark found her attractive, but not to the extent that Jacob did. In her blacked-out state she was like sleeping beauty. She wore a brown coat over a short cut blouse that complimented her tanned and copious cleavage. Her body wasn't what stood out the most, though. Her face had the best features by far. Her lips and nose were small and her eyes had a mysterious look about them. Her hair was blonde and cut short just below her ears making her look more like a little girl than a young woman.

Could this girl be a local whore? Jacob found himself praying that the things those men said about her weren't true, but by the way she dressed, it likely was.

Jacob cleared his head and lifted her up into his arms. She whimpered like a puppy and wrapped her arms around his neck, then rested her head on his chest. All of a sudden, the only thing Jacob wanted to do was protect her from harm.

"Awww, she's a sleepy drunk," Mark said like an adoring Mother. "Come on, Jacob, let's get her to the inn."

"Yeah, she's been through a lot." He looked up at the sky, which had turned unusually dark for that time of day. Some would see it as clouds rolling in. Jacob saw it as much more. "Let's hurry up and find this Marci. I have a feeling something bad is about to happen."

As they walked into the inn, an older man with grey in his mustache stood behind the counter. He was writing on a piece of paper and it took him a few seconds to realize they were standing there.

"Oh, I'm sorry. Can I help you guys?" He looked at the girl in Jacob's arms. "Does she need a doctor?"

"Nah, this little lady just had too much to drink," Mark said. "We were wondering if you might have somewhere she could sleep it off?"

"We'll pay of course," Jacob added.

The stranger reached to take the girl from his arms. "I think we can find a place for her. I'm sure she'll appreciate you guys bringing her."

"Thank you," Jacob said.

"No problem."

"Perhaps you can help us with something. Do you have a young woman staying with you by the name of Marci?"

"Yeah, that's her sitting over there," he said pointing to a table in the corner. Marci had heard her name mentioned and turned her head toward them. They walked over as the innkeeper took the girl upstairs.

"Can I help you guys?"

She was what you might call a plain girl; not homely, merely simple looking. She had long red hair down her back and small freckles on her face. She was properly covered up with a robe skirt combination and she had a thin white bandana tied across her head. Jacob and Mark looked at each other, not knowing how to start the conversation. It was Jacob that started things off.

"Marci, we were told that you are a fighter."

"Yes, I do fight, but only for the right reasons. I do not fight for money, or beat people up for it either, if that is what you're wanting."

"No, it's nothing like that. This is kind of hard to explain."

"Let me take a shot at it, Jacob. Let us introduce ourselves. I'm Mark Raven, a fighter from Bruton. This is Jacob Cross, a preacher from a small town to the west."

Her eyes widened and she became more interested in them. "You are a man of God?"

"Yes."

"I am so sorry. I meant no disrespect by what I said before." She kneeled down and kissed his hand. He had never been more uncomfortable in his life.

"That's really not necessary, Marci. I know you meant no disrespect. Please sit down."

"Thank you. Please, sir, tell me what you need. I'll do whatever I can to help you."

"Tell me, Marci, are you a religious woman?" He already knew the answer to that question, but wanted to find out the extent of her beliefs.

"Oh, yes, sir. I've been taught the scriptures since I was a young girl. I pray to God every day and night. I never drink or take part in sins of the flesh. I am a virgin."

"Wow! Kain is good. But, didn't he say something about wings and a halo?"

Marci looked at Mark confused, unfamiliar with his odd sense of humor.

"The reason I ask is that our need concerns religion," Jacob said softly, asking with his eyes for Mark to give it a rest.

"What do you mean?"

"Since you believe in God, then you must also believe in Satan and hell?"

"Certainly."

"This is going to be hard to believe, but I promise it's true. Mark has witnessed this as well." Mark nodded. "A great evil has been unleashed on this world. Satan wishes to make it his own. All of the sin and evil in the world today has motivated him to take it all for himself."

Marci looked as if she believed every word without question.

"He has sent one of his servants to cause as much pain and misery as he can. I have been chosen to fight this demon and so has Mark. We're supposed to find two more people to fight with us and we believe the next one is you."

"So, how much of this do you believe?" Mark asked.

"Every single word. Jacob, I've known for a while by the way the winds have changed that something horrible was going to happen. I don't feel worthy to fight with you, but I would be honored. Together we will show Satan that this world belongs to God and God alone. When do we start?"

Jacob listened closely and heard the familiar silence outside. He had been through this once before. Suddenly an enormous clap of thunder interrupted the quiet. All three of them nearly jumped out of their skins.

"It may be sooner than you think," Jacob said in almost a whisper.

"What's going on?"

"I don't know, Mark, but we're about to find out."

Running outside they saw that the sky had turned black as midnight. The sky lit up every few seconds with lightning, but there wasn't a drop of rain. All over town, the people shouted with alarm.

"What's going on? Is it a storm?" a voice from the street called out. More calls erupted until finally, they heard a shout that was their cue to fight. It began as screams of terror.

"What are those things?! They're going to kill us! We have to fight!"

"Come on!" Jacob said motioning for them to follow.

It wasn't difficult to find the center of the commotion. When they arrived near the town entrance, everyone was pale and looking on in terror.

Jacob followed the direction of their stares and at the town gate was none other than the hooded demon as he had been in Bruton. The monster sneered and growled at everyone in his path.

He must have smelled Jacob; as soon as he came into view, it glared straight at him, shining its canines. The aching in Jacob's head began again so he knew the demon was about to speak.

"Jacob Cross! I promised that I would feed on your flesh and now I will fulfill that promise! Behold! My children of darkness! They will do as you threatened me and bring your head as a trophy! You will regret ever crossing my bloody path! Then after you and your friends suffer a slow and agonizing death, the world will know my master Lucifer as the one and only God!"

Forced to his knees, Jacob clutched his head. He felt powerless and entranced until he heard words of Satan being the only God.

"NOOOOOOO! Spawn of hell! You dare speak of your master as God?! Know this. Your master is a whimpering dog in the sight of Jehovah! Your master doesn't have the power in his body or in all of hell that God has in one finger! You have stepped out of line and come beyond your borders! We will be the ones that put you in your place as the swine that live in the depths of the world and your master, the King of all swine, will know our mighty sting! Demon be gone! You have no power over us! We will send you back to the fiery pits of damnation where you belong!"

Mark and Marci stared in awe at Jacob as the fiery spirit of God radiated from him.

"Insolent fool! I will tear off your hide and wear it as a garment! I have absolute power over you! Die!"

In his fury, Jacob had failed to notice the small army of minions around the demon. Thcsc appeared to be twice as dangerous as the ones he had faced before. They hunched down and waited for their signal to attack. They were miniature versions of the hooded demon, minus the hood and their most dangerous quality by far was that in place of arms they had glimmering blades.

"Jacob? These things don't look as wimpy as you described them."

"These aren't what I fought before, Mark. These are upgraded minions, probably higher-ranked."

"***Go, my children! Bring me the head of the preacher!***"

"This is it Marci," Mark said. "All we can do now is fight." She nodded and raised her sword.

The demons charged in like wild animals and they seemed to be smarter than their low-class counterparts. Not all of them came straight at them; some branched off to the left and right to sneak up behind their prey.

Thankfully these people were more prepared than the people of Bruton. There was hardly a person who walked down the streets without a weapon of some kind. Jacob looked to see chains, knives, swords, and bows and arrows. At least these people had a fighting chance.

Jacob took long range action as they charged them. He was going to be a sniper in the night until they were close enough to battle with melee weaponry. He took aim and with every shot he got a one hit kill. One fell with an arrow through its left eye, another with a gut shot. One got dangerously close, but Jacob took it out with an arrow through the throat. The things were fast. He only managed to kill six or seven before they were forced to fight at close range.

"Be careful!" he yelled to Mark and Marci.

They slashed with furious blows left right and overhead. Jacob blocked each blow until he found an opening to run them through. After disemboweling a couple, he slashed one's head and learned they came off as easy as the others had. One of creatures managed to sneak up and slash his side.

"Ah!"

He turned to see a snarling face hissing and growling. Now that he was hurt, it smelled blood and was going in for the kill. It swung violently with both blades, knocking Jacob to the ground. Pinned down, the best he could do to block its blades. It pushed harder and harder until his own blade was inches from his throat. Thinking fast, he saw the carcass of one of the dead ones. He grabbed its arm and used it to run through his attacker's throat, spraying blood everywhere. It made a hissing gargling sound before falling down dead.

Jacob looked behind him to see how Mark and Marci were faring. He had told them to be careful, but they were doing better than he was. Neither of them had a scratch on them and they seemed to be in a competition to see who could butcher the most. There was a literal pile under each of them. Marci fought with a serious look on her face. Mark grinned uncontrollably. He seemed to take pleasure in destroying these things.

Looking past them, the townspeople weren't doing so well. Bodies lay all over the streets. A few were doing well, but the most part were being slaughtered.

He saw one man getting double-teamed and his left arm slashed off. Another was beheaded before he could lift his sword in defense. Whoever wasn't dead was rolling on the ground in agony. He couldn't stand seeing this, but he was doing all he could to protect them.

In the few seconds he had turned away, three of the creatures had snuck up on him. All he could do was block each attack that came. If all three of them attacked at the same time he was a dead man. Jacob pulled out his crossbow, but it was quickly knocked away from him.

Mark saw the situation he was in. "Hang in there, buddy! I'll be there in a second!"

True to his word, after finishing off one last blade arm, he was right there by Jacob's side.

"Hey! Three on one isn't very fair is it boys?" Mark slit one's throat to make it two on two. Now that it was even, the creatures were on the defensive. Mark and Jacob were the ones charging like animals.

The one on Jacob raised its right limb. Since the blade only went to where the elbow would be, he slashed it off. It hissed and squealed before he ran his sword through its heart. Mark, meanwhile, hacked his opponent to death.

"Thanks, Mark."

"No problem, but how many more of these things are there?"

"I don't know, but if the town's people keep dying, it's just going to be us versus them."

"I don't like those odds."

"Me neither. Let's just take out as many of them as we can before anyone else gets hurt."

"Got it."

They stayed side-by-side working as a team, hacking off limbs and heads alike. They both had their own style; Jacob was partial decapitating the beasts while Mark fancied simply running them through.

Before they knew it the number of blade arms was getting comfortably low. There were only about ten left that they could see, though some might still be lurking in the shadows. All of them seemed to be trying to kill a group of townsmen. They got their attention and led them in different directions to try and even things out. Two of them pursued Mark and three Jacob.

For once, the beings were moving slowly and stalking their prey. They hunched low, ready to strike at any moment. Jacob glanced behind him and caught sight of his crossbow. It appeared undamaged.

He slowly paced backwards and coaxed them to follow. When he was in reach, he knelt down with one hand behind his back. Drawing the weapon, he put an arrow between one of the creature's eyes. While the other two looked in surprise, he sheathed his sword, reloaded, and put another through one's heart. The last one charged in with both blades raised in the air. Jacob dropped to his knees, drew his sword, and spilled its insides.

Mark led his stalkers in different directions. He was purposely trying to put himself between them. As he had hoped, they charged at him at the same time. At the last second, he jumped out of the way, letting them impale themselves and they stood there like conjoined twins. Taking a page out of Jacob's book, he took their heads off.

The more skilled fighters of the town had managed to team up and stab, beat, or strangle the remaining enemies to death. Seeing that there were no more, Mark and Jacob dropped to the ground to catch their breath.

"Well, we did it again, buddy," Mark said

"Yes, we did. Nothing can stop us when we work as a team."

"Yeah, I just hope these things don't get any harder. I thought the armored freak was a challenge, but good God! Every time I turned around, I nearly had a pointy object crammed down my throat."

"It doesn't matter, Mark. There's nothing the enemy can throw at us that we can't handle."

"Yeah, three down and one to go." Mark looked around. "Hey, where's Marci? Hey, Marci! Let's go celebrate!"

Jacob went pale. "Mark…look behind you."

"Huh?...Oh, my God." Marci lay on the ground with one of the creature's blades plunged through her stomach.

"No," Jacob whispered and walked over to her body. She was gone. Mark shadowed above him with his fists clenched together.

"God…darn it!" he said, restraining himself. "She was a good girl!"

"I know, Mark. She fought her best."

"I know, I was right there beside her! She had a major body count going. Why is it that all the good ones get taken? Those jackasses over there wouldn't spit on you if you were on fire, yet they aren't even scratched!"

"There's nothing I can say, Mark. There's a purpose to everything that happens." Jacob closed her eyes and rested her head back on the ground. There was still faint signs of life in the blade arm that got her. It made light groaning sounds. In a fit of rage Mark stomped its skull in.

"Die, you filthy beast!" Mark looked back toward the gate breathing heavily. The hooded demon stood there staring ominously at them.

"You bastard! She was an innocent girl! You'll pay for her death! Just keep sending your little dogs! We'll slit their dirty little throats again, or maybe you're finally man enough to take us on yourself! Huh?! You're going to feed on my insides? You'll have to pry my sword from down your throat before you do! I'm not afraid of you anymore! Come face us like a man, you coward!"

The demon only sneered at him and vanished.

"Arrrgh! Come back, you spineless pig!"

"Mark," Jacob said putting a hand on his shoulder, "you'll have your chance to avenge her. Right now we have to move forward."

"Alright, but we're making sure she gets a decent burial."

"Don't worry, we will."

"Hey, if she's dead, then what about our third fighter?"

That was a good question. Jacob hadn't thought about it. "She must not have been the one." She was the perfect image of what

Jacob saw as a soldier for God, but what could he do?

"What do we do now?" Mark asked.

"I suppose we should go back to the inn and plan our next move."

"Yeah, I guess you're right. Do you think we could take a nap first?"

Jacob laughed. "That does sound nice doesn't it?""

Walking down the alley they found the dead bodies of even more creatures.

"Man, there were more of them than I thought."

"Be careful, Mark, they might not be all dead."

"Hey, do you think we should talk to that first guy Kain told us about?"

"You mean Rock?"

"Yeah, that guy."

"Well, that is the best lead we have. It can't hurt just to talk to him."

"Okay, then," Mark said. "We'll take a quick rest then look for this guy."

"Sounds like a plan."

When they walked through the door of the inn, the place was turned upside down with broken glass and papers strewn all around. For a second Jacob thought they had wandered back into Kain's house. The innkeeper was on his knees behind the counter peeking out.

In the center of the room, an attractive young woman stood among several dead blade arms, holding a wooden Bo. Jacob didn't recognize her at first because she was up and moving about. It was the same girl they had rescued and put to bed.

"Did we miss something?" Mark asked, scratching his head.

"Man! Am I glad you guys brought this little lady here!" the innkeeper said standing back up. "I thought I was a goner, but luckily she woke up and saved my rear end! I've never seen anything like it in my life. Those things didn't stand a chance. She was busting skulls left and right. One of them even tried running from her! It was like she had some kind of force backing her up."

Jacob and Mark looked at each other knowing what the other was thinking.

"The drunk chick?!" Mark exclaimed.

CHAPTER 4

"So, you're the guys who brought me in, huh? I appreciate it. Most guys would be trying to get into my pants."

"So we've noticed."

"Mark!"

"Sorry."

"I normally don't drink, but I was having an overly crappy day and the bar appealed to me. These two creeps came up to me and couldn't keep their hands to themselves. They made me a very indecent proposal and I told them to get lost. They didn't get the message and offered to buy me a drink. I'm not rich by far so I accepted. One turned into about five, then after that I blacked out. I don't know what happened after that."

Jacob looked uneasily over at Mark.

"When we found you, you were unconscious and those men were trying to rape you."

This girl seemed like the tough type, but the look on her face turned into one of anger and vulnerability.

"RRR! I can't believe I put myself in that situation. Excuse me, I have some bad dogs to castrate."

"No need, Miss. We took care of it."

"Yeah, the last time we saw them they were whimpering on the ground like wounded animals."

"Hmmm, well not only do you give me a place to stay, but you defend my honor as well. My heroes."

She gave Jacob a seductive look and grabbed the collar of his shirt. She had been gorgeous asleep, but now she was a walking symbol of beauty.

"I'll have to thank you later in private," she said with her lips inches from his.

"Hey, I helped too," Mark said like a jealous kid.

"What's your name?" she asked.

"Jacob… Jacob Cross." He could barely speak from all of the awkwardness.

"You're cute, Jacob. You know there's nothing like a night of hot passionate sex. Don't you agree?"

"*What happened to lead me not into temptation?"* he thought.

"Oh! Oh! Can I tell her?" Mark said like a school boy who had to go to the bathroom. "I would like you to meet *Reverend* Jacob Cross."

"Reverend? Oh, my God, I just came on to a preacher. That's it. I'm going to hell. Uhh, sorry. Is this the part where I say hail Mary's or something?"

"That's a priest."

"Oh, I'll say my prayers before I go to bed. Well, I'll be going since I've officially made an ass out of myself."

"No. wait. Ahh!" He went to his knees clutching his side.

"Jacob, you're hurt!" Mark said seeing about him.

"No, I'll be fine."

The girl kneeled down with him.

"Let me see."

He took his hand away from the wound.

"Yeesh. That's pretty deep. You're going to need that sewn up."

Jacob's eyes widened. "No way! I've never had stitches and I don't plan to."

"It's okay, Jacob," she said. "All you have to do is drink a bunch of whiskey and...oh, I forgot."

"I'll get the doctor," the innkeeper offered.

"Thank you. Okay, let's get you up to my room," she said helping him up.

"What's your name?" Jacob asked.

"Sarah Mist."

"I'm Mark, by the way," He said helping her get Jacob up the stairs.

"I need to talk to you about something," Jacob said out of breath.

"Okay, but it can wait until after the doctor takes a look at you. Then we'll talk."

When they reached the room, they laid him down on the bed.

"There we go," Mark said. "You'll be all patched up in no time."

Sarah looked Jacob over carefully. "How old are you Jacob?"

"Twenty-three."

"You're the same age as me. How did you become a preacher so young? I thought they were all only grey-haired old men that walked around telling people they were going to hell if they breathed wrong."

Jacob grinned. "That's a bit of a stereotype. I've just always been a faithful person and got called to preach at an early age. That's part of the reason I need to talk to you. Well, that and the creatures you just fought."

"What were those things, anyway? I've never seen anything like them in my life."

"Do you feel like hearing a long and weird story?" Mark asked.

"I don't guess I have anything better to do."

"Should I start or you?" Mark asked.

"I guess I will. Tell me, Sarah, are you a religious woman?"

"Ahhhh, religion isn't exactly my thing as you can tell by my earlier proposal. I'm kind of a slut. I'll be the first to admit it."

"Well, those creatures you fought were demons."

"You mean those things that serve the devil? I never really believed in any of that stuff, but I guess there aren't many other explanations. Wow, so there really is a God and a heaven? A Satan and a hell?"

"Yes, it's all real."

"I always thought it was all just stories made up to keep little girls and boys from misbehaving. What does this all have to do with me?"

"Satan wants to take this world for himself. He has sent this hooded demon to kill anyone who stands in his way. It has tremendous power and it's what sent those things. Mark and I have been chosen to fight it and I believe you have, too."

"Me?! Hold on a minute. I'm only a pretty face that's pretty good with a stick. I'm not cut out to fight demons."

"You already have."

"Well…yeah. But, why would your boss choose me? I know I've done plenty of stuff that book of yours says not to do."

"I don't know why you have been chosen, Sarah. God has a purpose for everything."

Mark stepped in. "I know how you feel, Sarah. I know we haven't known each other long, but I'm far from perfect myself. I don't have a clue why God would want me, but when Jacob and I fight together, it just feels right."

Sarah thought for a moment. "Can I really help?"

"I think you can."

"Okay, I'll do it, but I don't want you quoting scriptures at me every step of the way. Don't think for a minute that I'm just going to turn into a nice dress-wearing churchgoer."

"Agreed."

"Did someone call a doctor?" A tall lanky man with a greyish beard said walking in.

"He's all yours," Mark said pointing at Jacob.

"Let's take a look. Oh, yes, that is a nasty wound. We had better disinfect that."

Before Jacob could so much as blink, the doctor pressed some liquid to a cloth and put it to his side. "Gaaaah! What is that stuff?!"

"Heh, did I forget to mention this might burn?"

"You might have forgotten that detail, yes."

"This might burn a little."

Jacob's nights were getting remarkably worse. Now he was cut and left with a smart aleck doctor.

"Now that that's done, let's get some sutures in you."

"It'll be okay." Sarah said by his side.

"Rrrrrr. I feel like I've been beat in the head with a stick." Jacob said standing outside of the inn. His side hurt, he had a stress-induced headache, and he felt like he was going to vomit.

"You really should be resting you know," Mark said holding him steady. "Are you sure you don't want to take the innkeeper up on his offer? A free room and meal is pretty tempting."

"Yes, I'm sure. I feel like putting as much distance between me and this town I can."

"I honestly can't blame you for that," Sarah agreed. "This place is like the trashcan of society."

"How do you live here anyway?"

"I just got used to it over the years."

Getting used to that place was a disturbing thought and it made Jacob want to leave twice as bad.

"So, what's the plan Jacob?" Mark asked.

"Go pick up a few camping supplies and food. We'll travel forward a couple of hours then set up camp."

"Where are we going anyway?" Sarah asked.

"One time, about a year ago, I held a revival and I sent word to towns all around telling them they were invited. We got a handful of people from every town, but one entire town came. I asked them where they were from and they said it was a town north of here. I had never heard of it, but they weren't surprised. They said they mainly kept to themselves and tried to live peaceful lives. Perhaps they may be able to help us."

Sarah and Mark looked at each other.

"It sounds like we won't be having any fun for a while," Sarah said with a smirk.

"I guess not."

"No bars," Sarah said.

"Yeah, and no men with raging hormones to seduce," Mark said. They looked back at Jacob giving them a death stare.

"Uhhh, not that we need any of that stuff, right, Sarah?"

"Right, Mark."

Jacob sighed. "Just get the stuff," he said shaking his head and walking away.

The cool night air caused Jacob's head and stomach troubles to fade away. Sarah and Mark set up camp and chit chatted while he rested under the stars. This scenario was one hundred percent better than the den of iniquity they had just left. The only thing that troubled him was the thought that if the hooded demon attacked now, they were two miles away from anywhere.

They would have to take turns keeping watch, and he hoped they chose him last because he was desperate for some rest. With the pattern his nights were taking as of late, he hesitated to think what tomorrow might bring. He thought of his cozy little bed in his cozy little house back in his former village. It wasn't the fanciest place in the world, but it was home. He also had his resting chair where he could relax and read his bible. He was homesick for a place that no longer existed.

This was all before his dreams of rotting houses and bladed demons that tried to tear him to pieces. He was saddened by the thought of never sleeping there again, then he began to think of the people. They were all important to him and he tried to help them in every way he knew how. The older people ridiculed him, but they never really mistreated him. The children were hellions, but in the end he thought he had gotten through to them. Even though he was close to these people, he had always felt distant and out of place somehow. He had felt that way anywhere he ever lived. He could honestly say he never really knew what a true friend was. The closest thing he had ever had to a friend was Mark. He wasn't sure about Sarah, yet. He knew she wanted to be *really* good friends with him, but that wasn't the kind of friend he needed.

He watched as the two of them laid down blankets and laughed with every step they took. He wondered just as he did with other people just when it was they walked down the wrong path.

He knew with Mark it was the guilt over his Father that drove him to pick up the bottle. But, when was it that the little girl in Sarah die? She must still live somewhere deep down. What was it that made her take that next step with a man and never stop? Was it the curiosity of a young woman? Did her friends pressure her? What was it that made her lose all of her self-respect? He wanted to know so much more about her than he did.

"Well, that does it," Mark said wiping his hands. "Who's ready to turn in?"

"Well," Jacob said, "I was thinking. Weird things have been assaulting us left and right. If something comes while we're asleep we'll be slaughtered."

"You bring up a good point."

"I'll take first watch if you want me too," Jacob volunteered.

"No way," Sarah said. "You're hurt and need to rest. Mark and I can handle it, right?"

"That's right. I'll take the first hour, then you can take the next seven."

"Ha…ha."

He was glad to see that Mark and Sarah were becoming friends. "Okay, then, I'm going to lie down now."

"I'll take first watch," Sarah said walking away.

"All right," Mark said. "But wake me if you see or hear anything suspicious."

"Will do. I'll see you in two hours."

"Okay, it's a date."

"Goodnight, guys."

"Goodnight, Sarah," they said simultaneously.

Jacob crawled into his tent carefully, trying not to disturb his stitches. He said his prayers lying down opposed to on his knees for the second night in a row. He prayed for the strength to go on fighting and for protection against his enemies. Last of all, he prayed for Mark and Sarah, that they would overcome their problems and come to him. After his amen he laid his head down and went to sleep.

His rest over the next hour was limited and miserable, tossing and turning the entire time. He didn't even dream. What images he did see were like still pictures with no sound. He finally awoke with a dull ache in his side and his nausea returned. It was a hot night and even hotter inside of the tent. He was drenched with sweat as he sat up and he thought some fresh air might relax him.

The night was unusually bright when he stepped out. The moon was full and in the horizon looked only a few yards away. There were countless stars in the black sky. The air was much cooler outside than it had been in his confinement and felt incredible against his skin. If it weren't so late, it would have been a perfect night for a walk. The gentle breeze blew through the trees and the noises all around were relaxing enough to put him in a coma.

Looking around, he realized Sarah was nowhere to be found. His first thought was that something happened to her and he got worried. It took him a moment to remember that they had set up camp near a small lake. She might have gotten tired of standing in the same place and went down for a change in scenery. He decided to go look and make sure she was okay.

He walked down the small sloping hill toward the glimmering body of water. The bright blue moon reflected in the water creating an odd double universe. The wind made small ripples that disturbed the image. He looked across the lake and, as he had assumed, stood Sarah in the middle of the water.

She stood there glowing in an almost supernatural way, like a Goddess out of a legendary myth. Jacob stood watching, mesmerized by this symbol of beauty. Every move she made was majestic and awe-inspiring. She cupped her hands and picked up water and releasing it into her hair. She ran her hands through it repeatedly giving herself an odd, yet still beautiful wet hairstyle. Taking a cloth in hand she rubbed it delicately against her skin. Not once did she ever open her eyes. She breathed deeply with every stroke of the cloth, as if the water was her source of life and she was feeding on it.

Jacob couldn't take his eyes off of her. That was until he came across a detail that he had somehow missed until that point; she was totally naked. When he realized it, he jerked his head away and blushed.

"Now I know how David felt," he said under his breath. He tried to erase what he had just seen from his memory, but it was to no avail. The image stayed and he was ashamed to admit it, but part of him didn't want to forget it.

"*What is happening to me? I'm not supposed to be having these kinds of thoughts. I'm a man of God carrying out his work, and I'm standing in front of a lake lusting over a woman I'm not married to. She isn't even a Christian woman. She has admitted to being a harlot, yet I can't take my eyes off of her. She represents fornication and desecrates the act of lovemaking by performing it out of wedlock, and I'm finding myself completely attracted to her.*"

He began quoting a scripture that he had always felt was

perfect for overcoming lust. It was proverbs 7:6 through 23.

"For at the window of my house I looked through the casement and beheld among the simple ones, I discerned among the youths a young man void of understanding passing through the street near her corner and went the way to her house. In the twilight of evening, in the black and dark night. And behold there met him a woman with the attire of a harlot and subtle of heart.(She is loud and stubborn; her feet abide not in her house. Now is she without and, now in the streets, and lieth in wait at every corner. So she caught him and kissed him and with an impudent face said to him, I have peace offerings with me, this day have I paid my vows. Therefore I have come forth to meet thee and I have found thee. I have decked my bed with coverings of tapestry, with carved works, with fine linens of Egypt. I have perfumed my bed with myrrh aloes and cinnamon. Come, let us take our fill of love until morning: let us solace ourselves with love. For the good man is not at home, he is gone a long journey he hath taken a bag of money with him, and will come home at a day appointed. With her much fair speech she caused him to yield, with the flattering of lips she forced him. He goeth after her straight away as an ox goeth to the slaughter or as a fool to the correction of the stocks, til a dart strike through his liver, as a bird hasteth to the snare and knoweth not it is for his life. Hearken unto me now, oh ye children, and attend to the words of my mouth. Let not thy heart decline to her ways; go not astray in her paths. For she has cast down many wounded; yea many strong men have been slain by her. Her house is the way to hell, going down into the chambers of death."

The second he finished he heard Sarah's voice calling to him.

"Jacob? Is that you?"

He turned and saw her shielding her eyes with one arm and covering her breasts with the other.

"Yes, it's me. I…I wasn't watching you bathe."

"Well, I'm not exactly shy you know," she said walking toward him.

"I know, but I still shouldn't be looking at you...naked."

She giggled. "You know, you're cute when you're embarrassed."

That he was.

"Can you hand me my clothes?"

"Ummm, sure." He covered his eyes with one hand and held out her clothes with the other.

"Jacob, I'm over here. You're handing my clothes to a tree." She giggled once again and took her clothes from his hand. "I've never met a man like you," she said slipping into her top. "If I had been taking a bath in front of any of a hundred other guys they would be killing themselves to get a look. You're different."

"I believe there is a lot more to a woman than her body."

She looked at him with a wide-eyed grin. "Tell me again why you're not married."

"I just haven't met the right woman yet."

"If you keep that attitude up you could be married tomorrow. Okay, I'm decent. You can open your eyes now."

He uncovered his eyes, glad to see her dressed.

"Better?"

"Yes."

"Most guys, before I even tell them my name, have their hands up my skirt."

"Doesn't that bother you?"

"Not really. Over the years, I've gotten used to it. Besides, if a woman doesn't give a man what he wants then he has no use for her. Sex is what makes the world go round."

"You don't have to let men do whatever they want to you."

"I'm not that easy, but what else am I supposed to do?"

"You could wait for a man who loves and cares for you without forcing you into a sexual relationship."

She raised an eyebrow at him. "Honey, what planet are you living on? The world doesn't work that way. If I did that, I would be eighty before I had another man."

"The world isn't supposed to work that way."

"Yeah, but it does, so I have to do what the world does to keep up. It's the only way to get what you want in life."

Jacob was saddened by her view on life. He only wished she could know how much more there was to life and how much happier she could be. "Sarah?" he asked softly.

"Yes?"

"Can I ask you something?"

"Sure."

"Why are you with so many men?"

She smirked. “Because there’s no sense in setting your sights on just one. Do you really think any man out there besides you and a few other holy men want only one woman to love and care for? Men don’t think that way. They want cheap, meaningless sex with as many women as possible.”

This thought was inconceivable to Jacob.

“After a man has been with me he sets his sights on another woman, so I think the same way.”

“But doesn’t it bother you what people call you?”

“What? Slut? Whore? I don’t give a damn what other people call me, because I know I’m not the only one. There are women out there everywhere, just like me.” She laughed. “Isn’t it funny, though? If a woman is with a bunch of men, then she’s a whore, but a man can be with as many women as he wants and be respected for it. Tell me that’s fair.”

“It isn’t. In the Bible those men are called whoremongers and it doesn’t matter if it’s a man or a woman, sin is sin.”

She looked solemn and bitter. “Well, at least that book of yours got one thing right. Why are you asking me this anyway? What are you thinking? I’m just a poor lost girl drowning in sin? If only I would read the Bible and ask Jesus for help my life would turn around completely and I would find a man that loves and honors me for nothing but my mind and personality and considers lovemaking the most sacred thing in the world? I told you before, I don’t buy into that stuff and you’re not going to turn me into a sweet little church girl. Let’s change the subject.”

Jacob looked to the ground disappointed in the progress he was making.

“Anyway, what are you doing awake? I thought the doctor told you to get plenty of rest.”

“I couldn’t sleep. It’s too hot and my side is killing me. I thought the night air might relax me enough to get back to sleep.”

“Oh, so what brought you over here? Were you looking for me?”

“Actually I was. I thought something might have happened to you when I didn’t see you and I wanted to make sure you were okay.”

“Awww, you’re so sweet. Yes, I’m okay. Jacob Cross, do you have a crush on me?”

The redness came rushing back into his face. “I…I just don’t want you to get hurt.”

“You know, Jacob, I really do want to thank you for defending me against those jerks,” she said taking his hand. “No man has ever stood up for me in the past.”

She stared at him for a moment, then kissed him. At first Jacob kept his hands free. He then got caught up in the moment and embraced her. The put one hand behind her head and kissed her more deeply and passionately.

“*This is all I’ve wanted to do since I first laid eyes on her.*” He glanced at the water and saw his reflection. He saw a dirty man carrying out the lusts in his heart. He was disgusted by what he saw. This was enough to jerk him back to his senses. He pushed her away.

“No. I… I… can’t do this.”

“What’s wrong? Can’t you just ask for forgiveness when it’s over and everything will be okay?”

“It doesn’t work that way. If I did this with you, then how could I stand up and preach against it to other people?”

“Because you’re human and you have urges.”

“But the Bible teaches us to resist those urges.”

“Are you going to go through your whole life letting a book tell you what to do?!”

“That book is the meaning of life!”

“Wrong! All it is is a bunch of stupid rules keeping people from doing anything that feels good! Nobody wants to hear it and I think you’re a fool for living by it! Who in their right mind would go through their whole life without experiencing sex, drinking, or gambling? That’s what the world is, not the mumbo jumbo in that stupid rulebook! It isn’t waking up every morning, saying your prayers, and being perfect and nice to everyone.”

“We owe it to God to live for him because he blesses us every day.”

“Blesses us?! I haven’t seen a blessing in my life! God never did anything for me!!!” At that she broke down crying. “It seems selfish to me. God is up there in heaven and one day he decides to make humans and force them to worship him.”

“ He doesn’t force us.”

“Oh, gee, like there’s much of a choice. Do it or burn in hell.”

"But…"

"Just go away, Jacob! Leave me alone! I don't need you standing here judging me and telling me you can help."

"Sarah…."

"Go away!" He turned to leave and then sighed, "You're in my prayers, Sarah."

"Gee, I'm touched," she said sarcastically.

"I'll do everything in my power I can to help you."

"I don't need your help."

"No, you need God's." At that he walked away. She rolled her eyes and sat down under a tree, wrapping her arms around her knees like a pouting little girl.

When he got back to camp he was greeted by Mark standing outside of his tent.

"Mark? I didn't know you were awake."

"Well, I wasn't until the holy war by the lake woke me up."

"Oh…I'm sorry about that. I didn't mean to wake you."

"Don't worry about it. So, what was that little scene all about? Sarah seemed all happy and cheerful before I turned in."

"Yes, well as you heard, that changed dramatically."

"What happened?"

Jacob rubbed his eyes because he was starting to get drowsy. "Oh, she wanted to…thank me again, but when she kissed me I pulled away."

"Hey, maybe I should have watched instead of just listening. Let me get this straight. That voluptuous creature down there came on to you for a second time and kissed you and you pulled away from her? Are you sure you're not hiding a halo under that hat? I'll say it again, you're a better man than I am."

Jacob nodded. "She exploded when I told her that I had to resist all temptation. For some reason she's as anti-religion as they come. She claimed that God has never done anything for her and then she broke down crying. I get the feeling that she's been hurt somewhere down the line and she's blaming God for it, I just wonder what it was. I wish she would open up to me so I might have some idea how to help her."

“You may just have to leave her alone and wait until she’s comfortable talking about it. You got everything out of me pretty quickly, but not all people can trust so easily.”

Jacob thought about it and realized that Mark was wiser than he was at the moment. “You’re right, Mark. I shouldn’t try to force it out of her. Well, you had better get to sleep. She’ll be waking you up soon for the next watch.”

Mark shrugged. “I can’t help but feel sorry for the poor girl. She’s down there all alone wanting nothing more than someone to hold her and kiss…uhhhhh! If you need me I’ll be down by the lake.”

“Mark!”

“Okay, okay. I’m going to bed, but you get there, too. You’re hurt and need rest.”

Jacob nodded and headed for his own tent.

“Oh, Jacob?”

“Yes?”

“I, uh, read some of those verses you wanted me to. I didn’t understand half of it, but I still read it. Could you answer a few questions for me in the morning?”

Jacob smiled. “First thing. Goodnight, Mark.”

“Goodnight, Jacob.”

CHAPTER 5

The next morning, Jacob and Mark woke up to the enticing aroma of a well-made breakfast. Besides being a killer fighter, Sarah was also a killer cook. She served them their separate meals and began to walk away.

"Thank you," Jacob said smiling.

"You're welcome," she said flatly, still harboring hard feelings from the night before.

"Aren't you going to eat, Sarah?" Mark asked with a mouth full of food.

"I've already eaten." She walked away.

"I guess she's still steamed from last night, huh?"

"I suppose so. Maybe she'll be in a better mood later."

"Yeah, so how long do you think it will be before we get to this town?"

"Oh, I would say about two hours if we don't run into anything along the way."

"Let 'em come with everything they've got. We'll cut off their arms and legs and beat 'em with them. There hasn't been anything so far we couldn't handle."

Mark's enthusiasm was refreshing. It was a lot better than someone constantly screaming, "We're all going to die!"

"I hope it stays that way, too. Anyway, from what I've heard a lot of people stop by there along the way to wherever they are going. It's not much for sightseeing, but they have a nice comfortable inn where we can rest up."

"Do you think we'll find our fourth partner there?"

"I don't know, but it's the closest town around. It's worth looking into seeing as how we'll pass it no matter where we go."

"Yeah." Mark looked a little uneasy. "So, you say this town is full of church people?"

"Yes, but don't worry, Mark, we won't be in church every minute we're there. They're not fanatics, just good people trying to live for God."

"Hmmm, it might be a nice change from some of the dumps I've been around."

"Yes, it might. I'm sure you will like it. Who knows? You might meet a nice Christian girl."

"I'm taking baby steps here, Jacob."

"I'm just teasing, but they are good people."

Mark frowned. "Yeah, it sounds like just the kind of place the hooded idiot would like to burn down."

Jacob's eyes widened. He hadn't thought of that. "That's a good point. Let's finish eating so we can be on our way."

Both men found Sarah's cooking delicious. Although, Jacob was a lot quieter about it than Mark who moaned with every bite.

Jacob saw Sarah in the distance listening to Mark's good review, trying to remain stone-faced. She giggled a couple of times which gave him hope that she wasn't seriously mad. When they were finished they took up camp and went on their way. As they walked it was dead silent over the next half hour. Mark finally broke the silence.

"Okay, why do I get the feeling that I'm in school again? Will somebody say something?" Neither Jacob or Sarah responded. "Okay, I'll get the ball rolling. How is your side Jacob? I forgot to ask at breakfast."

It was feeling so much better that Jacob had forgotten he was injured. "It's much better now, thank you. I guess I just needed some rest."

"Good. Now, Sarah, that breakfast was delicious. Where did you learn to cook like that?"

"I taught myself. You have to learn a lot of things when you're on your own."

Jacob glanced up. She must have been an orphan. That might explain some of her problems.

"Very good. Now, do you two have something to say to each other?" They both gave Mark a dirty look. "Okay, maybe not. Hey, didn't you tell me you would answer some questions for me this morning?"

"Oh, I'm sorry, Mark. You should've reminded me. What did you need to know?"

"First of all, what the heck is *pulse*?"

Jacob was puzzled a moment, then nodded his head.

"Oh! Pulse is kind of like rice, it's real bland and flavorless. It was something people ate back then."

"Oh, then why did Daniel, Shadroh, Mecasa, and Abenigosh want to eat it instead of good meat?"

It was everything Jacob could do not to burst out in laughter.

"You mean Shadrach, Meshach, and Abednigo."

"Yeah, where did they come up with these names?"

A few feet away, Sarah was holding in her laughter as well.

"Well, Daniel didn't want them to eat it because it was unclean."

"You mean it was dirty?"

"No, no. It wasn't right to eat it, because it and the wine were from the table of a man that had attacked God's people and stolen from his temple. Therefore they asked to be given pulse and water which was okay to eat."

"Oh, then why did they get so much healthier than everyone else?"

"Because the food they ate wasn't unclean." Jacob thought for a second about how he was going to explain it. "There is a message in what happened. You see the meat and wine from the King's table represents all of the bad things in the world. Daniel and his friends didn't eat the King's meat and stayed faithful to God. So they became three times healthier than the other slaves."

"So if people don't do all of the bad things in the world like steal and drink and also stay faithful to God they'll end up with a life three times better than anyone else's?"

"Exactly."

"Okay, that makes sense. But why did the King want to kill them? Because they couldn't tell him what his dream meant?"

"He was angry because his great wizards, magicians, and wise men couldn't tell him what he needed to know. They weren't as powerful as they claimed to be."

"So, Daniel actually could tell him, huh?"

"It wasn't Daniel himself. It was God who told them what the dream meant because he and his friends were also to be killed."

"So, because they were so faithful to God he saved them?"

"That's right. How much did you read last night?"

"I read up until he interpreted the dream and I'll be honest I didn't have a clue what it meant. All I understood was a big statue with a golden head and then I got lost."

"Don't feel bad, Mark. It takes a lot of practice to understand it. Like I told you before, there are some things I don't understand."

"Can you explain it?"

"Yes. King Nebuchadnezzar dreamed of a giant statue with a head made of gold. Its breast and arms were of silver, Its stomach and thighs were of brass, Its legs were of iron, and its feet were part silver and part clay."

"Wow, and I thought I had weird dreams. So what did it mean?"

"Each part represented different kingdoms of the world. The head of gold meant his kingdom was the greatest of all. The silver meant that a kingdom would rise up after his, but not as powerful, the brass meant a kingdom would rise after both of them, but not be as powerful as the other two. The iron represented a fourth kingdom. It would be a nation as strong as iron. The feet were a fifth kingdom. It would be partly strong, but partly separated, which is why it was part iron and part clay."

"Ohhh, I get it."

"Then a huge boulder came down and busted the statue into pieces. It then spread out and covered the entire world. This represented God's kingdom. In time, all earthly kingdoms will fall, but God's kingdom will cover the world and reign forever."

"Wow, that's deep. Are all of the stories in here this good?"

"Oh, yes, there are many of them."

"I kind of like this Daniel guy. I'll have to read more on him tonight."

"You're not going to like it when they try and kill him," Sarah added.

"Huh? They try to kill him?"

"Yeah, but don't worry, it has a happy ending."

Jacob looked at her in surprise. “You’ve read the bible Sarah?”

“Not all of it. What? Just because you read it doesn’t mean you heed it. I had a friend once that heeded it and he didn’t get any help from God. Mark, I won’t tell you how to live, but if you want to drink, then drink. Think hard before you get caught up in all these rules on how to live.” At that she took a faster pace. Jacob and Mark didn’t say anything for a second and watched her walk away.

“I agree with you, Jacob,” Mark offered. “Something bad happened to her.”

“Yes, it seems she’s giving us another piece of the puzzle every time we speak, doesn’t it?”

“Maybe she wants to talk about it, but she doesn’t know how.”

“Yes,” Jacob said. “Perhaps these clues are her way of telling us.”

“Makes sense,” Mark agreed. “We may have to play investigator tonight, huh?”

“Ha, maybe. She’s a complicated person.”

“Yeah, but you have to admit she is cute.”

That was one thing Jacob did have to admit.

There was a moderate amount of activity in the small town as they entered.

“Well, here we are,” Jacob said looking around for a familiar face.

“Perky bunch of people, aren’t they?” Mark asked noticing the painted on smiles surrounding them.

“I saw your bottle, Mark,” Sarah said staring at everyone. “You’re almost on empty. I think you’re in trouble.”

“Well, sister, I hate to break it to you, but most of these guys look afraid to even look at a woman.”

“Will you two quit it?” Jacob said. “Come on, let’s find someone who can help us.”

Before he could take a step, a man with red hair and a mustache came up smiling like a mad man.

“Brother Jacob! What in the world are you doing here?” He took Jacob’s hand and shook it vigorously. “This is an unexpected pleasure. Tell me, who are these fine looking people?”

"This is Mark Raven and Sarah Mist."

"A pleasure to meet both of you," he said shaking both of their hands. They nodded politely, feeling about as out of place as a snowman in the desert.

"You're Ben, right?"

"Yes, that's right. I was one of the deacons you had at that big revival last year. I tell you what, that was a spirit-filled night. Five people were saved and two rededicated. You sure did work wonders."

Jacob smiled modestly. "I'm just the messenger, it's God that works the wonders."

"Well, he couldn't have picked a better person to work through. What brings you all the way out here? Are you here for a friendly visit?"

Jacob's face became more serious. "No, I'm afraid it's a little more serious than that. Tell me, is there any way I can speak to your reverend?"

"Well, that's not really possible. We don't have a minister anymore."

"Oh, I'm sorry. Did he pass away?"

"No, you might say it was worse than that. You see, his daughter was raped and murdered one night. The next morning, when he found out, he took it very hard. She was his only child and he lost his wife very early in life. He blamed God for letting it happen. He renounced his religion and left shortly after."

"I see. It's so sad when something like that happens."

"It sounds like he was pretty smart to me," Sarah said. "I'm going to look for some fun, Jacob. Call me if anything happens."

Jacob gently shook his head as she walked away.

"It appears your friend has lost her faith as well. She'll be in our prayers."

"I appreciate that."

"Um, you never did say what your reason was for traveling here."

"Oh, yes. Since the reverend left do you have a town leader of any kind?"

"Well, I guess you could say it's me. Is there something we need to discuss?"

"Yes, something very important. Is there somewhere we can go talk?"

"Oh, of course. Come over to my house. My wife can cook you and your friend a nice warm meal and we can discuss whatever you need."

"You don't have to go to any trouble."

"Oh, it's no trouble. Cindy's pleasure is cooking for other people. Plus, we're glad to welcome good people into our home."

Hearing that made a small pang of guilt run through Mark. He was quicker to admit his faults than Sarah was by far. Inside the house Jacob and Mark enjoyed the meal they were promised. Afterward they told their rather fantastic story to Ben and his wife.

"Dear God," he said staring blankly. "I knew the world was getting bad, but I had no idea it was that bad."

"Yes, and it's up to us to stop this thing. I don't know how we're going to do it, but we have to. This town might be next on the list because it's filled with good God-fearing people."

Ben paled. "You mean it may come here?"

"Yes, but we'll do everything we can to protect everyone."

"Is there anything we can do to help?"

"Well, as I said before, we're trying to find a fourth fighter. Do you know of anyone it could be?"

"Hmmm, I'm afraid not. We don't fight around here. The only reason we have weapons is if wild animals or thieves attack."

"I understand." Jacob gave Mark a look that said *What now?*

"I guess we head for Victory Castle," Mark said reading his mind. "That place is full of armed guards and fighters. We may be like a bunch of kids in a candy store."

"I suppose you're right," Jacob agreed. "That would be the next logical place to stop."

"When do we head out?"

"We'll stay the night here and see if anything happens. If not, we'll set out for Victory Castle."

Mark nodded. "Hmm, shouldn't we try to find Sarah before she tries to start up a bar somewhere?"

"Probably."

"Oh, Reverend?" Ben said before he got to the door.

"Yes?"

“Since you’ll be here anyway and we haven’t had the pleasure of a minister in sometime, would you mind giving a sermon tonight?”

“I’d be honored. Do you mind having an outdoor service? Anything could sneak up on us if we go indoors.”

“Yes, that’s fine. I’ll inform everyone right away. I’m sure they will be very happy to hear it. Is seven okay?”

“Yes, that will be fine. Come on, let’s go find Sarah, Mark.”

They didn’t have to look far, as she was standing right outside the door.

“Oh, there you are. Who’s your friend?”

Sarah stood wrapped in the arms of a young man. Not a day over eighteen. He was tall, broad shouldered, and muscular. He looked down at her and kissed her forehead.

“This is my new friend, Steven. I finally managed to find someone who isn’t a church freak and likes to live life.” She rubbed her hand down his cheek and to his chest. “Steven isn’t afraid to be a man,” she said then, staring straight at Jacob.

“Yeah, but won’t his teacher be mad if you keep him out of school?” Mark teased.

“Shut up, Mark!” Sarah barked. “If you’ll excuse us,” she said turning away, “we’re going to the inn to become better friends.” At that, she and Steven walked away hand in hand.

Jacob didn’t watch them go. Was she trying to make him jealous?

As they reached the door to the inn she turned around gave Jacob a smirk. He merely tilted his hat over his eyes and lifted his bible to her. This made her even more irritated than she was before. As they disappeared through the door he could only imagine what was going on behind it.

Mark could clearly see that this was troubling him.

“Hey, don’t worry. I’m sure it’s not as bad as you think it is. They could be sipping tea and sharing a stimulating conversation.”

Jacob rolled his eyes.

“Ummm, you’re not buying that, are you? Tell you what, I’m going to leave you alone here to stare vengefully at the inn. How’s that?” Mark walked off to leave Jacob to his thoughts.

Jacob was indeed troubled, but not because he was jealous. Rather because she was hurting herself so much. During his pity party, a small hand tugged on his coat. He looked down to see a beautiful black-haired girl with pigtails.

"What can I do for you, little one?"

"We're raising money to build a club house. Can we sing you a song for a gold piece?"

He smiled at her. "Of course." Then a sneaky idea popped into his head. "Tell me miss..."

"Jessie," she said looking up.

"Jessie, do you and your friends know any church hymns?"

"Uh huh, that's what we mostly sing."

"That's good. Tell you what, can you do me a favor?"

"Sure."

"Do you see that window over there?"

"You mean the one at the inn?"

"Yes, that's the one. I'll give you *five* gold pieces if you can sing a song for me under that window. Okay?"

"Thank you!!" she said her eyes wide as saucers. She then ran to tell her friends the good news.

Meanwhile, in the room, Sarah wasted little time spiting Jacob. She kissed her newfound friend, Steven, passionately, barely even taking time to breathe.

Young Steven was speechless and paralyzed with excitement. He was a young rebel, and had not yet been outside the village. Consequently he rarely had the pleasure of meeting a woman like Sarah. Once in a while, a semi-wild girl would pass through the village, but he had always been too shy to speak to them. Besides, none of them were as beautiful as Sarah. He closed his eyes as she kissed him. Deep down, he was thinking that God had answered his prayers.

Sarah was driven by a hurricane of emotions. Spite, lust, and anger powered her forward. She was barely aware of who she was embracing because in her mind, it was only to get back at Jacob. She also hoped to make him jealous. She was dead-set on the thought that deep down Jacob wanted to be in the place of the young man. Part of her couldn't deny wishing it were him. She didn't know why, but she *really wanted* to be with Jacob.

She ripped her young companion's shirt off, still not really aware of who is was or what he looked like. She was completely lost in thought. Visions of Jacob outside torturing himself over what was happening filled her mind. She pictured him clenching his fists and seething with anger. In her mind, he was praying, "Oh, God, why is she doing this?" as he stared at the building with only his imagination going wild.

Sarah finally snapped out of it and realized her time and place. She pried her lips away from Steve and smiled seductively his way. "Are you ready to become a man?"

With a look of amazement, he nodded. Sarah laid him on the bed and continued kissing him. Amidst the foreplay, a small voice echoed in the background."

Sarah listened closer; it was *many* voices, the voices of children. They were singing outside of the window.

"Stupid kids!" Steve yelped in irritation. "Don't they know people need privacy. They've been doing this all week to raise money."

Sarah continued to stare at the window. "This is seriously breaking my concentration."

"Do you want me to get rid of them?"

"No, wait." She listened more closely and recognized the song. It was a song her friend had taught her. Her desire to ravish young Steve faded away. Suddenly against her will she felt a huge wave of guilt fall over her.

"What's wrong, Sarah?"

"I…I can't do this."

"No! You're my only chance to do this!"

"Yeah, tough break kid."

Steve growled in anger at her sudden burst of virtue.

"Was that okay mister?" the little girl asked Jacob shining her pearly whites.

"Perfect, Jesse." He handed her the money and watched the door of the inn. Ten seconds later, Sarah stormed out. If looks could kill, the one she was giving him could wipe out a countryside. He grinned at her. "Back so soon?"

"Oh, shut up!"

Later in the day, the three of them gathered at Ben's house while he was spreading the news about the upcoming service. They had been sitting in the same place for nearly an hour nary a word said. Jacob sat at one end of the kitchen table thumbing through his bible and preparing for the night. Sarah, still unhappy to say the least, sat in a chair in the corner of the room. Poor Mark, not knowing what to do, sat opposite of Jacob thinking of different foods because his first meal was wearing off.

About five minutes into the second hour, Jacob looked up at Sarah pouting with her arms crossed. She was cute in her own way. Like a three year old having a tantrum. Jacob broke the silence.

"Sarah? How long are you planning to stay angry with me?"

"That depends. How long is this demon hunt going to take?"

"It could take a while. Don't you think we would feel a lot better if we settled this?"

"Thank you, God," Mark whispered to himself."

"There's nothing to settle. We just see things differently."

"Yes, but I don't understand why you're so angry with me. Is it because I rejected your advances?"

"As I recall, you were kissing back for a minute before you decided to go holy on me."

"I mean we didn't….you know."

"Have sex? Ohhh, I said the horrible S-word. Oh, wait I forgot, you say make love right?"

"That's what it is supposed to be called."

"Call it what you want; it's the same thing."

"No, my dear, I'm afraid there is a big difference in the two. One is done out of lust. The other is done by two people that love each other."

"RRRR! There you go again! You're living in a fairytale! That's why I'm so mad! The world doesn't work that way. The world doesn't go by all of these stupid rules."

"No they don't, but they're supposed to."

"No one gets anything from listening to that stuff."

"I have."

"What?"

"I have peace of mind, a friend to talk to when I'm alone, and someone who is always there for me."

This seemed to enrage her even further.

"God is not always there!! He has never been there for me! I have been alone since the day I was born! You stand there and judge me for the things I do and tell me Jesus loves me. You don't know what I've been through! You can't possibly understand!"

"I would if you would tell me."

"You want to know why I have sex with every man I meet? It's all I've ever known. I was a damn prostitute!" This came as a shock to Mark and Jacob, even though it made sense.

"Can I ask you something, Jacob?"

"Of course."

"What kind of family did you have? Were you happy?"

"Well, my parents died when I was sixteen, but before that we were happy."

"Hugs and kisses every night? Telling each other you loved them? A mother to tuck you in at night? That must have been nice. But let me tell you something, not everyone has that kind of life. I grew up in a place where nobody cared whether you lived or died and that included my parents."

"Tell me about it," Jacob said putting a hand on her shoulder. He expected her to tense up or pull away, but instead she relaxed a fraction under his touch.

"My mama was a drunken whore and my daddy was just… evil. Every night she would just stand back and watch him beat me for whatever reason he could find. He didn't even have reasons to hit me. He just did it for enjoyment. I actually cried tears of joy the day he got killed. I thought I might finally get to have a life. I was wrong. My stupid mother grieved over my Dad and killed herself. She left me alone with nothing or nobody. So I was forced to go around begging for food. I got scraps here and there, but I was still hungry.

"One day I walked up on three men having a big meal and one of them called out to me. He told me I was the prettiest girl he had ever seen. I told him thank you and began to walk away. One of the other men asked me if I wanted something to eat. I said yes and walked over."

Jacob began to get a sick feeling in the pit of his stomach because he had as good idea where this story was going.

"When I got there one of the men took me by the shoulders. He said I wasn't going to get any food for free, but I was so hungry I was willing to do anything for food." Sarah began to weep uncontrollably at the next part. "They made me do the most horrible things with them and only for a piece of ham!"

Jacob hung his head and wrapped her arms around her. She buried her face into his chest. He began to pray for guidance as the thought of those men's heads on spikes sounded very appealing.

Mark sat in silence and shook his head. "I'm sorry, Sarah. I do have the bad habit of judging people before I know their story. I'm starting to understand."

"Why did God do that to me, Jacob? I was only a little girl. Why did God do that to me?"

"Sweetie, it wasn't God. He would never make anyone go through something like that. It was the evil in those men's hearts that did that to you. Those creatures, the evil we're fighting, all of it is what is in people's hearts and that is what we're fighting against. Don't be angry at God for it."

"I had to have sex with those men just to get money and food."

"I know, I know," Jacob said stroking her hair. Jacob thought for a minute then asked, "Sarah?"

"What?"

"Who was your friend you kept speaking about?"

"Huh? Oh, you mean the one that taught me the bible?"

"Yes."

She sat up straight and wiped her eyes. "His name was Angus; he lived on the streets, too. I think he saw a man coming on to me one day. He was so angry that he beat the crap out of the guy and sent him packing. I was mad at first, because he was going to be how I got my dinner. But Angus told me that I didn't have to do things like that to live. He started telling me stories from the bible. He said that if you live for God, everything will be provided for you. He said that even though he lived on the streets."

A true Christian Jacob thought.

"I can honestly say that was the first time in my life I was ever truly happy. Angus was like a Father to me, a real one. Every night he told me a bible story. My favorite was David and Goliath. I liked how David was so brave even though Goliath was three times his size. Then we would say our prayers. He hugged me and kissed me every night before we went to sleep. No matter what he always found us something to eat and a place to sleep. He was the first man that never wanted to hurt me or touch me." Another stray tear creased her cheek.

"I loved him so much. He taught me everything I needed to know. Besides the bible, he taught me how to fight; that's where I learned how to use my Bo. He said I needed to learn to protect myself. It ended up being the best thing anyone ever taught me."

Even though he pretty much knew, Jacob asked, "What happened to him?"

She took a deep breath before continuing. "One day I came back to give him the food I had gotten, but when I got there he was covered in blood. Three worthless cowards stood around him and one of them was holding a knife. They couldn't even fight him fair. I guess two of them held him down while the other one stabbed him. He was already dead by the time I got to his side. I screamed at them, but they laughed at me. I remember every word they said. *'Well, aren't you a pretty little thing? If you don't want me to cut your face off, then you'll do everything I say. Right boys?'*

"I don't know exactly what happened, but something inside of me snapped. I took my Bo and beat all three of them until they lay in a puddle of their own blood. I took the knife and stabbed the one who killed Angus at least fifty times. I don't know if the other two were still alive, but from that day on, no man told me what to do. I got my own food, my own clothes and my own place to sleep. I was in control."

"So, that's why you said he wasted his life?"

"Yes, he served God every day. He did everything he was supposed to even though he was homeless, yet God let him be murdered like a dog! What good did it do him?"

"Sarah, I can't say why bad things happen to good people, but I know he's in a better place with plenty of food to eat and a place to sleep. Even though he was homeless, he was happy. Didn't you say you were the happiest you had ever been when you were with him? Yes. That's because you were both living for God. That's the joy of being a Christian."

"But God took my only friend from me."

"Yes, but he gave you *new* friends."

"Who?"

He looked at her with a smile. "Us."

Mark walked over. "Yeah sweetie, we're your friends."

"I'll protect you in any way I can." Jacob said.

"I thought you didn't like me because of the things I did."

"Sarah, there's a saying. 'Hate the sin and love the sinner.' I hold true to that saying. I like you and want to be your friend even though I don't like the things you do. I want you to see that and maybe want to stop what you're doing. Didn't you tell me you slept with men, because that was the only way they would want you?"

"Yeah."

"I care about you, but you don't have to sleep with me."

"That goes for me too," Mark added. "Though I wouldn't complain if you did."

"Mark!"

Sarah giggled. "You really like me for me?"

"Yes, and we'll be here if you need food, shelter, or just someone to talk to."

"Thank you, guys."

"You said God was never there for you, but he gave you Angus who befriended you without expecting anything in return, and who taught you how to fend for yourself. Now he gave you us to help you in any way we can."

"Jacob, you're the sweetest person I've ever met."

"Hey, what about me?"

"Oh, you, too, Mark. I like you even if you are a pervert," she said hugging him.

As she hugged Jacob a thought came to her. It was actually more of a feeling. Though she would never say it out loud, at that moment she fell in love with Jacob Cross.

In the middle of their emotional breakthrough, Ben burst through the door.

"Oh, I'm glad you're still here! Everything is all set up and everyone is looking forward to hearing you. It's been a long time since we got to hear the Gospel preached. Some are already gathered at the church. Many would like to see you again, so would it be too much trouble to see them before the service?"

"It would be no trouble at all. I'll be there in a couple of minutes."

"Thank you. Oh, by the way, a few men volunteered to stand guard while everyone is at the church."

"Good, but I hope it's not necessary."

After gathering their belongings the three went to the church and mingled with the townspeople. By the time he was ready to preach, Jacob had shaken every hand in town.

Sarah and Mark didn't know how to feel with everyone greeting them with warm smiles and thanking them for watching over the town. They were relieved when everyone began to spread out to prepare for the service.

Jacob took his place in front of the makeshift altar. Before turning everything over to Jacob, everyone sang a couple of hymns with no music. He had done this not three days earlier, yet it felt like much longer. Nevertheless, it didn't take long for God to build his confidence.

"Hello, everyone. It's great to see all of you gathered here under the stars tonight..." The night was beautiful. There wasn't a cloud in the sky and it seemed a million stars burned brightly. "I wasn't expecting to preach tonight, but I believe God has led me to a message that will bless each and every one of you. Now, I usually don't give titles to my messages, but tonight a title is in order. It is 'Satan will always be brought down.'

"You know, just that thought by itself gives me a blessing. It's Satan that lives in the hearts of people and causes them to hurt each other. It's Satan that turns our innocent children into unruly rebels. It is Satan that can cause a good man or woman to be a murderer a drunkard or an adulterer. It is his evil inspiration that causes people to do these things in the sight of God, but the comforting thing is that he will always be brought down.

"Most of the time, I base my message on one book or verse or biblical character, but tonight's message will involve many books, verses, and people.

"When I read through the scriptures today, I found one thing in common with everything I read: Satan. He was there in each and every scripture. He may not have appeared flesh and blood, but he was there in one form or another. The other thing I found in common was that always—with God's help—he was brought down." Jacob heard an amen from the center of the crowd. "You wouldn't believe how many times in this holy book that he was brought down by a prophet or God himself. Let me give you some examples of what I'm talking about."

Jacob thought of everything he had discussed with Sarah and Mark. "It was Satan who lived in Goliath and challenged one man to fight him. The people were too afraid, but David wasn't. God worked through David and, without even flinching, the young man cast that stone right through Goliath's skull. That may have been David-versus-Goliath on one level, but it was God-versus-Satan on another. In the end, it was David standing over Goliath's dead body and Satan was brought down.

"Let me give you another example. It was Satan working through the jealous hearts of the men that wanted to kill Daniel. He was doing such a good job that it made them look bad, so they wanted to get rid of him. But Daniel had a weapon they underestimated: he had God.

"So, they tricked King Darius into signing a law that made it forbidden for anybody to pray to anyone except the King. They knew Daniel prayed three times a day to the God of Israel and they wanted to use it against him.

"When they told King Darius that Daniel had broken the law, he was heartbroken. Daniel wasn't just his servant, but his friend, and he had been tricked into signing his death warrant. The punishment for breaking the law was to be cast into the lion's den and be ripped to pieces. Even though he didn't want to, he threw Daniel into the Lion's den, hoping and praying that Daniel's God existed."

Into the crowd, Mark and Sarah were mesmerized by his words. Jacob continued.

"That night, the King didn't eat, he didn't sleep, and he didn't have any music played. The only thought on his mind was whether or not his friend was dead. Early that morning, he went to the mouth of the lion's den and had the stone taken away. Scripture then says with a lamentful voice he cried, 'Oh, Daniel, has your God delivered you this day?' Daniel's voice came up and said, 'Oh, King, live forever, my God hath sent an Angel and shut the Lion's mouths!'

"God was watching over Daniel. Those men tried their hardest to get rid of him, but God said no! He didn't want Daniel to die, so he didn't die. The King ordered that those men and their families be cast into the lion's den, for their bones to be crushed and their flesh ripped. Once again it was Satan lying dead on the ground and God standing up in victory.

"Friends, this is how it will always work. No matter how hard Satan tries to ruin God's plan, he will always be stopped dead in his tracks. I know he's down in hell listening to me right now and I don't really care if I'm upsetting him."

"God holds all the power and in the end it will be Satan bowing down before the throne of God and his son, Jesus Christ! The problem so many people have is that they don't have enough faith. They know God is there for them, but in the eye of the storm and their darkest hour, they forget to look to the one who is protecting them. We're just like Peter when he walked out on the water to meet Jesus. We look away and we begin to sink. Friends, that's what each and every one of us are doing every day of our lives. We're going down the right path, and we have our eyes on Jesus, but somewhere down the line, we take our eyes off of him and we start to sink.

"We'll try every way we know how to make ourselves happy. We'll pick up a bottle of alcohol and try to drink our way to happiness. We'll take someone we don't even love and commit fornication in hopes of it making us happy. We'll lie, we'll curse, some will even commit murder in hopes of making themselves happy, but the emptiness is always there. Nothing we do that is of the devil will ever make us happy. Do you know when happiness will come? I'll tell you. Just as soon as we do what Peter did. As soon as we call for Jesus to pick us up from the water we are drowning in. It's the last thing we do when it should be the first. All you have to do is put your faith in God and his son Jesus Christ and I promise you, Satan will always be put down."

As the last word came out of Jacob's mouth, an earth shattering clap of thunder rang through the air accompanied by massive streaks of lightning.

"So, you've heard enough?" Jacob said looking to the ground. Screams began to peal from the town entrance.

"Demon!" a voice cried. "It's a demon! Help us!"

Mark and Sarah jumped up to where Jacob was standing.

"That sounds like our cue," Mark said looking on.

"Let's take this thing down!" Sarah cried with her Bo held high.

"Remember, stick together," Jacob reminded them.

"Got it," they said in unison. At that they ran to the center of the commotion.

As they arrived to the core of the chaos, flames blazed, creating countless silhouettes that flickered all around. The fire was the only source of light as everything had already turned black. They shielded their eyes and searched for the source. The answer wasn't hard to see and stood dead ahead. In the center of the street, concealed by flames, stood the most demonic sight any of them had yet experienced.

It stood tall, even larger than the armored creature Jacob and Mark had faced. Like all of the others, it had burning red eyes and a mouth filled with razor sharp teeth.

The thing snarled as it made eye contact with Jacob. Small flames shot from its nose and mouth as it snorted. Its hands were huge and its fingers long and slender. Glimmering nails stood on the tips. Its skin was a sickening green. Atop its head, on either side, ominous ram-like horns curved upward. This one was going to be the most dangerous of all.

"Oh, my God!" Mark yelped. "It's a goat from hell!"

"I don't think we're going to be able to simply charge this one," Jacob said holding them back impulsively.

"What do we do?" Sarah asked.

"I don't know, but if we go running straight in we'll end up barbecued."

"Then how are we going to stop it if we can't get near it? By the time we come up with a plan that thing will have burned the whole town to the ground."

She was right and Jacob thought fast. It was time to try long range combat. He aimed for an easy place to hit the thing and test how strong it was, choosing the left pectoral. It was large, and if he was lucky, he might hit the heart. Holding his breath, he pulled the trigger and sent the arrow flying. It hit dead on. As the sharp point penetrated, the creature cried out, a sound more of aggravation than real pain. It then unceremoniously yanked out the arrow and slung it back at them. Jacob and his partners jumped for cover as the barb buried itself in the ground only inches away.

“Here’s a tip,” Mark said looking at the arrow stuck in the ground. “Don’t do that anymore!”

Jacob nodded in agreement.

“Look!” Sarah cried looking forward.

Some of the townspeople were trying to fight the thing head-on and were paying dearly for their mistake. A couple were engulfed in flames and others were being mercilessly stomped upon. Jacob winced as he saw their insides practically rushing out.

Gasping, he realized a much smaller person was in the eye of the storm. It was a little girl who had become separated from her parents. Looking closely, he realized it was the same little girl who had asked to sing a song to him for money.

“Oh God no!” he cried as the demon inched its way toward her. “Jessie!” he called out, remembering her name. “Run to us!”

It was no use; she was frozen in fear. She crouched upon the ground hiding her face and crying hysterically. Jacob ran toward her as the demon raised its foot to stomp her like a bug. Jacob could swear he saw the thing smiling.

“No!”

Before he could move, Mark blocked him with his hand.

“I’ll take this one buddy!” he said sprinting to the rescue.

Thinking quickly, he pulled his sword and slid across the space to cover the girl while holding his blade in the air. As the creature stomped down, the sword acted as a giant nail impaling its foot. The demon howled again and jerked back its foot. Losing its balance, it fell to the ground.

This seemed to hurt it more than the arrow had and furious, the demon sat up. It sent Mark a death stare as he continued to cover the girl. Its eyes glowed even redder and he had a good idea of what was about to happen.

“Oh crap!” he yelped as his prediction came true. A massive wave of flames poured from the monster’s mouth, straight at him. With the reflexes of a cat, he rolled back toward Jacob and Sarah, doing his best not to hurt the girl. He escaped unscathed though a bit singed. Standing up he handed the child to Jacob.

“Are you okay, Jessie?”

“Uh huh,” she said with tear-filled eyes.

“Where are your parents?”

“I don’t know!” she cried becoming hysterical again.

"Shhh, it's okay," Jacob said even though he feared the worst. "Go, run to the people at the church, you'll be safe there."

"Okay."

As she ran off, Mark grunted in anger. "Okay! Trying to crush little girls is where I draw the line! This thing is going down!"

"No, Mark!" Jacob yelled after him as he charged for the thing.

"Are you insane?!" Sarah yelled.

His charge and battle cry were short-lived. When he reached the creature it kicked him like a soccer ball. Mark flew through the air and landed between Sarah and Jacob.

"Mark! Say something," Jacob said slapping his face.

"Ouch. Another tip, Jacob. Don't do what I just did either. That thing has a mean right foot."

They both took a hand and lifted him to his feet.

"So, what the....ow......do we do now?"

"One of us should distract it while the other two come at it from behind."

"I volunteer Mark to distract it," Sarah said raising her hand.

"Why me?"

"Hey, you're already hurt, why should the rest of us suffer?"

"Whatever. Go ahead, you two. I'll distract it, but make it quick."

"Okay, let's go."

Mark hobbled in front of the thing and began waving his arms around in the air. "Hey! Over here! Come and get me! You don't have the guts, you goat-looking, ugly, son of a.....demon!"

The monster growled and gazed directly at him. Either it was angry or thought he was a complete idiot. Maybe both. He glanced behind the thing to see if they had gotten close. They were almost there. They just needed a few seconds.

"Hey! Goat head! Come fight me like a man! What? You don't pick on anything but little girls?"

It was definitely understanding his taunts because it picked up an entire front porch and hurled it at him.

"Uh oh." Mark managed to leap to the side just in time. "RRR! How did I go from sitting happily in a bar to this?" Jacob and Sarah were finally right behind the thing and Mark sighed, relieved.

"You take one leg and I'll take the other," Jacob whispered, hoping to cripple it. Sarah nodded in agreement and they prepared to strike. Jacob gave the signal and rammed his blade straight through the monster's femur. At the same time, Sarah struck the opposite leg with enough force to break a human bone in half. The demon cried out and went to its knees. They had it right where they wanted it, or so they thought.

Sarah struck it in the back of the head, sending it to its stomach. Jacob saw his chance and jumped on its back. Instead of easily killing it by plunging his sword through the back of its head, the creature slung his fist backward sending Jacob flying. As Sarah helped Jacob up and the creature rolled over onto its back, eyes burning bright.

"Down, Sarah!" he cried taking Sarah and rolling away from the flames as Mark had earlier. "Hurry! In the house!"

Getting up quickly, she followed him through the door.

"Ummm, Jacob? Why did we come into a house? If it catches on fire, aren't we sitting ducks?"

"Yes, but out there we're even more of a target. There's no way we can fight it head-to-head. Maybe Mark can get its attention again for us to sneak out of here."

"Do you have a plan?" Sarah asked impatiently.

"At the moment, no."

"Well, I feel safe."

"Have you got any ideas?"

"Well, we could....Ahhhh!" Sarah shrieked as a giant clawed hand burst through the window nearest to them and took her by the hair. "Owwww! Its ripping my hair out!"

"Hold on!" Taking his sword, Jacob began slicing her hair from the demon's grip.

"What are you doing?"

"Would you rather that thing have some of your hair or your whole head?"

"Point taken." After he cut her loose, she put her hand to her head and could only imagine how lopsided her hair must look. "Arrrgh! I'm going to kill that thing!"

It was still moving its hand from side-to-side feeling for them. Jacob raised his sword high in the air and slashed the hand off. He heard a roar as it pulled a bloody nub back.

"You couldn't have done that first?"

"I didn't think about it."

"Ugh!"

Meanwhile, outside, taking advantage of it being wounded, Mark hacked away. He was able to cut it a couple of times, but every time he began to do serious damage, it would shoot its flame breath and force him to dodge out of the way.

"Could I get some help out here?!" he called out.

Still feeling of her hair and imagining how horrible she must look, Sarah heard everything going on outside. Finally, everything inside of her burst free.

"That's it! I've had enough of this! That thing is going down!"

"Sarah! Wait!"

Jacob attempted to hold her back, but in her rage she easily shoved him to the ground. Mark jumped in surprise as the house door came flying open.

"Hey, Sarah, what are you.. unf!" Sarah pushed him out of her way as he tried to slow her progress.

In moments, the half-crippled one-handed demon and Sarah were standing toe-to-toe. Considering the mood she was in everything was about evened out. Growling, it took her by the waist, lifting her up.

"Sarah!" Jacob and Mark called together.

Sarah waited until it had lifted her all the way up. It was powering up to burn her into a scorched piece of charcoal. But its glow-eyed ritual was cut short as she rammed her Bo into the demon's forehead with all her strength. On contact, its eyes returned to their normal eerie color and it dropped to one knee. Although stunned, it still hadn't let go of her. Performing her own angry battle cry, Sarah twirled the stick around and made another direct hit into its forehead. This time the thing loosened its grip.

Over and over again, she beat the stick into the beast's head. With every hit there was more and more damage. Finally, there was a small cut and with every slam of the bo, it grew. Eventually, blood flowed from the gaping wound. Finally, after a dozen swings, the creature's brains were all but protruding. With the last blow, it fell flat on its face, a pool of blood forming under its head.

Jacob and Mark's jaws dropped open. Sarah single-handedly beaten the thing to death. Neither of them knew what to say, but if there was any doubt that Sarah was one of the chosen ones she had just erased them before their very eyes.

“That was the most amazing thing I’ve ever seen in my life,” Mark said. “If I were you, Jacob, I would think twice about ever pissing her off again.”

Jacob nodded.

Sarah looked back at them and they took a step back in fear. They had no way of knowing if she was still in kill mode until she smiled.

“Hey, what can I say? Don’t mess with a girl’s hair.”

They both sighed with relief.

“You did it,” Jacob said extending his hand to her.

She took it.

“No, we did it. Come here.” She pulled them both to her for a big group hug.

Mark laughed. “Hey, if we kick this much demon butt when there are three of us, can you imagine how bad we’ll be when there are four? ...Ahh crap!”

Looking into the fog that always followed the fall of a demon, Mark noticed there stood Mr. Unholy himself. This was the first time Sarah had ever seen him. She was rightfully frightened by his nightmarish face and put Mark and Jacob between them.

“Is that him?” she asked peeking over their shoulders.

Yes…that’s our enemy,” Jacob said returning its stare.

“Okay, Sarah, here’s the routine. It starts thundering and lightning and raining and getting all creepy when some ugly-looking creature or creatures show up. We kick its butt and then the hooded idiot shows up and says something stupid. Its kind of a pattern. Don’t worry, you’ll get used to it.”

Although Mark was wrong this time. The demon didn’t say that much. In fact it only said one thing. After staring at the three of them for a moment it growled and said, ***“When will you give up?”***

Jacob didn’t dignify that with an answer, at least with words anyway. Taking a step forward and lifting his bible in the air he returned a stare that said, *“Send whatever you want, fire breathing, blade armed, armored followers or all of the above and we’ll take them down piece by piece and one by one.”*

The hooded demon then disappeared as fast as it had appeared.

CHAPTER 6

"Ugh!" Sarah muttered in disgust. "There goes my peaceful night sleep for the next three months."

"Tell me about it," Mark agreed.

"Don't worry," Jacob assured them. "God will shield us from any power that creature holds."

"I hope so," Sarah said still shivering. "That thing wasn't like the others. It was more…"

"Evil?" Jacob asked finishing her sentence.

"Yeah."

"It was the face of evil. That is what lives in the hearts of every man and woman that lives in sin."

That statement made Mark and Sarah shudder. The thought of that thing living inside of them wasn't a pleasant one.

"You sensed it more because it is of higher rank."

"So in the end, *it* is what we have to defeat?"

"Yes. There will come a time when we won't fight the followers, but the master itself."

All of them, even Jacob dreaded that thought.

Jacob was relieved to see Ben come running up to them. You could tell he was saddened by the deaths of all townspeople. Though the tears in his eyes were of gratitude to them for saving the rest of the town.

"Thank God you came here. God bless you. I can't thank you enough for helping little Jessie and the rest of us."

Jacob looked to the ground. “Don’t be so quick to thank us, or me, at least. I’m not so sure it wasn’t me who brought this plague upon you.”

Sarah and Mark looked at him puzzled. “Huh?” they both asked.

“The hooded one is out for my head and seems to follow me wherever I go. I should have known a peaceful town like this wouldn’t have any skilled fighters. Yet, I came along and brought it along with me.”

“You had no way of knowing that,” Mark said.

“Yeah, you were just looking for the nearest place you knew of. It wasn’t your fault,” Sarah added.

“Look where you found us. You found Mark drunk inside of a bar and me unconscious outside of one.”

Ben wrapped both his hands around one of Jacob’s. “Your friends are right. We don’t blame you. As you said before, this is a good Christian town, we would have been a target anyway. We’re lucky we didn’t lose any more than we did. Besides your message meant the world to us. We haven’t been able to hear the scriptures in such a long time.”

“Thank you,” Jacob said managing a small smile.

“Now then, you have saved our town and been chosen by God to save the world. The least we can do is offer you free room and board and a meal in the morning.”

“That sounds wonderful,” Sarah said in exhaustion.

“Well, if you guys need me, I’ll be in bed,” Mark said yawning and walking toward the inn. “Wake me up for breakfast.”

“No,” Jacob chimed in.

“Huh?”

“I’m afraid we can’t accept your kind offer. If you want to give us food, give us some to travel with.”

“You’re kidding Jacob!” Sarah shouted in disbelief. “After all of that don’t you want to rest in a nice bed and get something in your stomach?”

“Yeah,” Mark agreed, “I think you’ve earned it.”

“Yes, I know, but it isn’t that late and we can still travel until midnight toward Freedom Castle. We don’t have any time to spare.”

“What do you mean?” Mark asked.

"It was what you said earlier, Mark. We fight well with the three of us together, but our opponents are getting stronger and stronger. Soon they will be more than just us can handle. We need to find our fourth comrade as soon as possible."

Sarah and Mark looked at each other rolling their eyes and sighing. He was right.

"So, what's the plan?" Mark asked.

"Like I said, we can travel on until around midnight. Then we can set up camp like we did before and take watch through the night. I'm not hurt anymore, so I can help tonight."

They both nodded and motioned for him to lead the way.

"I'm sorry you can't stay any longer," Ben said with a frown. "Stay right here, though. I'll gather up some supplies for you."

"Thank you. We appreciate it."

As he walked away, Mark looked longingly toward the inn. "Oh, what I wouldn't give for eight hours sleep."

"Don't worry, Mark. I hope this will be the last night. When we get to the castle we should be able to rest easily. There will be tons of soldiers guarding the place and if they need us they can get us."

"Well then, what are we waiting for? Let's get going."

After gathering a few gifts from the townspeople, they traveled toward Freedom Castle. Before leaving, Jacob heard the distressing news that one of the men killed was little Jessie's father. He had been trying to help her get away before being mercilessly crushed.

They were mainly silent as they traveled on. Mark felt bad for all of the people who had died, though he knew none of them personally. He chose to keep silent, because he knew there was a time and place for his wisecracks.

For the time being everyone was dealing with their troubles in silence. Even though it was usually best to talk about your problems, sometimes the best way for someone to cope was to just say nothing at all.

On a side thought, they all wondered what Freedom Castle was going to be like. Even though it was a well-known place, none of them had ever been there.

At one time, none of the neighboring towns were independent. The entire continent was one Kingdom. But that was a long time ago, before any of them were ever born.

The first King had been the great Curtis Caimbridge, the First. He was a powerful but fair leader who kept order throughout the land. Since the fall of the kingdom, crime had grown by at least seventy percent.

Towns like Bruton and Takkar were once a great pride of the kingdom filled with nobles and common citizens alike. Crimes such as thievery and prostitution were unheard of. It wasn't as if having a king was a bad thing. Things were definitely kept in place a lot more, but unfortunately King Curtis was the only fair ruler. When he died in his seventieth year, his dark-hearted son, Conrad, took the throne.

Conrad was an evil ruler who took the wives and daughters of the townsmen for his own. He took possessions that weren't rightfully his and punished people unjustly for their crimes. Among his many sins, he once beheaded a man who stole a sheep to feed his starving family. They were starving because of Conrad anyway. This Tyranny continued for two more generations. It was during the reign of Conrad's grandson, Brutus, that the people had had enough. They finally realized that between all of the neighboring towns, they had more than enough people to outnumber the King's guards and overtake the castle. They did just that and killed Brutus, ending the monarchy.

At that time, the towns became independent entities. Some became total dumps and looked like hell on earth, while others prospered and made great names for themselves.

As for the Caimbridge bloodline, it didn't end with Brutus. His wife had, a year earlier, bore him his only son, John. When John came of age, he took the throne and attempted to rebuild his great grandfather's kingdom with promises of fair treatment and freedom. His failed. The towns had experienced seventeen years of absolute freedom and they weren't about to go back under a ruler's thumb.

After that, years passed and John sat on a throne that held no power except over the people who resided in the town around the castle. A couple of close-by towns remained loyal for the sake of the late Curtis Caimbridge. John soon learned to let go of the other towns and be content. The only regretted that he had very little to leave his own son, Anthony. Unfortunately, John died on Anthony's seventeenth birthday, so his son took up the throne. Anthony now sat on the throne, and he was the one Jacob and his friends hoped to meet with to find the fourth warrior.

Everyone in the jurisdiction loved him, not because he was King, but because he was such a kind and gentle person. Jacob hoped those rumors were true.

“We’ve gone far enough,” Jacob said breaking the silence. “Let’s set up camp here. You guys get some rest. I’ll take first watch.”

“Sounds good to me,” Mark said yawning and setting up his tent.

“I’ll take second shift,” Sarah volunteered. “Even if the big bear over there took it, he’d be asleep in five minutes.”

“Then its settled. We’ll each take two hour shifts. Mark, we’ll see you in four hours.”

“Got it.”

“Are you sure you don’t want me to take first watch?” Sarah asked.

“Thank you, Sarah, but I’ve had the most rest of any of us. You two need some sleep.”

She smiled. “You’re sweet. Goodnight.”

“What time are we leaving?” Mark asked finishing up his tent.

“So we’ll all have the same amount of rest we’ll have breakfast at noon. We should arrive at the castle no later than two.”

“Maybe all of this will be over soon.”

“I hope so, Mark. I hope so. Goodnight, you two. I’m going to walk a little farther down the path.”

“Goodnight, Jacob,” they both said.

After walking further down the path, Jacob sat down and wrapped his arms around his knees. The night sky was brightly lit with thousands of stars shining. It was a relaxing sight, though he was careful not to become too relaxed. He couldn’t handle it if he fell asleep and Mark and Sarah were devoured by some hell hound as they slept.

Being alone made him think about the events leading up to this. At one time he thought he had found his place in the small community and trying to put everyone on the right path. He thought he had found his purpose, but he always felt empty inside. Even though fighting this battle for God was stressful and often heartbreaking, it was the most alive he had felt in ages. He had also been lonely for a long time. Though he had always been a respected member of whatever community he was in, he had never felt like he had any true friends. He never felt like he belonged. Now though, traveling together and fighting with Mark and Sarah, he had a purpose, and for the first time, true friends. Even with the circumstances of being chased by the hooded demon and God only knew how many minions to fight, he was happy.

Looking up at the sky, he truthfully said aloud, "Thank you, God." Shortly thereafter, Jacob fell into prayer. "God, I hope everything is going according to your plan. So far you have protected us from every enemy that has come our way. Tomorrow, we hope to find our fourth companion. I pray that you will guide us to them. Finally, when all four of us are together, we can face the demon that pursues us and send him back to hell. Then your great plan will be complete. I know that when I pray sometimes, though I know I shouldn't so often, it's to ask for something that I personally need or want. Tonight that is not the case. I feel like I have everything I could need or want right now. Tonight I would like to ask for something for someone else.

"Ever since I met Mark, he has been nothing but kind to me. He's been reading the Bible and I know he's trying his best to let go of his drinking. I ask you give him the strength he needs to overcome his problem. I know in my heart he can be a good Christian man."

Jacob was silent for a moment, trying to think of how to put the next part of his prayers into words.

"I would also like to pray for Sarah. Lord, I know she has committed many sins in her past and done many wrongs in your eyes, but every human, even I have sinned against you at one time or another. She has had a hard life and many of her sins were to escape from her hard life when she saw no way out. I know this no excuse and everyone is punished for their sins in one way or another, but I pray you will be lenient on her. I also pray that you will help her overcome her pain and bitterness, so that she may look to you for guidance. Today, I think she finally realized that it is possible for someone to genuinely care for her without wanting her body in return. Help her to learn that there are people out there that she can trust and that she can put her trust into. I know in my heart that she can be the person you created her to be."

He took another pause to think.

"I…I guess there is one thing I wish to ask for myself. Help me to know what is truly right and wrong. Help me to sort out my feelings. I don't know what it is I feel for Sarah. I don't know if it's strong friendship, lust, …or love. What should I do? Am I supposed to tell her of your forgiveness and only be a friend to her? Would it not be wrong to judge her for her sins in the past and have no hopes of an intimate relationship with her? I'm a preacher and sometimes that makes my life confusing. I am a messenger for you, but I know that I am not above anyone else. Do I try to find out if I indeed do love Sarah or do I wait upon a virgin to marry me and bare my children? I am so confused right now. Give me a sign or a dream or even have a tree speak to me, anything to shed some light on my situation. I guess what I'm asking is…guide me. All these things I ask in your loving name and in the name of your only son, Jesus Christ. Amen."

Little did Jacob know, but not ten feet behind him, with tear-filled eyes was Sarah. She hadn't meant to listen in, but it was so unusual for her hear someone saying such kind things about her that she couldn't resist. Feeling guilty for eavesdropping, she turned to walk back to her tent. As she did, a root caught her foot and she tripped to the ground.

"Umph!"

Jacob turned instantly to see her lying flat on the ground. "Sarah? Are you okay?"

"Yeah, I'm fine."

"What are you doing here? I figured you would be asleep by now."

"Nah, I wasn't that tired. I thought I would come keep you company for a while."

"Thank you, I appreciate it." He looked into her eyes. "Have you been crying?"

"Huh…Ummm, I…" She frantically tried to think up a lie, but it was no use. "Jacob, I heard your prayer. I'm sorry I listened, but you said such nice things about me. You really do care. I know people say they will pray for you, but I never thought they actually would."

Jacob smiled. "That's my job Sarah."

"No, the way you prayed for me, you sounded like a friend."

"That's because I am."

"You prayed for God to have mercy on me. That's the nicest thing anyone has ever done for me."

"I just want you to get your life back on track."

"I know. I'll try my best, but it may be too late."

"It's never too late, Sarah. Until the last breath escapes your body, it's never too late."

"I'm sorry, again. I know praying is a private thing."

"That's okay. I guess we're even."

She looked at him confused.

"Last night when you were bathing. I walked up and saw you…naked."

She blushed and giggled in embarrassment. "Oh, my God, Jacob, what have you done to me? I'm acting like a school girl because you saw me without any clothes on. That's never happened to me before."

Jacob looked down and began to blush as well. "Do you want to sit down?"

"Yeah."

Taking his hand, she sat down and looked up at the sky. "You might want to scoot over a little."

"Why?" Jacob asked.

"It's a clear sky. God has a clear shot to strike me down."

"Ha. God doesn't quite do things that way." Neither of them said anything for a moment. "So, you heard everything I said about you?"

"Yeah."

"I don't know how I feel," he said after an awkward silence. "How do you feel about me, Sarah?"

"I…I don't know. I think you're cute and sweet, but I don't know how to care about someone without trying to sleep with them."

"It's not that hard," he assured her.

"Ha, you're talking about a ten year habit, Jacob."

"I know, but with God anything can be accomplished. Weren't you listening to me earlier?"

"Yeah. Sorry if a horned, fire-breathing demon made me forget."

"Oh yeah, I almost forgot about him."

"Well, it was very good anyway. You're different from all of the other preachers I've heard. You weren't just telling me I was going to hell. You told everyone how to have faith like everyone in the Bible did."

"Oh, I can be convicting when I want to, but there are other things to tell people besides what they are doing wrong."

"I noticed you used David and Daniel as examples."

"Yes, well they were very important people in the Bible. You and Mark inspired me to use them."

"Hmph, I never thought I would see the day that inspired a sermon, at least not the positive part of it."

"You're too hard on yourself."

"Yeah, well since I met you, I've been having this nasty little thing called guilt."

"They say that guilt is God's hand pressing down on you to tell you when you have done something wrong."

"He has strong hands," she said.

"Are you sorry for everything that you have done in your life?"

"I…feel bad about them. If what you say is true about God always being there for us, then I haven't been very appreciative."

"Well, you did have a hard time growing up. You just had your anger misplaced."

"You know, not one time since you met me have you called me a slut or a whore."

"That wouldn't be very nice, would it?"

"Well, it's true. Now that I'm having this new feeling of …religion…I feel kind of dirty."

"If you ask Jesus to come into your life, he will make it as if it never happened. All of your sins will be covered in his blood. Erased."

"Is it really that simple?"

"Yes. Right now, he's calling your name. All you have to do is answer his call and you'll be home where you belong."

A strange warm sensation suddenly fell over her. Listening to Jacob's words, her guilt melted away. For the first time in her life, she wanted to be a child of God. She could feel the blood of Jesus covering every inch of her body.

"Thank you, Jacob," she said with tears flowing.

"Thank God. He deserves more praise than I do."

"Thank you, God."

"Now, don't you feel the emptiness inside of you vanishing?"

"Yes, but what do I do now?"

"Well, usually I baptize people when they give their life to God, but we're not near a lake right now." Glancing down he saw her canteen at her side. "Do you still have water in there?"

"Oh, yes." She handed it to him.

Jacob unscrewed the top and sprinkled water onto her forehead. "Lord God, Sarah has given her life to you. She has repented of her sins and realized the error of her ways. With this water I wash away the sins and guilt that lies within her heart. I pray that you be with her in times of trial and lead her and guide her in your ways. May she be covered with the everlasting blood of your son, Jesus Christ. I ask these things in your holy name and in the name of your son, Jesus Christ. Amen."

As Sarah opened her eyes, she felt like a newborn child seeing the world for the first time.

"Now you never have to wonder where you will be when you die."

"I don't know what to say."

"You don't have to say anything. This is a new beginning. You have a second virginity."

She stayed silent for a moment. "Jacob? How can a good man like you have feelings for someone like me. I've sinned so much in my life."

Jacob smiled. "What sin?"

Sarah was speechless. All she could do was hug him. She loved this man in a way she never thought possible. Letting go she wiped the tears from her eyes. "How do I have a relationship with a man without…you know?"

He took her hand. "Well, first you need to find a man that doesn't want you for your body. He will take much more pleasure in just holding your hand." Jacob stroked her hair. "Another thing he'll want to do is comfort you. He'll be satisfied by just holding you in his arms and gazing up at the stars. He'll put no pressure on you and finally when he takes your hand in marriage and only then will he want to express his love to you physically."

She looked down in shyness. "Is it okay for me to kiss him?"

"Yes, I don't think there is anything wrong with that."

She looked up. Staring into his eyes she placed both hands on his face and then pressed her lips against his. He didn't resist but rather wrapped his arms around her. There was more power and more passion in this kiss than any she had ever experienced. The feeling was the same for Jacob. When they pulled apart, she looked at him and her green eyes sparkled.

"Now I'm going to do something I've never done before. I'm going to walk away, because I'm saving myself for someone special. Goodnight, Jacob."

"Goodnight, Sarah."

⁂

The next morning, Sarah made them another wonderful breakfast that Mark gulped up and Jacob took time to actually taste. Unlike before, they sat around cheerfully and laughed. The memories of last night were much more enjoyable than those of the previous ones. Mark had no clue of what had taken place as he was practically dead in his sleep. Neither Jacob nor Sarah told Mark, making the moment even more their own. Though Mark had a feeling he was missing something when he occasionally caught them holding hands.

"I swear, Sarah, I will pay you to be my cook until I die."

"What will you pay me with?"

"Why my incredible good looks of course."

"I'm afraid my price is much higher than that."

"It was very good," Jacob added.

"Thank you. I saw you had seconds."

"That's nothing compared to Mark's fourths."

"Yeah, I think I would have to slaughter a whole cow to fill him up."

"Well, I need to walk off my breakfast. Are you guys about ready to head out?"

"We would have to walk seventy miles for you to walk off your breakfast," Sarah said.

"Yes, Mark, we're ready to go whenever you are."

"Okay. Let's go."

⋊⋉

Finally after traveling on for an hour and a half, they stood awestruck outside of their destination.

"Wow!" Mark said. "I knew this place was supposed to be big, but man! Look up – it will make you dizzy!"

"It's beautiful," Sarah agreed.

"Yes, and it's been here for over two hundred years. I'm looking forward to seeing the inside," Jacob said.

"Then what are we waiting for?" Mark asked. "Let's crash this place."

"Wait, Mark," Jacob said grabbing his shoulder. "I don't know how wise it would be to crash into a castle."

"Yeah, Mark. I don't think we can just go up to the guard and say, 'We have an appointment, get out of the way.'"

"Hmm, you could be right. Jacob, How about you handle the guards?"

"Yeah. I think you're less likely to get us hanged," Sarah concurred.

"Very well."

As they approached the gate, the guard eyed them suspiciously. "State your business," he said in a low tone.

"Excuse me, Sir. My name is Jacob Cross and these are my traveling companions, Mark Raven and Sarah Mist. I know we're asking a lot, but we are in dire need of speaking with the King."

The guard squinted at him. "That is a large request. If I'm going to let you in, I'll have to hear a good reason."

"Oh, God! We're doomed," Mark said covering his eyes, knowing that most people wouldn't believe their reasons without proof. Jacob gave them a nervous glance before turning back to the guard. He was trying, unsuccessfully, to think of a way to explain this without getting the three of them thrown into an asylum. Sighing he decided to start from the beginning.

"As I said, my name is Jacob Cross, and I'm a preacher formerly from a small…"

"Wait!" the guard interrupted putting his hand in the air.

At first Jacob thought he had said something wrong.

"You are a man of God?" the guard asked.

He wondered why that would make a difference. “Yes I am.”

The guard suddenly changed his attitude. “I…I’m sorry Sir! I didn’t know. P...please come in, your friends, too. Forgive me.”

Jacob looked at him confused. “Forgive you? You didn’t do anything wrong. It’s your job to guard the gate. You do your job well.”

“Thank you, Sir. I’m not worthy of such praise.”

His words were confusing Jacob more and more. He knew people respected him for his position, but this man was speaking to him as if he were royalty.

The guard yelled for someone to open the gate and instantly it began to rise. Jacob motioned for Mark and Sarah to follow him and they walked through. As Jacob walked down the long tunnel path, he thought more about the way the guard had spoken to him. The poor man almost seemed to fear him.

Jacob stopped at the large wooden doors open at the side of the path, assuming they led into the town. When the doors finished opening, a tall man walked through. He had long blonde hair down his back and a well-trimmed mustache. It was obvious that he took pride in the way he looked. His clothes were well-tailored, and his sword hung on his belt under his cape that barely kissed the ground. To Jacob, he was the epitome of a royal knight. Jacob got a strange feeling as he looked at him. Was this the one?

“What is it Jacob?” Sarah asked.

“That man. I was just wondering if he might be who we’re looking for.”

“Nah, it couldn’t be,” Mark said. “He’s sober.”

Jacob and Sarah both gave him a dirty look.

“Just kidding.”

The man seemed to be staring straight ahead at nothing, as if he were concentrating on a far off painting that only he could see. The only way they were going to find out if he was the one was by speaking to him. The man didn’t seem to notice them even when they were right beside him.

“Sir? Maybe you can help us.”

At the sound of Jacob’s voice the man snapped out of his daze. “How dare you approach me in such a way?!” the man barked.

Jacob blinked in confusion as the man continued to shriek.

“When you address me you had better be on one knee and

address me as 'My Lord'!"

This seemed awfully pompous to Jacob, but he continued to be polite nonetheless.

"I'm sorry, My Lord." The words tasted bitter coming out. "We're not from around…"

"Yes, I've heard it before!" he interrupted. "*I'm not from around here.* But, ignorance is no excuse! If you come here, you had damn well better learn quick or you'll be beaten in the town square as a welcome!"

Although these orders were very quickly beginning to irritate him, Jacob held his tongue . But even though Jacob held his peace, Mark, God love him, was ready to show off his uncanny ability to mouth off.

"Hey, Jack ass! Back off! He's trying to be nice to you! Who do you think you are?!"

The man's eyes widened and he gasped at Mark's audacity. He pulled his sword. "How dare you, you filthy peasant son of a whore!"

"You say one more word about my mother and that sword is going somewhere you're not going to like."

"Silence! Such insolence. I am a noble. Anyone of lower status than I should and will bow down to me! I am second only to the Church and the King! To you, I am God."

Now he was really getting on Jacob's bad side.

"A noble, huh?" Mark continued. "Isn't that best translated as spoiled rich brat?"

The man sneered. "You don't know when to shut up. I guess I'll have to cut some respect into you!"

He quickly took a swing at Mark. Sarah screamed and closed her eyes, but instead of hearing Mark howl in pain, there was only a loud CLINK! Sarah slowly opened one eye.

There was no blood. There was a cross of steel between him and the other man's sword as Jacob had pulled his own blade and also blocked his strike.

Jacob shook his head. "That's a no-no."

The noble jerked his head toward Jacob. "You raise your sword to a noble? I can kill you for this."

"My life isn't yours to take."

He stared at Jacob and then smiled smugly. "Okay. Have it

your way. I'll fight you, but I won't kill you. I'm just going to put you on your knees where you belong and then I will personally beat you in the town square with the thickest limb I can find. You first!" he said pointing at Mark.

"I assure you that the only time I'll be on my knees is in prayer." Jacob was slow to anger, but more than willing to fight when necessary. Noble or not, this man needed to be taken down a notch.

The man took a step back. "En guard!"

They slowly circled, each waiting for the other to strike first. Jacob would win this battle of patience as it was the noble who struck first. The stranger was well trained, at least for a one-on-one duel, but he seemed to be fencing more than fighting. His attacks were quick and powerful, and though he was quick, Jacob blocked every strike with ease.

The knight gave him a mixed look of surprise and admiration, surprised he was defending himself so well. He chuckled under his breath, "Not bad. Now let's see what you have." He stepped back awaiting Jacob to strike.

Jacob moved cautiously, never taking his eyes off of his opponent. He finally held his breath to strike back. Jacob's strikes were fast, but not as powerful as the noble's. The noble smiled as he defended every blow with little effort. With one powerful action, he knocked Jacob back and slashed his cheek.

"Ahh! No fair!" Sarah called out.

"Yeah! Don't let him take you down, Jacob!"

Jacob rubbed his hand across his grazed cheek. This guy knew what he was doing.

"Now peasant, do you wish to give up and take your beating like a good little dog?"

Jacob answered him with a swift kick to the gut and a fist to the jaw sending the cocky soldier to his backside. "No. Bark-bark," Jacob said.

"Ohhhhh...I am going to enjoy making you bleed!" The noble jumped up and charged him, but Jacob dropped to the ground, using his feet to flip him backwards and then elbowed him in the nose.

"Grrrrr!" The knight groaned in anger and kicked his feet. Standing up holding his nose he literally growled at Jacob. "I'm not going to bother beating you. I'm going to slit your lowly throat right now!"

He kicked Jacob in the stomach sending him flying into the stone wall. The impact knocked his breath away. He had little time to gasp as the noble's sword came slicing at his head. He dropped to the ground and rolled away.

"Hold still, prick!" he shrieked. While he was on the ground the noble kicked dirt into his eyes.

"Gahh!"

"Hey, you stuck up jerk! Are you afraid to fight fair?!" Mark called out.

"Silence, peasant! I'll deal with you next!"

While Jacob was trying to clear his eyes, the noble took his advantage. The first kick caught him in his injured side and he screamed as if his ribs were shattered. Surely, the stitches had been torn. Warmth flowed eerily down his side. Jacob rolled over and clutched the wound while the noble kicked him numerous times in the opposite side.

"Get up, you filthy dog!!"

"That's it. His butt is mine," Mark finally said.

Before he could move though, pain and anger overflowed in Jacob and he took a page out of Mark's book. Shoving his arm up, he caught the noble with a perfect low blow. The stranger moaned and fell to the ground.

Jacob didn't want to fight dirty, but the Bible says, "Do unto others as you would have them do unto you." The noble was begging for it.

"Ouch," Mark said in discomfort.

"That works," Sarah agreed. "I've done that many times."

"Remind me again never to tick you off."

Walking up to the knight, Jacob kicked his sword away and held his own over him.

"Grrrr! Go ahead. Kill me. You win, peasant. But know this. My death will be avenged tenfold. Killing a noble is far worse than assaulting one."

"I'm not going to kill you. Besides, you attacked us first."

"Yeah!" Mark chimed in. "Isn't assaulting a preacher a free ticket into hell?"

The noble's eyes widened as if he had seen god himself.

"Oh my God..." He managed to wriggle to his knees. "You are a...reverend?"

"Yes, I am."

"Jesus, help me! I didn't know! You should have told me! I beg of you," he said grabbing Jacob's feet. "Don't condemn me to the fiery pits of hell!"

Jacob looked at him baffled. Where were these people getting this? "Condemn you? I can't do that."

"So, you'll have mercy on me."

"Yes…I mean, no…I mean, it's not possible for me to do that."

"Man, Jacob. They must think you guys are ogres," Mark said.

"What's your name?"

"J…Jonathan. Jonathan Lancaster."

"Will you tell me something, Jonathan?"

"Yes, anything."

"Why are people here so afraid of preachers?"

"My Lord, don't you of all people know? You are messengers of God. You hold our way into heaven. With just a wave of your hand you can send us to heaven or hell. You hold our very lives in your hand."

Jacob couldn't believe what he was hearing. Even Mark and Sarah were giving each other confused looks.

"Who told you that, Jonathan?"

"Why, the ministers of our kingdom of course. Even the King himself lives in fear of them."

Jacob smelled a rat. "Jonathan, will you take me to these ministers?"

"Oh, yes, of course. Once again, I'm sorry, my Lord."

"Please, just Jacob. It's okay Come on, Mark, Sarah. Let's get to the bottom of this."

As they walked through the huge wooden doors, the sun temporarily blinded them. They shielded their eyes to reveal what looked like a lost city of legend, a beautiful town shadowed by a glorious castle.

"Whoa," Mark said under his breath.

"This place is incredible!" Sarah said marveling.

Jacob was speechless.

"Welcome to Freedom Castle," Jonathan said cheerfully.

"My, you do have a beautiful kingdom," Jacob finally said.

"I'm honored by your words, Jacob. My home is your home."

Once again, the confusion returned to Jacob. What had these so called men of God been teaching these people to make them afraid to even breathe in their presence?

"Tell me, Jonathan. How long have these holy men been here?"

"Oh, about two years now."

"I see. Was there any kind of religion in the community before they came?"

"Not for years. The church died out during the reign of my Lord's grandfather."

Jacob was no genius, but things were coming together. "So, these holy men are the first to be in this kingdom for over fifty years?"

"Yes, and we are eternally grateful to them. They saved us from ourselves. Before they came we were trapped on a path to hell. They showed us the error of our ways."

Jacob wanted to meet these people, but he was going to have to be careful not to get the three of them killed.

"Where are they now, Jonathan?"

"You should be seeing them any minute now and the King. A public beating is scheduled to take place any time now."

"A beating?"

Not five seconds after the words came from his mouth, there was a loud pop and a woman's scream filled the air. It continued three more times before Jacob looked toward the square to see a young woman kneeled over a platform with her bare back being beaten with a cane.

"I'm sorry!" she cried. "God forgive me!"

"What did this girl do, Jonathan? She can't be over sixteen."

"Humph!" he muttered in disgust. "The little whore engaged in sexual intercourse with a fine upstanding boy."

"Then why isn't he up there?"

Jonathan looked at him as if he were insane. "He's the son of a noble. He was born innocent. He was obviously seduced. The slut came from a low class house."

Sarah was ready to plant her Bo into the back of his head.

"What does social class have to do with anything?"

"Don't you of all people know? The rich are blessed by God while the poor are shunned?"

Jacob seen and heard enough. He couldn't hold his tongue any longer. "Stop that! Leave the girl alone!"

Everything went silent and there were whispers all around. In the middle of the square, there were three men dressed in white garments. One of them had blonde hair and was clean shaven. He had been the one beating the girl. The second man was heavyset with a wooly black beard. The last one was almost a unhealthily skinny with pale skin, black hair and sunken cheekbones. The man wearing a crown in the front row of the audience was obviously the King.

"Who dares to speak to us that way?!" the blonde one asked indignantly.

"Here we go again," Mark whispered.

"I dare!" Jacob shouted walking closer.

Jonathan not knowing what to think ran up to introduce him.

"My Lords, this is Jacob Cross. He is one of your fellow brothers."

"Brother?" the tubby one asked.

"He is a man of God as well."

All three of the men gave each other an uneasy look. The King looked at Jacob with great interest. The blonde one cleared his throat and gained his composure.

"Ah, I understand Jacob. You wish to do the beating of this lowly sinner? Is that why you wished for me to stop?"

"No, I wished for you to stop because you're out of control. Who do you think you are?"

"Humph!" the chunky one grunted. "I am Lord Featherton!"

"I am Lord Shian!" the sickly one said stepping forward.

"And I am Lord Dorin!" the blonde one said. "Together we are the three wise men!"

"So does that translate into dummy, fat, and oh my God eat something or you're going to die?" Mark asked.

Jacob hung his head and thought, *Mark, don't you ever think anything and not say it?*

"Insolent dog!" Lord Featherton cried.

"Are you guys getting déjà vu?" Mark asked.

"What are you doing?!" Jonathan yelled in a whisper.

"Setting things straight," Jacob said.

"What gives you the right to beat an innocent girl who made a mistake?"

"An innocent girl?" Dorin asked. "She's a lowly dog."

"There's another thing! Where is all of this lowly dog stuff coming from? Did Jesus not ride a donkey to lower himself to all men?"

The crowd gasped.

"Blasphemy!" Featherton cried.

Lord Shian raised his hands and calmed the crowd.

"Nonsense!" Dorin said. "We all know that Jesus rode a mighty steed and healed only the rich. Did he not say blessed are the rich and may the poor be beaten with a cane?"

"No, he did not say that! What Bible are you reading?!"

"Silence!" Shian said. "We'll hear no more of this evil! You!" he said pointing to a man in the crowd.

"Yes, my Lord?"

"Tell this false prophet the teachings of God!"

"Yes, sir!" The man stepped up nervously and spoke. "God is vengeful. He punishes all those who sin and if the sin is bad enough they are condemned to hell for all eternity. The rich are to be respected and all must obey the preachers of his word or suffer a horrible fate."

Lord Shian nodded in satisfaction and the man went back to his place. Jacob was stunned.

"...You people don't even twist the word. You're just liars."

"Liars?!" Featherton cried in insult. "I'll stick your head on a pike!"

Finally the King broke in. "You! Jacob, was it? If you are a man of God why do you mock your fellow brothers' teachings?"

"These are not my brothers."

"That is quite right!" Dorin cut in. "Your Highness, this is no man of God. He is merely a commoner posing as one of us to spread false messages."

"Your highness," Jacob said with a slight bow, "with all due respect, I know the Bible is sometimes hard to understand, but by reading it, can't you see that what these men say is a lie?"

"Read?" he said confused. "We are not allowed to read the Holy scriptures. To do so would result in instant death and damnation."

The three wise men gave each other an uneasy look.

"Ah, it all makes sense perfect sense now. I wondered how you could all get this from the Bible, but you haven't. These men came in one day deciding they wanted to rule a Kingdom, but not with swords. They did it with religion. They scared you into believing that only preachers could read the word of God. That way they could tell you that God was a tree and you would have to take their word for it."

The three wise men were sweating heavily now.

"Your highness, if that were true, could I hold the word?" Jacob pulled out his Bible. "This is the Holy Bible, so that must mean they are lying. Even if they were telling the truth then it means I am indeed a man of God."

Everyone began to whisper and the king looked suspiciously at the three wise men.

"Your highness!" Shian said. "He holds the scriptures with gloved hands! He could not hold them with his bare hands."

Jacob rolled his eyes, sighed and began to pull off his glove.

"Seize them!" Featherton shouted. "Kill them! They are enemies of God!"

This outburst made the king even more suspicious.

Mark and Sarah ran to Jacob's side.

"It's time to kick some royal guard butt!" Mark said in excitement.

"What's the plan?" Sarah asked.

"Try not to hurt them. They are merely confused men."

Six armed guards charged them. These were special elite guards loaned to the wise men to do their bidding, personally trained by Jonathan.

"Should my guards and I help my lord?" Jonathan asked.

The King watched on with great interest. "No, that won't be necessary. This Jacob interests me. He humbles himself as a normal person and did you hear him just now? He told his companions not to hurt the guards if they could help it. Besides, you personally trained these men. They shouldn't have that much trouble taking down two men and a woman."

Jonathan hung his head in shame. "The man named Jacob bested me in a fight."

The King looked at him wide-eyed. "He defeated you, Jonathan? The greatest swordsman in the kingdom? That interests me even more. Perhaps God is on this man's side. This fight may determine who is telling the truth."

Jacob branched off with the commander of the group while the other five moved in on Sarah and Mark.

"Ah, come on! This is hardly fair!" Mark pouted. "Jacob has one, you have two and I'm stuck with three! I'm good, but I'm not that good!"

"Okay I'll even things out," Sarah said walking to one of the guards in front of Mark. "You wouldn't hurt a lady would you?" she asked with puppy dog eyes while rubbing her finger across his chest plate.

"I ummm…"

The second he dropped his guard, she swung a direct hit across his jaw sending him to dream land.

"There. Are you happy?"

"What a woman!"

The remaining four moved in on them and it was all they could do to keep from being sliced to pieces. The best they could do was remain on the defensive until an opening came to strike.

Meanwhile, Jacob and the commander were merely circling each other much as he and Jonathan had earlier. Jacob was making sure to let him make the first move. Unfortunately it was going to be a slow fight, because his opponent was using the same strategy, Seeing as how they weren't getting anywhere, the young man began a battle of words.

"Give up now and the three wise men might have mercy on you. You seem like a decent person. I don't want to have to hurt you."

"I'm afraid not. I intend to prove that these imposters are filling your heads with lies and deceit."

"Then you leave me no choice." The young man charged at him with a series of slashes, left, right, and overhead. Like Jonathan earlier, he was shocked to see Jacob block every strike with ease.

"I'm afraid you will find that I have a lot more behind me than you do," Jacob said.

Behind them Mark and Sarah were practically running in circles from their attackers. They backed into one another once and almost killed each other. They blocked an attack here and there, but for the most part it was four guards chasing a man and woman running for their lives. If one hadn't know they were going to be slaughtered it might have been comical. Although, they were doing their part to keep the fight between Jacob and the commander one-on-one.

"You can't win, Jacob!" the young man yelled giving Jacob everything he had.

"We'll just let God decide that, won't we?" Jacob decided to go on offense since his attacker had tired himself out a little. When the commander came at him with an overhead swing, he kicked him in the stomach and sliced his chin.

"Ah!" He put his hand to his chin and stared. "You're the first person since Lord Jonathan to make me bleed."

"What's your name?" Jacob asked.

He looked at him puzzled. This was an odd question to ask in the heat of battle. Nonetheless he answered anyway.

"Andrew."

"Well, Andrew, why don't we quit fighting? We have no reason to hurt each other."

"Oh, I'm afraid we do. I'm under orders."

"Tell me, are your orders the most important thing in your life? If you were ordered to rape a woman and kill her baby would you?"

"I…Well, of course not."

"You said you didn't think I was a bad person. You told me that you didn't want to hurt me. Why don't you follow your feelings?"

"You're a blasphemer!"

"So they say. Don't you think it's a little strange that they tell you to live in fear of God and you aren't allowed to read his word yourself as proof? God meant for everyone to read his word. Look." He took his Bible from his coat. "Do you want me to take off my glove?"

Slipping off his glove, he opened the Bible and pressed his hand to the pages. Everyone gasped as they saw this.

"If I'm touching this, then I must be a man of God, or even if I'm not, then the three wise men are lying to you."

The three of them scowled. He had just checkmated them. Andrew looked at the three wise men, then back at Jacob.

"Men! Leave his friends alone!"

"Thank you, God!" Mark cried and hugged up to Sarah for dear life.

"Fools! Dorin cried. This man shows up out of nowhere and you believe him over us?! You'll burn in hell for this!"

"Save it!" Jacob snapped at him. "It's over. These people are closer to heaven than they have ever been." Jacob walked toward the King. "Here, your highness. Hold my Bible. I promise you won't burst into flames or melt into a puddle of flesh."

Hesitantly the King reached for it and took it in his hands. "You speak the truth."

"Read this scripture," Jacob said pointing. "Read it aloud."

The King read aloud John 3:16, the same scripture he had shown Mark their first day together.

"This speaks of love and forgiveness, not fear and wrath."

"Yes, of course. That is what God is. He isn't a bully up in heaven waiting for you to mess up so he can strike you down. He's a loving Father waiting to pick you up when you fall along the way."

"Curse you, Preacher!" Featherton cried. "We had this city in the palm of our hands! They obeyed our every word! You ruined it!"

"Silence!" the king yelled. "If it were up to me I would have you three beheaded. But I'll ask Sir Jacob what the proper punishment should be."

"Well, your highness, I agree that they indeed deserve the punishment you had in mind, but Jesus said it is not our place to judge. I think I have a suitable punishment though."

Walking up to Lord Dorin, he carved a cross into his cheek with his sword. He then did the same thing to the other two.

Now your highness, spread the word to every town of what these men have done. They can now be identified by the marks on their cheeks. If they ever try this again, the people will know who they are and I doubt they will have as much mercy on them as you have.

The king nodded and turned his attention back to the three of them. "Now be gone, you three! If I ever see your faces again you will find your heads on pikes!"

They ran away like whipped dogs with their tails between their legs. Smiling, the King looked back at Jacob.

"Sir Jacob, I can't thank you enough for helping us. We have all been fools for letting the blind lead us. I am the most ashamed for I am a King and I was made a fool. Please, honor my request and stay here with us and teach us the right way to worship God."

Jacob smiled and nodded.

"Of course, your highness. I would be honored. But I have something very important to…talk…to you…a…uhhh!" Before he could finish his sentence, Jacob collapsed to the ground.

"Sir Jacob!" Jonathan cried kneeling at his side. "Are you alright? Oh, no. It's blood."

"I…I didn't cut him!" Andrew said nervously.

"I know you didn't," Sarah said kneeling beside Jacob. "This is a wound he already had."

"Yeah!" Mark added. "It must have reopened when somebody went on a kicking fit."

"I…I didn't know."

"Well, you do now!" Sarah snapped.

"Quick!" the King said. "Get him to a room! Jonathan, you get the doctor."

"Yes, my Lord."

The King watched as they carried Jacob to the castle. "This is the least we can do for the man who saved us."

"My goodness!" the doctor said as he observed Jacob's side. Pushing seventy, he was short and balding with solid white hair. He had a funny little beard that matched the color of the hair. The funniest part about him was the monocle on his eye. You could tell by just looking at him that he was the richest person in town, next to the King, but not once did he act like it.

"This work is so sloppy! Where did he get this treated?"

"The slums of Takkar," Mark answered.

"I take that back. He actually got decent work considering the surroundings. I always figured there they gave you a bottle of whiskey and sent you on your way."

"Well, the doc there actually tries to treat people as professionally as he can," Sarah said.

"Well, God bless him."

"So, how bad is it?" Mark asked.

"Well, it's actually a good thing Sir Jonathan disturbed the wound. Do you see this odd color of red it's turning?"

"Yeah," they said at the same time.

"Pretty soon he was going to be suffering from a very nasty infection. Without the proper herbs and medicine that I doubt exist in Takkar, he would be a lot worse than he is now. All colored fluids would be leaking and draining out while he suffered on the ground. Soon after it would all turn green and decay."

"Yeesh!" Sarah said sluggishly.

"You really know how to paint a pretty picture, Doc," Mark said.

"Yes, but luckily we can stop it now. In a way Sir Jonathan did him a favor."

"Oh, I have a feeling it was someone of a lot higher authority looking out for him," Mark said.

"Yeah," Sarah agreed. "Jonathan was like as chess piece."

"Either way it should be okay. Put this ointment on him whenever you change his bandages. I'll look in on him tonight and tomorrow morning."

"Thanks, doc," Mark said shaking his hand.

"Oh, and whatever you do, don't let him overexert himself."

"Oh, God," Sarah said. "We might as well tie him to the bed."

"If necessary I would suggest that. Good day."

After seeing him to the door, the two of them sat back at Jacob's side.

"Oh, Jacob," Sarah said calmly. "How many times are you going to scare me like this?"

Mark watched as she gently stroked Jacob's hair. "You really like him, don't you?"

"Huh? Well you do, too, don't you?"

"That's not what I mean. I'm not that dense. I've seen the way you two look at each other and how you try your hardest not to sit or stand by each other."

"It really was kind of obvious wasn't it?" she said giggling.

"What gives? I thought you weren't going to be turned into a sweet dress-wearing church girl."

"Well, I'm not, yet. But Jacob makes me want to change. He is the only man who has ever been good to me besides Angus."

"I've been good to you."

"If I took my clothes off right now and asked you to jump in bed with me, would you refuse?"

"Yes, Jacob's in the bed."

"Be serious."

"Okay, you've got me there."

"I thought so." She looked back at Jacob. "He's the only man to never think of me as an object."

"I don't think of you just as an object."

"I know, you're just a typical man."

"Ouch. Well, I have to admit that he is the greatest guy I've ever known. I've never seen anyone who can resist all temptation. He doesn't drink, he doesn't swear, he doesn't...gulp...have sex. At least not until he's married."

"It kind of makes you feel ashamed doesn't it?" Sarah asked.

"Yeah. Hey, at least he sets a good example for us."

They turned as the door opened and Jonathan walked through. "Hello, how is he?"

"Unconscious, thanks to you," Mark snapped.

"Yes, I'm afraid I owe all of you an apology."

"You're darn right you owe us one you..."

"Mark! Hush!" Sarah interrupted. "Sorry, Jonathan, if you haven't noticed, he's a bit of a hothead."

"I see."

"Anyway, we accept your apology. You were only following the teachings of those three idiots anyway."

"...Yes, well, I hope I didn't injure him too badly."

"No, he's all fixed up. The doctor says if we keep putting medicine on him and keep his bandages clean, he should be fine."

"Ah, very good. I haven't properly introduced myself. I am Jonathan Lancaster, captain of the royal guard."

"I am Sarah Mist from Takkar," She said shaking his hand. "This is Mark Raven from Bruton."

"A pleasure to meet you."

"Mark?" Sarah asked. "How long are you going to be a jackass?"

"No offense, buddy, but it's going to take me a little while to warm up to you."

"I understand. Anyway, what is it that has brought you to our kingdom, Miss Sarah?"

"Uhhhhhh, that is a very long, complicated, and unbelievable story. I think it would be best if Jacob told you when he wakes up."

"Oh, well alright. I'll take my leave of you now. If either of you need anything at all don't hesitate to ask. You are welcomed guests here at the castle."

"Thank you, Jonathan."

As he walked out Sarah turned to Mark. "My, we're quick to hold a grudge aren't we?"

"Hey, you have to admit he was more than a jerk before."

"Yes, I know. But, he was misled, heck we both were."

"At least we…I wasn't a jerk to him."

"What is that supposed to mean?!"

"Hey, you said some pretty nasty things during your hissy fit."

"I…GRRR! Men! Well, the bottom line is that none of us are perfect. You keep saying you wish you could be more like Jacob, this would be a good place to start."

"Yeah."

"Besides, he could very well be our last comrade."

"Surely Jacob doesn't still think its him. Then again, you never know with Jacob."

"Yeah, if he's one thing, its unpredictable." Mark stared at him and began to laugh.

"What is it?"

"I was just thinking. What a group we would be. A preacher, a drunk, a harlot, and a prideful noble."

CHAPTER 7

Jacob woke with a pounding headache. The medicine had helped his side, but he still felt like death walking. All through the night he had slipped in and out of sleep. When he was awake he felt as if he were still asleep, but with pain and nausea. What little sleep he did have was haunted by nightmares.

In one, the hooded demon had cloned himself and surrounded Jacob, reaching for him. In another, there was an army of blade arms and others he couldn't begin to describe attacking him. Not once through the whole night did he have a peaceful dream.

Jacob muttered under his breath and opened his eyes. What little light there was in the room was like direct sunlight. He shut his eyes and squinted to let them adjust. Straight ahead of him sleeping in a chair was Mark with his mouth hanging open. Jacob moved his left hand and felt hair. He looked over to see Sarah asleep with her head resting on his arm. They had both stayed with him through the night. He smiled and tapped Sarah on the head. She made cute little sleepy noises before opening her eyes.

"Good morning," he said.

"Oh…Jacob," She said wiping her eyes. "You're awake."

"Yeah. Have you been here the whole night?"

"Yes, we wanted to stay with you."

"What happened? Where are we?"

"We're in the castle. After you showed everyone that the three wise men were phonies, you collapsed. Your side got ripped open again during your fight with Jonathan. The doctor said you were lucky to be treated in time. You were starting to get a really bad infection."

"Oh, have you talked to the king?"

"No, but Jonathan was here last night. He wanted to know why we had come here, but I thought it would be best if you explained it to him."

"Ha. Leave me with the fun part, huh?"

"Hey, you're the holy man. It will seem less insane coming from you."

"Were there any attacks last night?"

"No, not that I've heard of."

"Then we can't waste any time," he said sitting up. "We have to talk to the king."

"Hold your horses, minister," Sarah said. "The doc said for you to take it easy."

"The doc doesn't know what kind of situation we're in."

"You still need to slow down the pace. Come on, a guard last night told us to come get breakfast whenever we felt like it. At least get something to eat first."

He thought for a second. "That does sound nice. I'm starving."

"Me, too. Let's go."

"Don't we need to wake, Mark?"

"Oh, yes. I forgot about the human eating machine. The king had better be loaded. After feeding Mark a few meals, his food bill will be sky high. Hey, Mark! Wakey-wakey, sleepy head."

"Huh?"

Jonathan stood up from his seat to greet them as they entered the dining room. "Ah, Sir Jacob, how are you feeling?"

"Please, Jonathan, just Jacob, and I'm fine, thank you. My stomach is a little upset, but fine otherwise."

"Very good. How about you, Miss Sarah, and Mark?"

"Right as rain," Sarah said cheerfully.

"Yeah, me too," Mark said yawning. "Although I'm starving completely to death."

"Please, sit down and order whatever you wish. Our chef Martin is a master of cooking and can make just about everything in existence. Steve, everyone is seated."

"Coming, Lord Jonathan!" The door to the kitchen opened and

a happy-faced, skinny man came walking out in a traditional chef's hat and apron. "Yes, sir? May I take your orders?"

"Man, you guys have a regular restaurant here don't you?" Mark asked.

"Ha. Yes, anytime between the hours of eight A.M. and 8 P.M. you can find Stephen here to whip you up something in a flash. There is always someone in the kitchen, but none as talented as Stephen."

"You flatter me."

"I only speak the truth. Now, Stephen, I will have four pancakes smothered in syrup, butter and powdered sugar with a cup of coffee, cream and sugar."

"Very good, sir. Now what will our guests be having?"

"Can you make me a deer burger like this big?" Mark said circling his hands to the size of a plate.

"For breakfast?" Sarah asked.

"Hey, we slept late. It will be lunch before long."

"Ha, no problem, sir. Would you like anything with that?"

"How about a side of mashed potatoes?"

Sarah stared blankly at him. "How do you not weigh six hundred pounds?"

"And what will you have to drink with that?"

"A big frosty glass of be—I mean…Win…" He caught eyes with Jacob. "Ah, heck, a glass of water."

"Okay, and for the lady?"

"I would like sausage, bacon, and scrambled eggs, please. And could I have a glass of milk with that?"

"Of course, madam."

"Okay, and you sir?" he asked looking to Jacob.

"Ummm, my stomach isn't feeling the best in the world, so I think I'll have soup."

"Ah, what kind?"

"Do you know how to make chicken and rice soup?"

"Soups are my specialty, sir. I have made every soup known to man at least once. I have a special blend of herbs and spices that will make your mouth water."

"That sounds nice. I'll have water with that."

"Okay, it will be about half an hour. I have plenty of help back there."

"Oh, Stephen? Can you go ahead and bring me my coffee?"

"Yes, my Lord, right away."

"Now, Jacob, I know we got off to a rocky start."

I wonder whose fault that was? Mark thought, and for once, didn't say.

"I apologize for the way I treated you and hope we can start fresh."

"Of course, Jonathan. All is forgiven. Those three fake preachers were misleading you."

"…Yes. Anyway, now that we have a chance to talk, tell me what it is that brought you to our kingdom?"

Jacob hung his head low and opened with the question he asked many times before. "Tell me, Jonathan, are you a religious man?"

He seemed surprised by the question. "Well, yes. I believe in a higher power."

"Then you believe in heaven and hell?"

"I've always heard of them, but I've never really thought about it."

"I promise you, Jonathan, they exist. I have seen the inhabitants of both places."

"I don't understand where you're going with this."

"Let me ask you another question. What is your definition of religion?"

"Well, I suppose it would be to serve the said higher power that created you the best way you can. The three wise men taught us that God is vengeful and that he is always looking for a reason to strike you down. You however teach of a God that forgives and is always there when you need him most."

"That is how God is. I promise I will teach everyone the truth and erase their false teachings. Did the three wise men ever talk to you about Satan?"

"You know, as a boy growing up, my mother spoke of him as our enemy and said he was the one out to get us, but not once did the wise men ever speak of him. I always found that odd."

"Your mother was right, Jonathan. He is our enemy and he is always out to get us…now more than ever."

Jonathan looked confused.

"As I said, there is a heaven and a hell and…all of hell is being unleashed on the world."

"What do you mean?"

"Just as there is a Satan and a hell, there are demons, and during the past two days I have fought my share of them."

"You mean there are demons here on earth?"

"Yes, and they want to take the world as their own. I know this sounds crazy and I don't blame you if you don't believe me, but Mark and Sarah have witnessed this just as I have."

They both nodded in agreement.

"But, I thought God was in control."

"He is, but for some reason he is allowing this to happen."

"Why?"

"We may never know. But, during my first encounter with the demons I was knocked unconscious and an angel appeared to me. He said that God has chosen me to rid the world of this evil. He also told me that I would find three companions in three different cities to help me. I have found two of them and I believe you may be the third, Jonathan."

"Me?" Jonathan asked as Stephen brought him his cup of coffee. "What would make you think that it's me?"

"I just get a feeling when I look at you. Plus, did I not hear the king say that you are the greatest swordsman in the kingdom?"

"Yes, but I don't think that qualifies me to fight beside you. I do believe in God, but I'm a far cry from a good Christian man."

"Hey, buddy, we aren't anywhere close to perfect," Mark said.

"That's true," Sarah agreed. "Jacob found Mark drunk inside of a bar and me lying unconscious outside of one."

He gave them a puzzled look.

"I know it doesn't sound like we're the ideal people to help a preacher save the world, but when we fight together there is just…a connection."

"Yeah," Mark added. "It's like it was meant to be."

"Yes, when I look at the three of you, you do seem like a team. I suppose it's because it really was God's will for you to be together. But, I still don't think I am the fourth member. I don't see myself saving the world from demons."

"No offense, Jonathan, but do you think it was exactly our childhood dream?" Mark asked.

"Ha. Yes, well I couldn't possibly leave the kingdom anyway. It is my sworn duty to stay at the king's side and protect him at all costs. I made that vow before everyone, including God. I don't think he would want me to break that vow, would he?"

Jacob nodded in agreement, but still felt that he was right about Jonathan.

"Although, I think I know who it might be."

"Who?" Sarah asked.

"Young Andrew. The man you were fighting against with the three wise men."

"Oh, yes," Jacob recalled.

"I trained him in all of my skills. He is almost my equal in every way. Besides, he isn't part of the special forces anymore so he may better serve you."

"Are you sure?" Jacob asked.

"Yes, quite sure. I'll inform him of the news after breakfast."

"There is one other thing, Jonathan."

"Yes?"

"I don't mean to question the way you post your guards, but is two men all that ever watch the front gate?"

"Well, there hasn't been a war in years and I doubt anyone would ever want to invade us, so we usually keep minimal security at the gate. Why?"

"Well, the leader of the demons seems to follow us wherever we go in an attempt to annihilate us. We needed to come here, but by doing so we may have put everyone in danger."

"Ah, I see. I'll take care of it."

"I hope you'll tell your men exactly what they're up against."

"I'm not sure I can do that, Jacob. I myself do not know exactly what we're up against."

"He has a point, Jacob," Mark said. "Unless you have seen what we have firsthand you can't possibly have a clue what they are."

"I suppose you're right."

"Well, enough talk of demons, devils, and goblins, and such. Let us all enjoy a fine breakfast and get to know each other better."

As he had read his mind, Stephen and his assistant brought out all of their meals. As he sat each meal in front of them they were captivated by the addictive aroma. None of them were displeased.

Mark's deer burger was even bigger than he had envisioned. Sarah's sausage and bacon were cooked to perfection and her eggs were especially fluffy. Jacob took a sip of his soup and almost moaned in delight. It was definitely on the top five list of things he had ever eaten. That one sip seemed to settle his stomach completely.

"MMMMM!" Sarah said taking a bite of eggs. My compliments definitely go to the chef.

"Thank you, madam. It's always great to see the look of pleasure on the faces of people who eat my food."

"See?" Jonathan said. "I told you he was the best cook around."

"I believe you."

"Man!" Mark said. "Jonathan? Is there a way for me to become a knight so I can eat this food every day."

"Everything is wonderful, Stephen," Jacob added.

"My pleasure, Lord Jacob."

Jacob could not get used to everyone calling him Lord.

"Thank you, Stephen." Jonathan said. "Everything looks delicious."

"Very good. I'll leave you now."

"So, is everything to your liking?"

"Oh, yes," Jacob said slurping soup as politely as he could.

"Yes, Jonathan. Everything is wonderful."

"Well, there is one thing that could be better," Mark said.

Everyone looked at him as he took a sip of water. He looked at Jacob.

"You just had to take my beer away, didn't you?"

They all laughed and continued on with their breakfast.

Mark moaned and held his stomach as after finishing his meal.

"Jacob? Can you and Sarah carry me up to my room?"

"Everything was great, Jonathan," Jacob said.

"Yes," Sarah agreed. "I haven't had a meal that delicious in a long time."

"Yes, well your thanks should go to Stephen. I'll tell him you enjoyed it," he said sipping down the last of his coffee. "Now then, you may have an audience with the king later in the day. In the meantime, why don't the three of you take a tour of our grand town? We have plenty to see. Weapon shops, book stores, and later if you get hungry, restaurants."

"Ohhh, I don't know if I'll be eating anymore today," Mark said.

"Yeah. That will last about forty-five minutes," Sarah said grinning.

"Okay then, you just go enjoy yourselves and I'll take care of the gate situation. I'll also inform the king ahead of time some of what he needs to know."

"Sir Jonathan! Sir Jonathan!" a voice cried out. Suddenly the door busted open and Andrew came running in. "Sir Jonathan! Oh, there you are. Thank heavens!"

"My God, Andrew, calm yourself. You act as if you've seen a ghost."

"It's much worse than that, sir! It's a demon! It has the face of the devil himself!"

"Oh no," Mark said. "Why do I get the feeling I know who that is?"

"Doesn't he ever give up?" Sarah asked.

"No," Jacob said. "Come on! We have to protect the people!"

"Whoa, whoa, whoa!" Mark said jumping in front of him. "Didn't Doc say for you to rest and not over exert yourself?"

"I don't know. I was unconscious."

"Well, he did."

"Yeah Jacob," Sarah pleaded. "You can't fight. You'll only make yourself sicker."

"I appreciate your concern, but I don't think the doctor quite understands our situation. Have you forgotten that we have to fight these things together?"

"Yes, but we can't if you kill yourself."

"I won't, Mark. Besides, I have a higher Doctor on my side."

"He has a point," Sarah said.

"Oh, brother," Mark said covering his face. "What the heck! I wouldn't feel safe without our sharpshooter anyway."

"Will you help us, Jonathan?"

"Of course, Jacob."

"Let's go then."

"Where is this demon, Andrew?"

"At the town square, Sir Jonathan."

"You…go lie down. You're pale as a ghost."

"Yes, sir."

Jonathan turned to Jacob.

"What are we up against, Jacob? That's normally one of the bravest soldiers I have. Now he's white and shivering, looking like he's going to wet himself. What on earth does that?"

"Nothing on earth, Jonathan. Something in hell."

They ran down the concrete stairs and out the door into town. Arriving at the square they all saw what Andrew had spoken of. Jonathan gasped. It wasn't the hooded demon as Mark had thought, but a minion none the less.

It hissed and drooled at the sight of them. Like all the others it's skin was a sickish color and looked like rubber. There was no skin on its head, but rather sported a large exposed human skull with sharpened teeth. Besides it's claws and rather large size it seemed like no more than a mindless zombie, until it spread its wings.

"Oh, crap," Mark yelped.

The demon's wings gleamed in the light and were covered with glimmering blades.

"Sir Jonathan!" a soldier called out. "Thank goodness you're here!"

Jonathan looked around to see blood splattered all over the pavement. Many of his men looked like they had been in a war.

One man clutched the place where his right arm used to be. Another was sprawled out and decapitated. Others were still in one piece, but crimson gushed from cuts and gashes. It had been no wonder that Andrew had looked so terrified. At this sight Jonathan was tempted to back away.

"My God. What is it, Jacob?"

"That, Jonathan, is an inhabitant of hell. This is what we fight every day."

"How do we kill it?"

"Good question," Mark said. "Sometimes you can hack them to pieces and sometimes an army can't put a dent in them."

"There's only one way to find out," Sarah said stepping

forward. "We go in for the kill."

"Hold it," Jacob said grabbing the back of her shirt. "Those sharp things on its back and the mangled men lying around make me think otherwise."

The creature began hissing and screeching before taking flight.

"On the ground!" Jacob shouted.

Mere seconds after they hit the ground, the creature dove down in an attempt to cut them in half. Seeing that it had failed it circled around again for another shot.

"It's coming back!" Mark yelled.

As it missed them by inches. Jonathan stood up.

"Jonathan! What are you doing?!"

"Stay down, Sarah. I'll take care of this thing."

"This guy is nuts!" Mark said with his head still down.

"Jonathan! Watch out!" Jacob called.

The creature came in for a third dive and straight at Jonathan. As it got within inches of him he dropped and slashed at the same time. The creature hissed as he sliced it's shoulder.

Jacob saw that the blade had done damage. Jonathan rolled back to their group.

"So, it can be injured," Jonathan said.

"Yes," Jacob said. "The only problem it attacking it without losing our heads."

"But, the thing is so darn fast. How do we do that?" Sarah asked.

"Hey!" Mark said as an idea came to him. "There is only one of us that can hit things from a hundred yards away."

"Yes, Jacob, your crossbow."

"I'll try, but it's not easy to hit a moving target no matter how good you are."

"Right now, it's the only idea I've got," Mark said still burying his head into the ground.

Taking a deep breath Jacob aimed at the creature. He pulled the trigger and sent an arrow flying. It hit, but only went through its foot.

"See? It's almost impossible to hit. I think I only made it mad."

"Just keep trying until we think of something else," Sarah said.

Jacob kept shooting blindly at the aerial bomber, but only hit two out of seven shots. On hits its thigh while the other managed to hit it in the gut. It was a nice shot, but didn't seem to even slow the thing down.

"This isn't getting us anywhere!" Jonathan yelled.

Once again he jumped up ready to take another charge from the thing.

"You're right Mark. This guy is nuts," Sarah said.

As it came down, Jonathan tried the same thing he had before, but missed this time slashing as he went down.

"My, Jonathan, you're just full of bright ideas aren't you?" Mark asked sarcastically.

"It was worth a try. If only we had a way to keep that thing still."

"Well, you could jump on its back and hold it for us."

"Quit it, Mark. He's right. We're never going to be able to take that thing head on. It's as quick as lightning."

"Well, then what's plan B?" Sarah asked.

"Pray. That's all I have right now."

"Yeah, if we're lucky lightning will strike the thing," Mark said.

Jonathan rubbed his chin and thought about what he could do to help stop this thing. He finally saw the answer twenty feet away.

"There we go!" he said pointing at a rope. "I'll be back in a minute."

"Jonathan! Wait!" Jacob cried.

"This guy has a death wish," Sarah said shaking her head.

Jonathan could see the thing coming for him as he ran at full speed ahead. He jumped for the rope at the last second.

"Whoa!" Mark said. "He needs a haircut, but that's a heck of a bad way to get one." After grabbing the rope, he used his arms to slide like a snake back to the others.

"Here, this should help."

"Has anyone ever told you that you're insane?!" Mark asked.

"Putting your health at risk is part of being a soldier."

"What's your plan?" Jacob asked.

"Give me an arrow."

Taking the arrow, Jonathan tied the rope around it and handed it back to Jacob.

"Oh, I see what you're thinking."

"Can you do it? Can you get me a clean body shot?"

"I'll try, but Jesus himself is going to have to guide this thing."

"Given our current situation I think there may be a good chance of that."

Taking aim as carefully as he ever had, he held his breath and let loose the home made harpoon. It missed the creature by mere inches.

"That's okay," Jonathan assured him. "Try again."

This time he held his breath even longer. Once again it flew by and barely missed.

"Darn it! I wish that thing would hold still," Mark said.

"It's okay," Sarah said. "Just concentrate."

He nodded and took aim again. This time he took a deep breath and prayed before pulling the trigger. It flew right into the demon's stomach and through its back.

"Bull's eye!" Mark yelled. "It doesn't look so tough now!"

Unfortunately Mark was wrong as it began shrieking and flapping its wings violently.

"Help!" Jacob cried. "I can barely hold on!"

All three of them grabbed Jacob to help hold on to the creature, but even with all of their strength they were still being dragged.

"Um, Jonathan?" Mark asked. "Now that we have him, what do we do with him?"

"I didn't think it would be this strong!"

"Well, somebody had better think of something or this thing is going to drag us across the whole continent!" Sarah said.

"Rrrr! One of us is going to have to kill it while the other three hold on," Jacob finally said.

"He's right. I'll do it," Jonathan said walking away.

"Be careful!"

"I will, Miss Sarah."

"Okay, demon! I'll show you what happens to intruders in my kingdom!"

Jonathan braced up and began to swing hard enough to cut the beast in half when the arrow pulled free.

"It's loose!" Jacob said.

Jonathan had seen the arrow pulling free and at the last second grabbed the creature's foot. It now had him airborne and going no telling how fast. Not wanting to let go of the demon or his sword either, he sank it down into the demon's thigh. It cried out and began to violently trying to shake him off.

He slowly inched his way up the creature's back. Once he was securely riding the horse from hell, he took his sword back. Being careful not to get thrown off, he sank the blade into the creature's neck and turned it completely, decapitating it. Unfortunately he didn't think about the fact that this was going to cause a very painful crash landing. Seeing that he was about to make impact with the concrete wall, he braced himself and closed his eyes. The body hit with what looked like enough force to go through the wall.

There was a loud thud and the carcass plummeted to the ground. Luckily for Jonathan, it halfway cushioned his fall. When he landed, Jacob, Mark, and Sarah ran to see if he was okay.

"Jonathan!" Sarah cried. "Are you okay?"

"Do you need a doctor?" Jacob asked.

"No, no. I'm fine. I probably should have planned that better, but I'm fine."

"Wow!" Mark said. "He really is one of us. He killed the creature with a stunt that was effective, yet half-killed him. Good work, Jonathan!"

They all smiled before the silence was broken by screams. Jacob knew what was behind them without even looking. The usual screams of, "No! It's Satan himself!" and "God help us!" filled the air.

He turned to face his hooded nemesis, which scowled more angrily than ever. It wasn't just because another one of his minions had failed to bring him the head of the preacher. It was because there they stood united. The team was finally completed and stronger than ever. Just by looking at them he could feel power radiating like he had never felt before. He almost feared them.

"***Preacher!"*** he cried sounding as confident as ever." ***I can rip your heart out at any time!"***

"Have you ever noticed that bad guys always say things like that when they're losing?" Mark said.

"What… What is that thing?"

"That's the enemy, Jonathan," Sarah said.

The demon began to laugh frantically. It started as a chuckle, but evolved into a howl of laughter. He acted as if they were the funniest thing he had ever seen in his life.

"***Oh, how amusingly pathetic! Do you believe for a second that the four of you can even hit me with the air from a swing of your weapon? Fools! With the blink of an eye I could turn you into dust."***

"Doesn't it look like he would have done that by now?" Mark asked.

"Yes, Mark. Empty threats."

"***Don't you dare mock me!"*** he shouted with fire practically exploding from his eye sockets. They all shuddered as a forked tongue shot from his mouth. "***I'm done playing with you! It's time to show you my true power. Die!"*** He clutched his hand in the air and began squeezing something imaginary.

"What's he doing?" Sarah asked.

Suddenly they heard someone coughing. They looked over to see a man clutching his throat. His eyes looked like they were about to pop out of their sockets. His throat then collapsed and he fell dead.

"Dear, God," Jonathan whispered.

"***Hmm, hmm, hmm. Do you wish to see more?"***

This time he merely snapped his fingers and a man folded completely in half. Everyone shrieked in terror.

"Ugh! That's not right," Mark said turning away.

"***Oh, foolish dogs, I'll show you even more!"***

Picking up a hand full of sand he blew it into the wind and a man caught fire.

"Enough! Demon, begone! You have proven nothing, but that you are a cowardly swine, just like your master."

The demon's eyes glowed brighter than ever.

"***Insolent…dog!!!! You still fear me not?! You still do not bow to me?!"***

Jacob laughed. "If you had any power over us, we would have been dead long ago. Why don't you crush our throats or set us ablaze?"

"Whoa, Jacob," Mark jumped in. "Let's not push him."

"Don't worry, Mark. Look at him. He's standing there frightened with his hands tied. He can't touch us, at least not with his powers. He merely tried to scare us into giving in with his little demonstrations."

"***You will all burn in damnation!"*** he cried waving his hand toward them. There was a huge gust of wind that knocked them to the ground.

"Ha, you see? He can only knock us down, but we will always get right back up. Now, go back to the fiery pits from whence you came!"

He shot an arrow and it went through the palm of the demon's hand. He stared blankly and faded away.

"Is he dead?" Mark asked.

"I'm afraid not, though I wish it were that simple."

"My, God." Jonathan said in nearly a whisper. "I had no idea creatures of that kind really existed."

"Yes, and that's why we need your help. If you don't fight with us he and I'm sure things ten times as horrifying will rule over the earth."

"You still believe that I'm the chosen one?"

"Yes. Now more than ever. Wasn't this fight proof enough? You helped us take down one of the minions. Did you see the look on young Andrew's face? He was petrified. He looked as if he might throw up at any moment. I'm not saying that to be disrespectful, but he isn't much more than a child. He can't handle things like this…but you did, bravely and head-on. We don't need the student, we need the teacher."

Jonathan hung his head. Sarah walked up to him and put her hand on his shoulder.

"Jacob's right, Jonathan, you're the one we need, not Andrew."

"As much as I hate swallowing my pride, they're right," Mark said.

"But…what about my oath?"

"I'm ordering you to forget your oath," A voice called out.

"Huh? Your Highness! What are you doing out here? You shouldn't be here. There may be more creature's around. Get back in where you will be safe."

"I'm fine, Jonathan. There are more important matters at hand. The fate of the entire world is at hand."

"But your Highness, it is my job to protect you."

"No, Jonathan, not anymore. You have a new job now."

"My Lord, are you sure this is what you want?"

"Yes, Jonathan. I rule over two, maybe three towns. If the world is taken over I won't have even that."

"But who is going to watch over you in my absence?"

"I will!"

"Andrew?"

"Yes. You taught me everything there is to know about being a swordsman and a knight. I'll gladly take over for you in your leave."

Jonathan smiled. "Thank you Andrew."

"Yes, besides it wouldn't be the end of the world if I died, Jonathan."

"My Lord, don't say that."

"Come now, Jonathan, I'm no true King. You know that as well as I do. My lineage ended a long time ago."

"You're still our King."

"Yes, but you will better protect me by going with Lord Jacob." He turned to Jacob. "Speaking of which, this kingdom owes you and your friends everything. You haven't just saved us once, but twice. You first run off the false prophets and now save us from the creature. I should pour your pockets full of gold until they can hold no more."

Jacob smiled and waved his hand. "No your Highness. You give us thanks enough by giving us good food to eat and a place to sleep."

"I'm telling you, he's hiding wings under that coat!" Mark said. "Here, Sarah, help me look."

"You are a great man, Jacob. You've done so much for us, yet I have one more thing to ask of you."

"What is it your Highness?"

"Teach us. Teach us about God. Tell us the true teachings of Jesus. We would all like to know the truth. We'll pay of course."

Jacob hung his head. "Your highness, I would gladly pay you to let me teach. Nothing would please me more. Of course I'll do it."

"Thank you, Jacob."

"Will tomorrow evening be okay?"

"Yes, perfect. Since the church won't hold everyone, we'll have the services here in the town square."

That night Jonathan sat on his bed thinking about everything that was happening. Only yesterday he had been serving the king and following the teachings of the three wise men. Then out of nowhere Jacob had appeared and revealed them as frauds. Now that he was here, his job was now to serve Jacob and fight off whatever hellish demons stood in their way.

Standing up, he looked at himself in the mirror. Part of him wished the three wise men were still around. He had thrived on their teachings. When they were the only truth he had no reason to feel guilty about his past.

Jacob spoke of all men being equal and peace and love. It was the exact opposite of the wise men's teachings. He was very uncomfortable with how good of a person Jacob was. Now there was no place for him to hide. He turned around as he heard a knock at the door.

"Come in."

Jacob entered.

"Lord Jacob, what can I do for you?"

Jacob smiled and gently shook his head. "Please, Jonathan, just Jacob."

"Ah yes. I'm used to calling the men I serve *Lord.* I'll try to break the habit."

"Jonathan, you don't serve me. I'm not your master, I'm your friend. We are equals."

He felt ashamed hearing this.

"We are all a team," Jacob continued. "Together we will destroy the darkness that threatens us."

"Y…Yes Jacob." With his head still hung low Jonathan turned back toward the mirror.

"Is something wrong, Jonathan?"

"No, it's just that everything is moving so fast."

"You're afraid."

Jonathan looked insulted. "A knight does not become afraid!"

"You're lying, Jonathan. You're lying to me and to yourself."

He fell silent.

"It's nothing to be ashamed of, Jonathan. I would call you a fool if you weren't afraid. All of us felt the same way, but that fear is replaced with anger and determination to beat the evil one. Once you see this creature brutally massacre villages and watch him try to kill innocent children that fear will go away. Wait until you look into the crying eyes of a child that lost her father or mother or both."

"Yes…I am afraid. How can we fight this thing?"

"Together, as God intended."

"But, why me Jacob? I'm no good Christian man."

"Neither was Mark, but he was chosen. God has a purpose for you."

"You're a good man, Jacob."

"I'm no better than anyone else."

"Yes, you are. I've done such horrible things in the past. You called me your friend. I'm not worthy to be called a friend. I treated you terribly and disrespectfully at the gate. I hurt you when you did nothing wrong."

"I forgive you of that."

"You forgive me that easily?"

"You apologized. That was enough."

"If only everyone thought like you."

"Besides, you were being misled. I can't hold that against you."

Jonathan closed his eyes and sighed deeply. "No Jacob, I wasn't misled."

Jacob looked puzzled. "What do you mean?"

"I have acted that way since I was twelve years old. The three wise men were only here for two years. I'm twenty-seven."

It took a moment for Jacob to realize what he was saying.

"I see. So you have always thought yourself to be above all people and lower class people were like animals even before the false teachings."

He nodded. "Yes, I was raised that way. In fact it was law in my house. If that law was broken, the punishment was severe. I learned that from my great father."

Jacob did not judge him. He realized that much like Mark and Sarah, there was a story at the root of this problem.

"Do you understand now why I don't feel worthy to fight with you?"

"You have a problem. So did Sarah and Mark. I helped them and I think I can help you."

"I think I'm a lost cause."

"What makes you say that?"

"Jacob, I look at lower class people and they are disgusting in my sight. I believe myself to be better than them in every way. I feel like they should bow down and shine my boots."

His thoughts were irritating Jacob, but he stayed patient.

"But, you Jacob, are a great man of God. You serve the one who created all men and the earth and you truly are greater than any man. You are greater than I am, yet you lower yourself to them. Why?"

"Jonathan, high class, low class, middle class, these things don't exist. They are all created in your mind and in the minds of all who believe in them. Peasants? Nobles? God doesn't know the difference. I don't treat anyone as if they are lower than me, because no one *is* lower than me."

Jonathan looked at Jacob as if he were speaking a foreign language.

"All men were created equal. It was men themselves that separated into groups. You are a noble right?"

"Yes."

"If you and a so called peasant were standing before God, you would be treated as equals. You would be an equal sinner or an equal Christian. He loves you just the same. No one, not even a King is high enough to mistreat another man rightfully."

"That is inconceivable to me, Jacob. Let me tell you a story about my childhood.

"When I was twelve years old, I was a shy and sheltered child. One day my Father told me to go out and find some friends. It would do me good to get out of the house. I did as he said and walked around town looking for somebody to talk to, when I heard a young boy crying. I looked and saw three boys in clothing like mine beating and kicking this young boy on the ground and calling him things like Dummy and retard. I went over and shoved one of the boys to the ground and told them to leave him alone. They looked at me like they wanted to kill me and ran off. I helped the boy off the ground and helped him dust himself off. He was wearing old and tattered clothes. It was obvious the boy wasn't quite right. He thanked me and said his name was Tommy.

"We played all day long and I went back home. My Father asked if I made any friends and I told him I met a boy named

Tommy. He asked who his father was and I told him I didn't know. Mind you, at this time in my life I knew nothing of the whole noble and peasant thing.

"A couple of days went by and Tommy and I still played together. Then one of my father's friends saw us and ran to tell him about it. My father came up to us and looked furious. He looked at Tommy as if he were a leper. He then turned to me and slapped me to the ground and began screaming at me. Tommy, as I said wasn't quite right, tried to defend me like I did him. He yanked on my father's cape and told him to leave me alone. My father looked like a man possessed. 'How dare you, you little disease!' he screamed. He punched Tommy to the ground and began hitting him repeatedly. I still remember hearing Tommy screaming for him to stop. I tried to stop him, but he only pushed me away. I think he was going to kill him. That was when Tommy's Father jumped in and knocked him to the ground.

"'Enough, Lucas!' he said. 'You have taken this noble thing too far! This ends now. How horrible it must be for you to find out your son is human. He has more class and heart than you could ever have. He doesn't deserve a father like you.'

"He stared blankly at him. 'You know you die now don't you?' he finally said. 'You will be put back in your place before you stop breathing.' They began sword fighting. It went on for nearly fifteen minutes. When Tommy's father began getting the upper hand, one of my father's friends threw dirt in his eyes blinding him. That was when father cut his arm off. He screamed in pain and fell to the ground, bleeding profusely."

"My God," Jacob said with his mouth agape. "What a horrible childhood memory."

Jonathan didn't seem to notice he said anything and continued on.

"'Now you lose your head!' my father shrieked. Finally, albeit too late, a guard showed up. He asked if my father did that and he answered proudly that he did!

"My Father was in shock as the guard backhanded him, closed fisted, to the ground. 'You scum sucking pig! Do you know who I am?! I own you! I know who you are. You're the piece of garbage noble that wreaks havoc on the other townspeople. Yes, when they are out of line. They are not your servants! Are you insane? They are peasants and don't deserve to live. They're better than you will ever be. You say that again and I'll kill you! I'll slit you from head to toe!'

"He pulled his sword and held it to my father's throat. 'You're good, but guarantee you, I'm better.' 'Wait,' my father said. 'I know who you are now. You're that beggar that became a soldier. A pathetic mistake. Keep talking and I'll have *your* head. Now come with me. We're going to have a nice talk with the king about what you have done.'

"My father grinned at him. 'He'll take my side one hundred percent and I'll go free. Unfortunately for you, I'll have your head mounted on my wall,' he sneered. Tommy's Mother was kneeled over her husband crying and trying desperately to stop the bleeding."

"Did he live?" Jacob asked.

"Yes, but he's a cripple. He couldn't work or support his family. Of course, he received money for his suffering. But, not even money helps some things."

"What happened to your father?"

"He was wrong about the king, which was our king's father. He didn't take his side. In fact he totally supported the actions of the guard. He told my Father he had gone too far this time and had him caned publicly. The peasants thought it was a holiday. The nobles thought it was the most shameful moment in history."

"So, you think your father didn't deserve the punishment?"

He didn't answer.

"That night, he walked in and beat me within an inch of my life. He told me that if I ever tried to be friends with a peasant again he would kill me."

"You were his own son and he threatened to kill you?"

He nodded. "My mother tried to stop him, but he beat her, too." Jonathan lifted up his shirt and revealed an array of scars on his back.

"Dear, God. He did that to you?" Jacob stood there not knowing what to say. "You describe this man as being so great, when he beat innocent children, crippled innocent men, and did this to his own child?"

"It's the way of life."

Jacob was sick of hearing this. "No! I have heard that until my ears are bleeding. This is not the way of life!"

Jonathan appeared shocked.

"It was *man* who made this a way of life! If you want to know the real meaning of life, read the book I hold in my hand!"

Jonathan hung his head down again.

"Tell me, Jonathan, did you love your father?"

"I respected him."

"That isn't what I asked. Did you love him?"

"I…I…He was my father."

"Yes, Jonathan, but just because a man has your blood, it doesn't make him a father."

"He said he wanted what was best for me."

"Best for you or best for him?"

"He was a highly respected man."

"By who? The innocent people he mercilessly beat? Was it by his son that he scarred for life?"

"Every man in the community respected him."

"All nobles, right?"

"Yes. Not a day went by that at least one of them didn't stop to tell me. 'Your father is a fine man. Always show him the respect he deserves' or 'You should thank God every day for having a father to teach you the way of life.'"

"Tell me, are any of these men still alive?"

"Yes, a couple of them. Why?"

"Don't you understand, Jonathan? You aren't this way because you want to be. You're this way because you're afraid of what the others might say. That little boy who befriended a peasant is still alive and well in you."

"No, that isn't possible."

"Yes, it is. Not once did you ever believe in the noble and peasant thing. You only believed it out of fear, the fear he put inside of you the day he gave you those scars."

Jonathan fell silent.

"When I asked you if you loved your father, you couldn't answer me. That is because you can't look me in the eye and honestly tell me you loved that man."

"But, he was such a great man."

"No, that is what all of his friends planted in your mind. He wasn't a great man or a respected man. He was a foolish man. No one respected him, but his fellow nobles. He was feared and despised by everyone else. You said the day he beat you he beat your mother, too. Was that the first time he had ever hit her?"

"No, he had little respect for women. He thought she was to be seen and not heard. She kept bruises on her a lot."

"Did you love your Mother?"

"Of course, I did!"

"See? You didn't waste a second telling me that. Now, can you tell me you loved your father?"

"I…I."

"He was a selfish man, Jonathan. He had his beliefs and if you didn't follow them, he beat them into you. He used fear in the place of love. All he did was hurt you and your mother."

"AAAAARGH! I HATED HIM!"

Jacob now fell silent as Jonathan burst into tears.

"I hated the bastard! My mother was a saint! All she did was love that man day after day! What did she get in return? He beat her! RRR! I was so small I couldn't do anything. I used to fantasize about growing up an beating him within an inch of his life for what he did to my Mother and me. I know it's horrible to say, but I pray to God he's burning in hell right now."

"You thought you would be free after he died, but you weren't were you?"

"No, I found myself fearing what the others might say or do. I…became my father."

"No, you're better than your father. You feel remorse where he never did. Your father could never totally convert you. He took your mind, but he failed to take your heart. He loses."

Jonathan sat beside him on the bed and buried his face with his hands.

"I became him more than you think."

Jacob looked at him confused

"I'm a sinner."

"Jonathan, we're all sinners. We were born that way. I'm a sinner, you're a sinner…"

"No," Jonathan interrupted. "About two years ago I did something terrible. It can't be forgiven."

"I'll be the judge of that. Tell me."

"One day I was walking through town and I was in a particularly bad mood. I don't really remember what I was angry about, but I was walking around in a trance like I do when I'm angry. Before I knew it I was on the lower class side of town."

He took a deep, regretful breath before continuing.

"There were some children playing with a ball and it got away from them. It rolled over to me and I picked it up. Then a…beautiful little girl with dirt on her face came up to me, tugged my cape and tapped my leg. She said, 'Mister? Can I have my ball back?'"

As he had with Sarah's story back in the church town, Jacob had a sick feeling where this story was going.

"I basically did the same thing as I did when I met you. I demanded she speak to me in a respectful manner. I screamed at her." He squinted his eyes in shame. "She didn't know what I was talking about. She was so little, she didn't understand. I lost my temper though and continued screaming and swearing at her. Then…"

This was the part Jacob had been expecting.

"I hit her."

Though he was trying his hardest not to, Jacob was feeling considerable amount of disgust. He tried to remember that Jonathan was trying to repent.

"I…didn't hit her just once. I beat her repeatedly in the face. I was enraged and couldn't stop myself. The last I remember I got up and she was screaming hysterically. She was clutching her face pouring blood and crying uncontrollably."

"What happened to her?"

"They rushed her to the doctor. Her face was shattered. She has to this day had four surgeries to repair it. Our doctor is the best there is."

"Jonathan, are you telling me you did this and weren't punished in any way?"

"Oh, I was punished. I was punished severely. The king was completely revolted by me. He told me that if I were any other man I would be beheaded. But since I was a friend, he chained me in the dungeon for seven days with no food or water. See? I told you it was unforgivable."

"I didn't say that."

"What? Don't stand there and tell me that a God as you say he is could forgive something like that."

Jacob smiled. "Did you hear what you said? Loving. He loves you and he will until the day you die. A man isn't beyond saving until he breathes his last breath. When Jesus was on the cross there were two men with him. The one to his right mocked him, but the man to his left asked him to remember him when he got to heaven. Do you know what Jesus said?"

Jonathan shook his head.

"He said, 'On this day you will join me in paradise.' You see, that man had sinned his whole life. He was dying, but he found mercy at Jesus' hands. A man can go through his life and murder ten thousand people, but God still loves him. It isn't too late until he dies."

Jonathan began crying again. "I'm not worthy of such mercy."

"None of us are, Jonathan. None of us are."

"How can I ever make it up to him? I've been a fool."

Jacob looked at him sincerely.

"Make it right, Jonathan."

Mark yawned and dragged his blanket across the floor like a five year old.

"Nighty night," he said to Sarah who was sitting on the bed reading a book she had borrowed from the royal library.

She looked quite elegant in her very expensive nightgown that had been supplied. It was light blue, ironically Mark's favorite color, and it covered her whole body. No one would ever know she had once lived a life of degradation.

"Goodnight? Already? It's only nine o'clock. What gives? You always seemed like the kind of guy that stays up until midnight burning up the town."

"Hello? That was when women an alcohol were involved. As you can tell, I have neither."

"Ha. You're getting along a lot better than I expected you to. This religion thing isn't easy is it?"

"You're telling me! And I must say you are doing very well yourself."

"Huh?"

"There are a ton of eligible guards around here and you haven't made goo-goo eyes at one of them."

"I've realized I don't need a man in my life. I've picked up new hobbies as you can tell by the book in my hand."

"Gee, this is great. To take the place of our evil desires you're going to get a pair of those cute little glasses and read every book in the land while I become the next Rip Van Winkle."

"Yeah."

"Besides, why do you need to flirt when you've already found the love of your life."

She looked stunned. "Excuse me?"

"Oh, don't you look all shocked and surprised. You know exactly what I'm talking about."

"Mark Raven, I'm sure I don't have a clue what you are talking about."

"Oh, yes, you do."

"Oh, no, I don't."

"Oh, yes, you do."

"Oh, no, I don't."

"Oh, no, you don't."

"Oh, yes, I… Grrrr! Go to bed, Mark!"

"Oh, come on, admit it!"

"I'm not admitting anything."

"Don't you think for one second that I'm turning into a sweet, dress wearing, church going girl," he said mocking her.

"What makes you think I have?"

"For one thing what you're wearing. You seem like the kind of girl that sleeps in the nude."

"How did you know that?"

"Lucky guess. But the biggest reason of all is that Jacob has you melting in his hands. I've seen the way you look at him."

"Oh, really?" she said walking over to him seductively. "Why don't I show you how smitten I am?"

She put her arms around him and put her lips less than an inch from his.

"You're bluffing."

"Yes, I am," she said sighing. "Of all of the people for me to fall in love with, it had to be a preacher."

Mark smiled. "I'm pretty sure he feels the same way about you."

"Yes, but for the life of me I don't know why."

"Hey, he's a good guy."

"Yeah, too good. I don't feel like I deserve to be with someone like him."

"You're too hard on yourself, Sarah. We all make mistakes. Haven't you been listening to him? You can't keep beating yourself up for what you did in the past. He says the big guy upstairs makes it like it never happened."

"Yeah…thanks. Goodnight, Mark."

"Goodnight, Sarah," he said hugging her and kissing her on the forehead. "Pleasant dreams. Oh, by the way, I could never sleep with you now."

"Huh? Why not?"

"Are you kidding? Do you realize how big of a thunderbolt it would be if I messed with a preacher's girl?"

She giggled.

"Besides, I'm starting to get that little sister feeling about you. Heh, I can't wait."

"You can't wait for what?"

"To see you in a fancy dress and sitting in a church pew."

"Oh, shut up."

Jonathan stopped dead in his tracks as he and Jacob walked toward a small cottage.

"What is it Jonathan?"

"I don't know if I can face him."

"Of course you can. It was your father that did that to him, not you."

"But I'm his son. I'm ashamed of what my father did."

"Then you have to make it right."

He took a long sigh. "Very well. Let's go."

As they neared the small house's door, Jonathan paused once more before knocking three times on the door softly. In a few seconds the door opened and an average sized man with a beard and one arm came to the door.

"Yes? Can I help you?" He stared as he finished his sentence. Squinting his eyes he said, "Jonathan?"

"Yes…sir. It's me."

The poor man became frightened and couldn't speak. "I…. ummmm… I… have I done something wrong?"

"Calm yourself, sir. It is I who have done something wrong."

He looked at him confused. "What do you mean?"

"It's because of my father that you lost your arm."

The poor man looked as confused as ever.

"Sir, I have come to make amends for what my father has done."

"B…But why?"

"I'm a fool. You know that as well as I do. Ever since I did that to that poor girl everyone has looked at me in disgust. I was a fool for letting myself become my father. I have seen the error of my ways and now I want to compensate for everything my father and I have done."

The old man looked a strange combination of happy and sad. "I'm glad to hear that, son."

"I know there is nothing that can ever repay you for losing your arm, but maybe this will help." He handed the man a cloth bag. He gasped as he opened it.

"Dear Lord. It's so much gold. Its 500 pieces."

"It isn't much, but it's the least I can do."

"Not much? This is enough gold to feed us for over a year. I can't accept so much from you. Just knowing that you turned from your father's ways is enough to make me happy."

"Please accept it. It will make me feel a lot better. I know because of your handicap that your family went without meals, without clothes and at times you were in danger of losing your home. Not to mention it was everything you could do to give your wife a decent burial."

A tear ran down the man's face. "God bless you, Jonathan… God bless you."

Finally for the first time since he had met him, Jacob saw Jonathan smile, although it was short lived.

"Jonathan! What the hell are you doing?!" a voice called out.

Jacob and Jonathan both jerked their heads toward the voice. There stood a crotchety old bearded man who dressed fancier than Jonathan. For a second, Jacob thought that Jonathan's father had risen from the dead in order to keep his son from repenting. With everything that had happened lately it would almost seem normal. Finally Jonathan spoke his name.

"Kilmore."

"Answer me, boy! What are you doing with this trash? I had better see you slap him to the ground."

Before Jacob could yell, "Away with you old man," Jonathan spoke up.

"Be silent, you old fool!"

The man gasped. "How dare you?! You once showed respect for your elders. Perhaps I should teach you once again the pride of being a noble."

"Pride?!" he cried. "Is it honorable to throw dirt in a man's eyes while another permanently cripples him?"

"He had to be put in his place."

"Enough! If I hear of any man being called a dog, a slave, or anything else that makes him unequal from you or anyone else I will personally cut their tongue out. It isn't up to us to put them in their place, because there is no place for them to be put in. The rich are no better than the poor."

"No better? Are you insane? Money is power! It makes us better. It's the way of life."

Jonathan thought of what Jacob had said and passed it on. "No. It was man that made these laws. God never intended for things to be this way. The way of life is in the book Jacob holds in his hand."

"You're speaking like a fool, Jonathan! What would your father say?"

"I couldn't care less what that dog thinks! He was a poor excuse for a man and he's burning in hell where he belongs."

Kilmore was speechless. Fumbling for words he looked at Jacob. "You! It was you that put these foolish ideas in his head. The three wise men knew the way of life, but you, a mere foolish child, came and ran them off so you could poison everyone's mind with your nonsense!"

"I speak the truth. It was the wise men feeding everyone lies. Perhaps if you read the holy book you would know that."

"I'll have no part of any religion where all men are treated as equals."

"Then you are doomed to the same fate as Jonathan's father, to die alone and loved by no one. I pity you."

"Don't you ever say you pity me!"

"Enough!" Jonathan chimed in."

By this time, all of the households had heard the commotion and come outside to see what was going on. Jacob noticed they were wide eyed and in surprise as they witnessed a war between their enemies.

"No more, Kilmore. I end it here."

"You end what?"

"I end this barbaric abuse of innocent people. From now on everyone will be treated equal."

"Shut your mouth!"

"Everyone!" he shouted through the town. "On this day I break the ties I had with my father and declare all of you free! Never again will you have to endure being looked down on by anyone else!"

"No!!! Stop! I'm warning you! If you peasants listen to this I'll see that you are beaten daily!"

"Silence, old man. It's over. If any man hurts anyone without cause I'll see to it that they receive fifty lashes or a week in the dungeon. It's your choice," he said looking straight at Kilmore.

"You stupid pathetic fool. You're ripping apart an ancient tradition! How dare you lift up peasants to our level?" Once again he shifted his eyes to Jacob. "This is your fault, you bible spouting dog! I'll kill you for this!"

Jacob was prepared to defend himself, but it wasn't necessary. Before he could move, Jonathan jumped in front of him.

"You'll have to get through me first. I won't allow you to harm a hair on this man of God's head. Do you really want to take that chance? Remember, I was trained by my father who was a much better swordsman than you were. Not to mention you are a lot older and weaker now."

Kilmore returned his sword to its place and literally growled before turning to walk away. Jonathan looked around and everyone was still open-jawed and speechless. He didn't know what to say either. Finally he saw someone he recognized and walked toward them. It was the little girl. As he approached, the child hid behind her mother. When he got to the door, he knelt down and spoke to the mother.

"What is the child's name?"

She hesitated. "A…Amanda."

"Amanda," he repeated. "Amanda, I know you're afraid of me, but I promise I'm not here to hurt you."

The little girl peeked from behind her mother with curiosity. Jacob noticed that the doctor had done excellent work. There was noticeable scarring, but for the most part she looked like a normal girl. Still hugging on to her mother's leg, she asked a question that tore at Jonathan's heart.

"Why did you hurt me?"

A putrid feeling erupted in the pit of his stomach. "Because I'm a horrible man. Amanda, I am so sorry I hurt you. I know there is nothing I can do to take back what I have done, but I want you to have this." He held out a white teddy bear. Her eyes brightened as she took the toy.

"He's pretty! Thank you."

"Here," he said to the mother, "I want you to have this as well." He handed her a bag. Much as the old man had before, she gasped as she looked inside. "It's 500 gold pieces. I want you to use it to buy her food and all the toys and clothes she wants. Hopefully it will help her forget the pain I have caused her."

"Lord Jonathan…I…"

"Just Jonathan, ma'am. I'm not worthy to be called Lord. I have also taken the liberty of eliminating all of your debts with the doctor and any time she needs to see him, even if it's for the common cold, I'll take care of the bill."

The woman covered her mouth and began crying. "Thank you, Jonathan. Thank you."

"With all of this I still haven't truly made anything up to you, but I hope it helps. Goodnight to you, ma'am."

As he stood up and began to leave, the little girl ran over and tugged on his cape.

"Hmmm?"

She motioned for him to kneel back down.

"Yes?"

"I forgive you, Jonathan," she said and put her arms around his neck. This was too much for Jonathan to hold in. He broke down into tears.

"Oh, please, God, forgive me. I am so, so sorry, Amanda. I was such a fool."

Jacob smiled looking at this. He thought of how Jesus said we must have the innocence of a child to enter into heaven. This innocence was a beautiful thing. He walked over to Jonathan, still embracing the little girl and placed a hand on his shoulder.

"Welcome home Jonathan. Welcome home."

CHAPTER 8

After a long day of demon slaying and burning bridges, Jonathan and Jacob went to their separate rooms for a well-earned rest. Jacob wrote down a few scriptures for him to remember in case he was ever tempted to go back to his old ways. Jonathan went straight to his room and was asleep by the time his head hit the pillow.

Jacob stopped to see if his remaining two friends had gone to sleep. It was obvious by the snoring he heard coming from Mark's room that he was dead to the world. When he peeked inside of Sarah's room, the light was on, but she was collapsed on the bed with one hand lying across her chest and a book in the other.

He figured she must have stayed up to see him before she went to sleep, but fatigue took her over. She looked beautiful in her night gown. He had really wanted to talk to her, but since she was resting so well he decided not to disturb her. He merely kissed her forehead and blew out the lamp beside her bed.

After taking care of her he went to his own room As he always had, no matter how tired he was, said his prayers. He thanked God for helping him find all three of his comrades. He thanked him for helping Jonathan to see the error of his ways and seeking forgiveness from the ones he had harmed in the past. He then prayed for each of his friends individually, After his amen, he lay down and was asleep in a couple of minutes.

XX

The next morning Jacob awoke remarkably refreshed. Whatever the doctor had given him for his side had worked wonders. He barely felt any pain, though he would have to get the bandages changed before long. The best feeling of the morning was the absence of wanting to vomit with every breath. He felt that this morning he could eat a hardy breakfast like everyone else. He was the last to wake. All three of his friends were waiting outside of his door when he came out.

"I wish I slept as well as you do," Sarah said smiling.

"Are you guys fighting the same things I am or am I just out of shape?"

"You're just out of shape," Mark answered mischievously.

"Okay, good to know."

"Well, do you feel like a big breakfast?" Jonathan asked.

"Yes, I'm starving. I think I'll be eating more than soup today."

"Alright then. Let's sit down and enjoy a meal before we fulfill our duties of the day."

"Lead the way."

"Oh, by the way, Jacob, the king would like you to deliver your message at noon. Is that okay?"

"Yes, that's fine."

At the table they had the morning before, the cheerful cook came out to take their order. Jonathan ordered a plate of bacon with a cup of coffee. Sarah had pork tenderloin with eggs and milk. Mark, not caring what he ate with what meal, ordered a steak well done with a glass of water.

Jacob thought for a second before ordering.

"I'll have four pancakes with butter and syrup, two pieces of sausage, grits, and I don't know if I want water or milk, so bring me a glass of both."

Sarah gawked at him with a surprised smile.

"Are you hungry, Jacob?"

"Famished actually, I don't know why."

"That medicine must have healed your side while draining your stomach. You're competing with Mark today for the title of biggest glutton."

"How dare you try to out eat me holy man!" Mark said feigning insult. "Everyone knows I am the biggest pig in the land. Add mashed potatoes and corn to my order good man. I must defend my title."

Jonathan laughed out loud. "There is never a dull moment with you guys is there?

"Not so far," Sarah answered. "I already have to keep these two men in line, since you're joining our group I hope you'll behave yourself so it won't be three."

"I'll be on my best behavior, Sarah."

After a few minutes the cook brought them their food. The four of them talked and laughed as if they were lifelong friends, which Jacob hoped they would be.

Sarah and Jonathan were the first to finish their meals. In the end, it was a contest between Jacob and Mark to see who could finish the fastest. Mark won, but he looked to be in far worse shape than Jacob. Mark was slumped back in his chair making noises like a man on his deathbed.

"Ohhhh…too much food."

"Wow. I never thought I would hear that from him," Sarah teased.

"No fair," Mark complained. "God expanded your stomach. I want a rematch tonight."

Jacob smiled and patted him on the back. "As much as you ate, you may be full until next winter."

"Yeah…uurrrgh."

"Well, shall we get everything in order now?" Jonathan asked.

"Yes. Let's go."

"Ummm guys?" Mark asked. "Can you guys carry me outside?"

Standing on a platform freshly built for the occasion and at a homemade pulpit, Jacob looked out at all of the people gathered around. They were gathered like sheep needing a shepherd. It appeared that everyone in town had appeared for the service, though Jacob figured that a few nobles were missing from the picture.

In the front, three chairs were set with a throne in the middle. The king had a front row seat and apparently the other three chairs were intended for Jonathan, Sarah, and Mark. Jonathan would be used to being put on a pedestal, but this would be a brand new experience for Mark and Sarah.

As they took their seats Jonathan seemed right at home. Mark and Sarah however kept giving each other uncomfortable looks.

"Jacob, we're ready any time you are," Jonathan said.

"Yes. Your Highness? Do you wish to speak a few words before I proceed?"

The king nodded, stood up, and turned around.

"People of my kingdom! May I have your attention!"

The silence was eerie.

"I want you all to listen carefully and take Brother Jacob's words to heart. The three wise men poisoned our minds with lies and deceit that we need to be cleansed of. Jacob has come to do this. Listen as he speaks the truth to all of you and listen with keen ears. I know I will."

At that he nodded for Jacob to proceed. Jacob thought for a moment before beginning.

"Hello, everyone. Yesterday I thought long and hard about what I was going to say to all of you today, but I had no idea. With everything the three wise men had told you I didn't know where to begin. I had finally decided to start at the beginning when God created the heavens and the earth. Then I realized it would take a hundred messages to get to the true message if I did that. I don't know how much you know of the bible, but I want to give you the greatest message in this holy book. It finally came to me when I remembered what one of the three wise men said. 'Blessed are the rich and Jesus rode a mighty steed,' he quoted. There is no greater lie than what they have told you. On this day, I am going to reveal the lies they spouted and tell you the true life of Jesus Christ."

Jacob went on to tell everyone the story of the nativity and Jesus' Birth. He then told of his coming of age when he was tempted three times by Satan. Next he told of Jesus meeting his disciples and the miracles he performed. He closed with the crucifixion and the resurrection.

"Why did Jesus do this? The answer is simple, because he loves you. Even when you are committing the most vile and horrible sins, he loves you. He knew that only his sacrifice would be enough to carry the sins of everyone to ever live. So I ask you, the next time you think about stealing, or killing, or committing adultery, I want you to picture this." He held out his hands to imitate a man hanging on a cross. "Just imagine a great man hanging, suffering, and dying just for you."

"Demons!" a voice cried from the lookout tower. "My God, its demons! There must be hundreds of them!"

Jacob ran over and climbed the lookout tower. The guard was right, there was an army of blade arms and low ranks alike charging for the castle. He looked in the back of them and as he expected was the hooded commanding officer pointing the way. Even at that distance he could swear that he made eye contact and sneered in anger at him.

"Dear God!" the soldier continued to cry. "There must be 1500 of them!"

Jacob pulled out his crossbow and began to target practice, dropping each demon with one shot.

"Don't just stand there, you fools!" the king cried. "Get up there and help him!"

At his command a group of archers climbed the tower and sent a rain of arrows over the hellish army which began to drop like flies. Jacob stopped shooting and climbed back down to meet the other three.

"It's no good! There are too many of them. We have them down under a thousand, but they'll still end up breaking in here eventually. Jonathan, how many men do you have?"

"Six hundred and fifty maybe."

"We'll still be outnumbered."

"Then what do we do?" Sarah asked.

"We fight them head on!" Mark shouted.

"Unfortunately, I think he may be right," Jacob said looking toward the town gates."

At that moment the sky became as dark as night and thunder boomed overhead.

"This is never good," Jacob muttered looking up.

"Guards! Get the king to safety! Andrew! Where are you?!"

"Right here sir!"

"Order the archers down and get everyone to the gate. We have to keep those things out of here."

"No," Jacob said grabbing Jonathan's shoulder. "If you send everyone to the gate they'll be slaughtered with nowhere to go. Those demons will charge in non-stop giving their lives to get the others in."

"He's right, sir."

"Then what do we do?"

"Get a handful of your men and get all of the townspeople into the castle, then let the demons in."

"Let them in?! Have you gone mad Jacob?"

"No, if we let them in, we will have plenty of open space to fight in instead of being trapped in an enclosed area."

"Ohhh, I get it," Mark said. "If they're out here we have plenty of room to stick and move without being trapped between a demon and a hard space."

"Exactly."

"Hmmm, are you sure you have never led an army before Jacob? All right, men! Get the townspeople to safety! Archers come down! Thomas! You stay up there as a look out! Everyone else wait at the double doors!" Jonathan waited impatiently for a moment. "Thomas! What are they doing?"

"Lifting up the gate, sir!"

"Okay, get ready men!"

"Here we go again," Sarah said standing in her fighting stance.

"Yay! More ugly hell rats to gut!"

"You have a morbid way of having fun, Mark."

"Stay together," Jacob reminded them.

There was a dead silence until the minions finally busted through the double doors and into town.

"Here they come!" Jonathan shouted to his men. "I know we're outnumbered, but fight with everything you have!"

A full front line of blade arms came charging straight in, hacking and slashing away. Some of the men got easy kills, but others were run through before they could even raise their swords. A few began to branch off to the four chosen ones.

The first one came at Jonathan. He stood firm and poised, showing no fear as he slashed its juggler vein. Jacob was quick to begin dismembering as he took three heads off. After a missed swing he gutted and beheaded his fourth.

Everyone was using their own styles of demon slaying. Mark was having fun dodging and running them through. Sarah was bashing heads and ribs in like a mad woman. Two came at her, one on each side, prepared to maul her. Thinking quick she jabbed them with two quick actions between the eyes and busted their skulls.

Jacob was surprised to see what a warrior Jonathan truly was as he watched him ram his sword through a low class minions throat, keep it there and break a blade arm's neck with his bare hands.

Jacob turned to a lower minion leaping at him. Without hesitation he cut it in half at the waist. Suddenly a large portion of the blade arms were gone and replaced by low minions.

"Jacob?" Sarah called. "We're surrounded. How do we fight these things?"

"Carefully. Their claws can disembowel you, but they are predictable. They love to leap at you, but it leaves them vulnerable. Just keep crushing skulls like you have been."

"I can do that."

Jacob barely ducked the attack of a stray blade arm and ran it through.

"Uh oh! Trouble behind you Jacob!" Mark called out.

Jacob looked back and saw a father and daughter that had failed to escape into the castle. He was giving everything he had to fend off a blade arm. His daughter was crouched down behind him, crying in terror. He had blood and cuts on him to prove that he wasn't having much luck.

"Time to save the day!" Mark yelled running toward them.

By the time he got there the man was on the ground holding his sword up and pushing desperately to hold off his nemesis. His own blade was coming toward his throat. Finally he saw a blade plunge through the creature's back and it began shrieking wildly.

Mark picked it up and turned its head toward him so he could look into its eyes.

"What? Afraid to fight someone who can fight back?"

"Look out!" the man cried.

He ducked just in time to keep the back of his head from being slashed off by a low minion. As it turned back around he plunged his blade through it as well making the two hellish partners give each other a hug of sympathy.

"You two get to the castle, now."

"Yes, sir! Thank you!"

After they ran away, a handful of low classes and blade arms encircled him snarling and growling meaner than ever. Apparently they were tired of watching their numbers dropping like flies.

"Oh, this is great."

Jacob saw that Mark was in trouble and started toward him before being tackled from the side by a low class. He struggled against it clutching its wrists to keep its claws from burying into his face.

Using his legs he flipped it over his head. He stood up prepared to defend himself, but Jonathan's blade came ripping through its back.

"Thanks. Now we have to help Mark. He's outnumbered."

"Wait. What about Sarah?"

Jacob looked over and saw her being held by two low classes while another charged at her. Using the two holding her to balance, she wrapped her legs around the charging one's neck and snapped it. Flipping backwards she escaped her captors and crushed in their throats and skulls with four quick motions.

"I think she can take care of herself."

"Obviously."

Jacob and Jonathan ran in full speed hacking and chopping away, turning Mark's circle of enemies into more of a crescent moon. They stood back to back so no surprised could come at them. Half the time they did their predictable leaping move and impaled themselves.

Now that it was only three on one Mark liked the odds better. It was to low classes and a blade arm. The blade arm ran in aggressively. Mark ducked a jab and back dropped it to the ground. After it hit the ground he stabbed straight through its mouth.

He motioned for the other two to come on. He slashed the first in the gut as it jumped toward him. The other one jumped into the air, landed behind Mark, and began choking him. He threw it over his shoulder and ran it through.

"No!" Jacob cried, looking toward the castle.

"What is it?" Jonathan asked.

"They're getting into the castle."

"What?! We have to stop them!"

It was too late. The demons had already mangled the guards at the door and broke their way in.

"The king is in there with the all the townspeople. I have to save them!"

"Wait! I'm coming with you. Mark! Back Sarah up!"

Mark looked over at the pile of bodies around her as she was busting yet another skull.

"Does she need back up?"

Jonathan froze as he reached the broke down door. There were at least twenty demons standing there hissing like rattlesnakes, guarding their lair. They didn't try to attack. They remained frozen in place to prevent anyone from entering or exiting.

"Jacob, we fight well together, but we can't cut through that many at one time with our heads still intact."

"Rrrr! They're keeping us out so we can't save the people or…."

"The king!" they both said at the same time.

"Gahh! I have to save them! It's my duty! I may die trying, but I'm fighting these beasts!"

"Wait! I may have an idea." Remembering Jonathan's idea before he tied a nearby rope to one of his arrows. He looked up to a broken window where a blade arm was standing with its back turned. "I hope this works."

Letting the arrow fly it went through the creature and it shrieked wildly. Pulling on the rope, the demon wedged against the small window and became a homemade grappling hook.

Jacob went up first, testing the waters and it proved sturdy. He knew it was the hand of God holding the arrow in place. He motioned for Jonathan to follow him. As they reached the top Jacob slit the creature's throat and they moved in unscathed.

Here there was another handful of demons. It wasn't as many as downstairs, but a formidable number nonetheless. They guarded the door to the throne room.

"How many of these things are there?"

"I'm afraid hell is quite over populated. So they aren't hurting for recruits."

They were in an enclosed area between the throne room and the window. To the left was a solid wall and to the right was a spiraling staircase that more unwanted company could come up any second. These too were standing firmly in place and hissing at them like they were trespassers on their territory.

"How are we going to get past them?" Jonathan asked.

"I have only one idea."

Jonathan, somehow knowing what Jacob was thinking, nodded. All of the demons were standing in a triangular formation in at the center of the door. They put their swords tip to tip, forming one huge blade like an Egyptian booby trap in a pyramid. They then ran at the demons at full speed. Their swords went through the demon flesh like a warm knife through butter. Blood splattered all over them. When they reached the door they looked behind them to see a pile of severed demon parts that only God himself could put back together. They then heard a blood curdling scream coming from the throne room. Jonathan pushed on the door, but it wouldn't give.

"Rrrr! They locked it!"

"We'll break it down," Jacob said.

Bracing themselves they rammed into the door shoulder first. It didn't give much. The second time it gave a little more. The third time it busted and they fell through to their knees.

At that moment, a blade arm was straddling the king with its blade two inches from his heart. The next few moments seemed to go by in slow motion. Pulling his crossbow as fast as he could Jacob took aim and put an arrow through its throat.

Although shots like this had previously given instant death to the miserable beasts, this one seemed stubbornly determined to cling to life. It wasn't the desire for mortality that kept him going though, it was the animalistic determination to slay the king. It raised its arm one more time prepared to disembowel the ruler.

Jacob reloaded instantly and let another arrow fly into the demon's heart. It had no choice this time, but to die, although not alone.

With its last ounce of strength it began to stab down. Jonathan leaped forward, willing to take the blade for him, but it was too late. It penetrated the king in a mortal area.

"NOOOOO!" Jonathan screamed, reaching the creature and cutting its head off with enough force to go through steel. Breathing frantically and in panic he kneeled down and cradled the King's head and begged him to speak to him. All he could manage was a short gasp an gurgle before dying.

"I'm sorry," Jacob said looking down at them. "I acted as fast as I could."

"ARRRRGH!" Jonathan had snapped. Jacob stood back as he walked toward the rest of the room's inhabitants. The other demons barely acknowledged that they were there.

Two other guards had been watching over the king. One laid in the corner bloodied and gutted while the second was sprawled in the middle of the room decapitated. Watching them made Jonathan twice as enraged.

They were making their own little game of kicking the guard's head around like a ball. Their cries, sounded like laughter, as if they were mocking how weak humanity was and easily they could take life from it. Unfortunately at that moment Jonathan had the same opinion of them.

"Servants of hell!" he yelled in a battle cry. "Allow me to send you back home…but not before you suffer."

One arrogant blade arm was brave enough to come face-to-face with him for a showdown. Jacob and it was shocked as Jonathan grabbed it by the shoulders.

The room was decorated with old suits of armor from past generations. There were three standing in a row with spears held out in front of them. He slammed the blade arm into one of the metal triplets and the spear penetrated through it with ease. It kicked and wriggled like a worm on a hook before letting go of life. As he turned a low class was bringing its claws down to rip his face off. He caught the arm in mid swing and snapped it. He then seized it by the throat and impaled it on the second metal triplet. Number three was a blade arm stabbing forward. Jonathan side stepped it and forced its own blade through its throat. He then made a three piece set making it look as if the three suits of armor were hunters coming home with their kill.

There were five remaining in the room and a blade arm was charging him from behind. Jacob made a quick shot and put an arrow through its head, sending it flying out the window.

Meanwhile on the ground Mark and Sarah had their hands full with more than five.

"Man!" Mark cried. "We're knee deep in these hell hounds and they're still coming!"

"I know, but all we can do is keep fighting until there aren't any left."

"When is that?"

"I wish I knew."

"Well, darling, I hate to bring you distressing news, but have you noticed that the soldiers are disappearing faster than the demons are?"

"Huh? Oh no."

He was right. She had been so busy fighting that she hadn't even bothered looking around. There were soldiers lying dead and wounded all over the place. There was a fair amount of demon carcasses, but a lot less by comparison.

"Oh, God. We're losing."

"Not to brag, but they are. We're kicking Satan's butt!"

Sarah looked up at the window on the top floor of the castle.

"I hope Jacob and Jonathan are okay."

No sooner than she finished her sentence, the blade arm came crashing through the window and landed with an arrow in its head.

"I would say their doing just fine," Mark replied.

"Arrrrrgh!"

Jonathan had gone mad with rage. Jacob would have been happy to help him fight off the remaining demons, but he didn't appear to need help.

One blade arm merely held its blades up in an attempt to shield itself from the barrage of Jonathan's attacks. It was no use as he found an opening and hacked it to death. It was actually in fear and crying. Another low class swung at him only to have its arm taken off. It then swung its left arm resulting in the same fate. He finished it by slitting its throat.

The last blade arm didn't have a chance to move before its head was gone. Now it was Jonathan one on one with one low class. It stared a hole through Jonathan before letting out a hissing growl. He answered back with a growl of his own. He watched the creature circling its claws and looked at his own sword. He threw it to the side. When the creature saw this, it charged in. It gasped as Jonathan gripped its throat with both hands. It choked while waiving its arms before finally going limp and falling to the ground.

"Are you still afraid?" Jacob asked watching him still breathing heavily.

He was silent for a moment.

"Not a chance in hell. You said it yourself. The fear will be replaced by anger when you watch innocent people die. There was no man more innocent than the one lying dead on that floor! This unholy bastard walks into innocent towns and takes lives as if they mean nothing!" He was silent another moment. "I believe it now, Jacob. I believe I am the fourth chosen one. Together, you, Mark, Sarah, and I will send this slime back from whence it came."

Jacob smiled, but then looked out the window.

"What is it, Jacob?"

"The demons…they seem to be pulling away."

"Why would they do that? They seemed to be winning."

"Yes, it's almost like their only purpose for being here was to kill the king."

"That doesn't make any sense. It looks like the kingdom of hell would have bigger plans than to assassinate a king that controls two, maybe three towns."

"It's strange. I guess we'll have to figure it out later. At least they're gone. Now comes the hard part."

"What is that?"

"Taking the bodies of brave soldiers from the streets to be buried and you breaking the news of the king's death."

"Yes. I suppose I am the best one to tell them."

Andrew came running through the door. "Lord Jonathan! Thank God you are okay. The demons are retreating and…Oh, my God." He became pale as a ghost.

"Andrew," Jonathan said putting a hand on his shoulder.

"Oh, my God," he repeated. He seemed more like he would throw up now than he had after the first demon attack. "No…"

"Andrew, calm down."

"No… no... no!"

"Andrew!"

"I was supposed to be guarding him. I… It's all my…"

"Don't you dare finish that sentence."

"But it is! It's my fault!"

"No, it's not," Jacob tried to assure him.

"Yes, it is! I vowed to protect him in front of Lord Jonathan, not twenty-four hours ago."

"I know," Jonathan said. "But, there is no way you could have prevented this."

"I should have been here guarding him."

"You would have died, too, Andrew. I know you're a great fighter. I trained you myself, but you couldn't have protected him if you had been here."

"It would have been better for me to have died trying to protect him than to have left and let him die."

"What happened?" Jacob asked.

"Well, the other two guards and I were in here guarding the king, waiting for anything to come through the door. That's when I heard screams. I walked outside and went a short way down the stairs and saw that the creatures had gotten into the castle. The guards were horribly outnumbered and I knew if they were killed, the townspeople wouldn't stand a chance. Some of them were down there with them, cowering in the corner."

"So you helped them?"

"Yes. I had to at least try to help them get the upper hand, especially when I saw a pregnant woman about to be run through. When I went down, some of them must have snuck in behind me and come up here. I got so caught up in killing the demons and protecting the people that I…forgot all about the king. I abandoned my duty, so it's my fault that he's dead."

"But Andrew..."

"You're right," Jonathan interrupted.

They both looked at Jonathan confused.

"You did abandon your duty."

Andrew buried his face in his hands.

"You abandoned your duty for a nobler one."

"What?"

"Andrew, you left to save innocent women and children. My God, you can't get any more noble than that. You know how the king was. He would have given his life to save one person. You left to save more than you could count. He wouldn't have blamed you and neither will I. He ordered me to forget my oath and help Jacob in his fight. You did the right thing."

"Thank you, Lord Jonathan."

Mark and Sarah then came walking into the room.

"Boy, it's a mess out there!" Mark said pointing. "There are a lot of guards down, but they took down plenty of hell hounds with them. I guess we finally scared them off."

"Oh no," Sarah said noticing the king on the floor.

"Huh? Uh oh."

"I am so sorry, Jonathan," Sarah said covering her mouth.

"Don't be sorry for me, Miss Sarah. Be sorry for all the people who looked to him for guidance."

"Jeez, he seemed like such a good guy."

"You don't know the half of it, Mark. He was the greatest man I've ever known."

"His death won't go unpunished, Jonathan. I promise you that."

"I appreciate that, Jacob."

"Gee," Mark said. "I guess this is the first fight we've really lost."

"We're still breathing," Jacob said. "He's won the battle. But we will win the war. Remember that the four of us have found each other now, so the final showdown can't be far away."

They all gave each other a nervous look.

"I know that deep down in you that there is still a small part that is afraid of fighting him. It's in me, too. But I want you all to remember what you have seen up to this point."

They all nodded.

"Mark? Do you remember your friend's daughter? Do you remember her crying in your arms because her daddy was dead? Sarah, do you remember all of the good people who were crushed and burned in the church village? Jonathan, there are God knows how many men you trained and are probably like sons and brothers to you lying dead in the streets. Aren't all of those people worth fighting for?" They all nodded again. "Now, let's show the hooded menace who is boss and send him back where he belongs."

“Yes, you’re right, Jacob,” Jonathan said sighing. “I suppose I should go tell everyone of the king’s death now.”

“Don’t worry, buddy. We’re going to be right there with you,” Mark said patting him on the back.

He smiled. “Thank you everyone.”

CHAPTER 9

It had indeed been a dark and grim day. Only God himself could count the tears that were shed. The families of all the soldiers mourned for the ones who died and pitied the ones that were maimed for life. Everyone, soldier or civilian, mourned the loss of the king. Though he didn't have any real power, they loved him as if he ruled the world.

Jacob sat on his bed thumbing through the bible, trying to find some comfort in any scripture he could find. Since the beginning of this journey he had never seen so much death in his life and hoped he had seen enough to where he would never have to see it again. He highly doubted it though.

He finally began to read the beginning of Genesis and found comfort in the verse, "In the beginning God created the heavens and the earth." Since he had the power to do all of this, Jacob trusted that whatever happened was his will and for the best.

The door to his room opened and Jonathan, Mark, and Sarah walked in with the most solemn faces you could imagine. They did have good reason.

"The town has finally grown silent," Jonathan said. "The people have gone from crying out in the streets, to mourning in their homes to themselves. This is the darkest day the kingdom has ever faced."

"Ever since we started fighting there has been nothing but dark days," Mark added.

"Jacob?" Sarah asked.

"Yes?"

"When will all of this be over?"

"Soon, Sarah. Soon."

Jonathan continued. "Since being here, the demon has wiped villages off the map, killed countless innocent people and destroyed a dynasty. When do we fight him, Jacob?"

"He'll come to us. He knows he can never accomplish his goal until we're dead. He needs us out of the way before he can do anything. It probably won't be long before he confronts us for the final showdown. Then…we destroy *him*."

Barely after Jacob finished his sentence a soldier came running through the door. For a second he thought the final fight would come sooner. But, for once it wasn't a demon sighting that had him excited.

"Lord Jonathan!"

"Yes?"

"We need you and Lord Jacob in the town square. A man from the village next door has collapsed. Before he lost consciousness he was begging for an audience with the king."

"I see."

"That's not all. He also said one other word, monsters. I assumed this would be in the reverend's category of expertise."

"Thank you, soldier. We'll be down momentarily."

Mark looked at Jacob. "Is this it?"

"I don't know."

"He must want us to come to him," Sarah said.

"So it would seem."

"The only way to find out is to hear this man out."

"Jonathan's right. Let's go."

The man had been moved into the doctor's office. The doctor greeted them as they walked in.

"Is he hurt, Doctor?" Jacob asked.

"No, just exhausted. The next town is a good five miles away and he ran the most part of it. His body eventually just shut down. He's resting now."

"When will he wake up?" Jonathan asked.

"Well, I don't know. Under the circumstances that what he has to say may be greatly important, you can wake him up. However I'm not sure how much you will get out of him."

They all walked over to the man lying in bed. His mouth hung open in fatigue. His face was pale and drained of all color. He was muttering unrecognizable words in his sleep. Jacob hated to wake him, but as the doctor had said, these were unusual circumstances.

"Sir?" he asked. There was no answer. He repeated himself a little louder than before. "Sir?"

The man's eyelids began to twitch and his eyes slowly opened.

"Sir, we need to speak with you."

His voice was weak and breathless. He could not speak in whole sentences. "The king…need to speak with him."

"We're the king's advisors." He fibbed to keep from having to tell the whole story. "You can tell us. We'll pass your story along to him."

He nodded weakly. "Children…in trouble."

"Children?" Sarah asked with her maternal instincts kicking in.

"Yes…children…were…taken."

"Taken?" Jacob repeated.

He nodded again. After a brief silence Jacob began asking questions again.

"Before you collapsed you spoke of monsters?"

At the sound of that word the man's eyes grew as wide as saucers and he looked as if he were about to begin convulsing.

"Monsters! Horrible…hideous monsters!"

He was overexerting himself.

"Calm down, sir. Now, slowly tell me what happened."

He swallowed and took a deep breath.

"We were all… having a party… outside of town. Everything got dark. Then… a monster wearing a hood appeared. He… had a… bunch of… smaller monsters… with knife arms."

Though he knew the answer he asked anyway. "He took the children?"

He nodded. "The…monsters…went into …our houses and… took the children… from their beds. Fathers…tried to fight… too strong… two died."

"Do you know where they took them?"

"Yes. They took…them to…our old cemetery. They said they would…sacrifice children…when the full moon was high."

"Full moon? That's tonight," Jonathan said.

"We tried to... get into… cemetery. Some kind of… magic… guarding it. Can't... get through… need King's… help."

"Rest now, sir. We'll save the children and make the ones who did this pay."

He was still restless. "Save my… little boy. He's all… I have left." At that he fell unconscious again.

"Grrrrrr!" Sarah growled. "I didn't think it was possible to hate that lapdog any more, but he seems to discover new ways to piss me off all the time."

"He's going to sacrifice innocent children?" Jonathan said shaking his head in disbelief. "It's hard to imagine that anything could be that evil."

Mark looked at Jacob. "Creatures that steal children from their beds and whisk them away to be eaten. I thought that was only stories our parents told to frighten us."

"This is no story, Mark. It's really happening. As Jonathan said, tonight is the full moon and the stars will be out in less than an hour. The doctor said this town is five miles from here. Is he right, Jonathan?"

"Yes."

"Then we have no time to waste. Jonathan, tell Andrew and the other soldiers where we're going. I doubt there will be any attacks while we're gone, but tell them to keep a watch out anyway."

"Yes, Jacob," he said sighing. "I hate to leave here with everything in chaos over the king's death, but we have no choice."

"Mark, you and Sarah go grab a few supplies and get some horses. We'll never make it there in time on foot. I'll meet you at the town gates."

As they all walked away Jacob looked once more at the man in the bed, then up to the heavens. "Please God, for the sake of those parents, don't let us be too late."

Night had come by the time they had arrived at the small village. Jacob prayed that it was a long ritual before the children were sacrificed. He looked up at the full moon to see it hidden ominously behind the clouds.

"What now?" Mark asked looking around.

"We should tell the people who we are and get them to tell us where the children were taken."

"I think I have a pretty good idea," Sarah said pointing. "Look."

She pointed to a gate where two men were desperately chopping away with axes. Walking over, Jacob called out to the men. He was wary of getting too close seeing as how they had axes and looked to be on the verge of a breakdown.

"Excuse me."

The two turned lightning fast toward them with their eyes wide and bloodshot.

"We're here from the kingdom. We came to save the children."

Disappointment clouded their faces. When they spoke it wasn't with the ramblings of mad men, but with sane, reasoning voices.

"You mean it's only the four of you?" one of them asked.

"Yes, I'm afraid so."

"What did Terry tell you?" the other man asked.

"Not much, I'm afraid. He had collapsed from exhaustion by the time he got there. He was very weak and barely able to speak. He did tell us about the children being taken by monsters, though."

"I'm sorry if we sound ungrateful," the second one said. "But we're expecting a battalion of the king's men to rescue the children."

"Don't worry," Mark assured him. "We've handled quite a few of these things. You might call us monster exterminators. We'll bring your kids back safe and sound."

New life came into the men's faces. The first man called into town. "Everyone! Help has arrived to save the children!"

After the word children, the townspeople poured from their separate houses. As they arrived one woman asked, "Where are they?"

The man pointed to the four of them. Like the men had been they all seemed disappointed.

"It's just the four of you?" a man asked.

"Yes, but don't worry we've faced these things before," Jacob said.

"I'm sorry." A woman apologized. "We were just expecting the King to send a bunch of soldiers on horseback to fight the monsters. Is he busy with matters of his own?"

"No." Jonathan said stepping in. "He would have been here to personally fight to save your children if he were able. Unfortunately circumstances can't allow that."

"Oh, then he's ill? Another woman asked?"

Jonathan hung his head not wanting to say it.

"He's dead."

"What?!" A man shouted.

Women covered their mouths and gasped. The men were shaking their heads and everyone was murmuring to each other.

"The King is dead?" A man repeated.

"Yes, it happened only a few hours ago."

"How?"

Jonathan looked at Jacob wishing for him to tell them.

"He was killed by the same creatures that took your children. They aren't monsters. Well.....they are, but that isn't the name for them. They are demons."

"What? What are demons doing in our town?"

"They aren't just in your town. They were in my town, which is now burned to ash. They were in Mark's town where good friends of his died. They were in Sarah's town where many were maimed and killed. They were in Jonathan's Kingdom where nearly two hundred soldiers died trying to protect it."

Everyone was shocked and confused.

"They are taking our world. Only the four of us standing before you can stop them. We were chosen by God himself to fight for earth before hell takes it over. Now, for your children's sake, tell us what happened."

A red bearded man stepped up to be the speaker for the group.

"We were all having a party, having fun and laughing. It was a beautiful evening, but out of nowhere the skies were taken over by the darkest clouds I've ever seen. We thought it was just a storm cloud that had shown up without warning. We began to gather up our stuff and take it to my house and that's when it happened."

"What happened?" Sarah asked.

"Silence. It became utter hear a pin drop silence. It was unlike anything I had ever felt before. Then Mrs. Stone looked into the distance and saw something. At first it was only eyes glowing in the darkness. She asked if it was wolves. That's what we all thought too, until one of them stepped into the light."

The man rubbed his shoulders as his own story chilled him.

"We all gasped at what we saw. It was like creatures from your worst nightmares. They had thick rubbery skin and no hair. Where arms should have been there were blades. We were all horrified. One by one about a dozen of them came walking into the light. They didn't attack. They only stood there. That was until their leader came walking out behind them."

"Gee, I wonder who that was?" Mark asked sarcastically.

"At first he merely sneered and stared at us. Finally he hissed something and they all came charging at us. We were armed and ready to fight, but they ran past us and into our houses. When they came out they were carrying our children kicking and screaming. We fought desperately to save them, but the demons were too strong. Even fighting with one blade they were too much. Two men died. Another one probably lies on his deathbed in one of our homes."

"Your messenger said something about the cemetery." Jacob said staring at the gate.

"Yes, that's where they took them. After they entered the head demon put some kind of cursed seal on the gate, so nobody could get in."

"That's what we were chopping at when you first came up." The first man added.

"I see."

The red bearded man continued hanging his head.

"He said your children will serve as lambs to slaughter as an offering to my master. Don't look so sad. They will give unlimited power to the new ruler of earth. Their blood will spill when the full moon is high in the sky."

"I've heard enough! Mark cried. Let's go kick some demon butt and save the children."

Jacob nodded and walked to the seal.

"You can't touch it." A man said holding out his hands. They were scarred and burned. "The fire of hell is in it."

It was pulsating with evil. Jacob held his cross high.

"Lord God who created the heavens and the earth. I call upon you in these people's time of need. Help us break through this evil seal so that we may be able to save these little ones. Lord God help us be in time and give us the strength to send these putrid dogs back to hell where you meant for them to be. Now, in the name of Jesus Christ may this barrier be broken!"

He kicked the barrier with all of his strength and it shattered like glass. Every shard melted as it hit the ground. The townspeople rejoiced at this sight.

"Let's go." He said walking through the gate and the other three followed.

"Good Lord!" Mark said looking around at the vast area and all of the tombstones. "Do all of these people live fifty to a household? Look at this place. There has to be two thousand gravesites here."

"These aren't all people who have lived here." Jonathan explained. "You see the majority of this town is its graveyard. They allow people from different parts of the continent to bury their dead here. That's why the cemetery is so big. In fact this is where many of the soldiers lost will be put to rest."

"Stop." Jacob said putting his arm up.

"It's them." Sarah said.

They watched as the hooded demon had his hands raised toward the full moon. He and all of the blade arms circled a huge bon fire, each of them holding a screaming child. Jacob didn't know what this unholy ritual was, nor did he want to know.

With his hands raised toward the heavens, which made no sense since his master lied in the other direction, he was muttering words in a language that none of them understood. With every word he spoke the fire grew and blazed as if it were a living thing feeding off every syllable.

After finishing his unholy speech he pointed to a blade arm holding a screaming little girl and motioned for it to throw her in the fire. Before it could move a muscle, Jacob had already cocked, aimed and shot. The arrow hit the demon in the neck, piercing all the way through. It let out a cry, dropped the girl, and fell backward into the fire.

"Honey! We're home!" Mark yelled into the night.

As usual the hooded demon sneered at Jacob in hatred. He expected him at any second to call out attack orders, but something strange was going on. Instead or charging in and attacking them or even showing signs of life, they merely stood frozen.

"What's going on, Jacob?" Sarah asked.

"Yeah, they're looking at us like we just showed up at a royal ball naked," Mark added.

"I don't know, but be ready for anything."

The hooded demon gave the blade arms a nod and they dropped the children.

"Run back to your families!" Jacob called to them.

They weren't hesitant to listen. He pointed back toward the shadows and the blade arms disappeared into them. Suddenly they thought this was indeed the time and place of the final showdown.

"I think we've been had," Jonathan said.

"It was a trap?" Sarah asked.

"Yes," Jacob said suspiciously, the demon's motives a mystery.

"Okay, little demonic riding hood!" Mark called out. "Are you finally man… or monster enough to face us?"

"Yes demon!" Jonathan yelled. "You and those vermin that serve you took the lives of men that were like my brothers! Also the life of a man I would have given my own to protect. For that I'll cut you into pieces and feed you to the buzzards!"

"I've watched you hurt too many people!" Sarah added. "Now all that is left for me to do is bash in that ugly skull of yours!"

Jacob stepped up.

"It's over demon. Look at us. We are four united now and that spells your demise. Together we will bring your dynasty of darkness to a tragic end."

There was a momentary silence, then the demon burst into laughter. "***Ha Ha Haaaaaaaa! I never grow tired of hearing you spill out nonsense like vomit. I should take you all back to hell and let you tell your speech to my master. It's been a while since I had a good laugh. Do you actually hear yourselves? Oh no, this is not the time for our last battle. Why are you so eager to die anyway? Do you know that I could…"***

Though they were all sick of this speech it was Mark who exploded.

"SHUT UP! We're the ones spewing out nonsense like vomit? All you ever say is 'I could breathe and kill you' or 'I could snap my fingers and turn you to dust'! Well, you ugly, yellow-bellied, sap-sucking, Satan-butt-kissing, hellhound ballerina, do it, or shut the hell up!"

You wouldn't think that an evil force of hell could lose its composure so fast, but leave it to Mark to cause just that. As the demon quivered in anger, its noticeably forked tongue shot in and out of its mouth like a snake having a seizure. At the peak of its shakes, giant bat wings jumped from under the cloak he wore, shaking wildly at the tips.

"Uhhhh, I think you successfully pissed him off," Sarah said.

"Arrrrrgh! You defy the serpent, so now you shall die by the serpent!" he cried and flew away.

"Wow. That was something new," Mark said watching him fly out of sight. "He just ran away."

Suddenly the ground shook beneath them.

"I get the feeling he left us a playmate, though," Jacob said trying to hold his balance.

"What is it?" Jonathan asked.

No sooner had the words left his mouth, than the creature burst through the ground, sending them flying in different directions. Jacob and his crew shook their heads clear to examine the newest monstrosity. It was the largest snake they had ever seen. For double the fun, it had two heads.

"Ah jeez! I hate snakes!" Mark yelped. "Do you think its poisonous?"

"Oh, gee, Mark, like we're not going to be dead after it bites us in half?" Sarah said.

As they watched, it hissed and bobbed its heads back and forth. A green liquid oozed down its fangs and fell to the ground, smoking and burning as it hit.

"To answer your question, Mark," Jacob said. "Yes, I think it is very poisonous."

"Of course, it is. He hasn't made us fight cuddly bunny rabbits yet, so why should he start now? As I say before every battle, does anyone have any ideas? Jacob? Sarah? Jonathan? Anybody?"

"We do the same thing we always do, Mark. We look for a weakness and try to kill it."

As they stood, the thing jumped into action.

"Run!" Marked yelled. As he turned to run, the serpent used its tail to sweep his feet out from under him. He landed flat on his back with the wind knocked out of him. He was as helpless as a rat in a cobra's grasp. The snake cocked itself to strike, but as it jumped forward it jerked, hissing. Jonathan had run through the snake's tail, pinning it to the ground.

"You and Sarah help Mark! I can't hold this thing for long!"

As they helped Mark up, the snake turned and snapped at Jonathan, narrowly missing. He fell to the ground and slid backward as each head took turns trying to devour him.

"Jacob, we had better do something or he is going to be a noble hors d'oeuvres," Sarah said.

Pulling out his crossbow, he sent a shot flying into the back of one of its heads. Not obviously injured, the thing did remove its attention from Jonathan and reversed, slithering back toward Jacob.

"I don't think taking turns playing tag is going to put this thing in the grave any quicker," Mark said.

"Have you got any better ideas?" Sarah asked.

"Unfortunately, no. We can't even use our usual distraction strategy because its guarded from both sides."

"He's right, Jacob. How do we get rid of one head without getting eaten by the other?"

"When I think of that, I'll tell you."

Jonathan had taken the long way back and rejoined them. "Urrrrgh! The beast strikes like lightning."

"Yeah," Mark agreed. "I guess he caught on that the big, dumb, and stupid approach wasn't working."

"What now?" Jonathan asked.

"Well, we… umph!"

Suddenly they were all knocked in the chest by the battering ram that was the thing's tail again. After landing, it took Jacob several seconds to catch his breath. "Everyone just take a direction and try not to get eaten!" he shouted gasping.

Jonathan and Sarah took the left and right, alternately, while Mark took the back. Jacob took the front. It faced Jacob and turned each head toward Sarah and Jonathan. The only one not in at least its peripheral vision was Mark.

Slowly Mark came up behind it and chopped off the tip of its tail. The demon snake released a hissing cry and used what tail it had left to send Mark flying.

"Is it just me or are we spending more time flying through the air than on the ground?"

The snake stood in place frozen like a statue. Each time one of them took a step forward, it snapped at their heads. Then, without warning, it hopped back into the hole from which it came.

"I guess hoping it ran away in fear would be too good to be true," Mark mumbled.

"Be on guard," Jonathan warned.

There was utter silence as they looked in all directions.

"Ahhhh!"

The silence was broken as it emerged right under Sarah and she began riding the left head like a bull.

"Hold on, Sarah!" Mark called to her.

"What else am I going to do?!"

"We have to get her down," Jacob said.

"But how?" Mark asked.

Sarah, not waiting for either of them to come up with a plan, took matters into her own hands. Taking her bo, she shoved it into the thing's mouth. It clamped down so hard that it went through its upper and lower jaw, pinning its mouth shut.

"Way to go, Sarah!" Mark said. "That takes care of one problem."

"Sarah!" Jacob called to her. "Slide down its tail!"

"What?!"

"Use its tail like a slide! I'll catch you!"

"I hope you know what you're doing!"

Closing her eyes, she slid down its tail and into Jacob's arms.

"Ha! Mark said mocking the beast. "Not so tough when you have only one head huh?"

The snakes demonic hissing roar grew. Whatever was about to happen, it couldn't be good. It finally spat a huge gob of green liquid at them.

"Watch out!" Jacob cried jumping to the side.

The liquid struck the ground in the middle of them and evaporated the grass, making a small crater. It spat three more gobs at them forcing them to dodge their way farther and farther back.

"Curses!" Jonathan said. "Every time we break through one defense it creates another!"

"We have to do something! Pray for a giant mongoose, Jacob."

"I don't think that's going to work, Mark."

"Then I'm out of ideas."

"How do we beat this thing?" Sarah asked.

"We can't get within thirty feet of it without taking a killer bath," Mark said. "Too bad *we* don't have a burning goo launcher."

"Wait," Jacob said. "That's it!"

"You mean you have a burning goo launcher?"

"No. I mean that gives me an idea."

"Do tell."

"Sometimes when two rattlesnakes get into a fight they get tangled up and snap at anything that moves. Sometimes one of them will accidentally bite itself. They aren't immune to their own poison."

"So, it kills itself?" Sarah asked.

"Yes."

"So we get it to commit inadvertent suicide?" Mark asked.

"Brilliant!" Jonathan said.

"How do we get it to bite itself?" Sarah asked.

"Well, as usual someone will have to be the bait."

They all looked at Mark.

"Hey, what happened to drawing straws? Bah, why break tradition? What do I do?"

"First you have to get close to it. Then stand near its lower body and tail. When it strikes, jump out of the way as fast as you can. If we're lucky, it will bit itself and that will be the end of it."

"Be careful, Mark," Jonathan said.

"Don't worry. I'm not ready for a harp and halo just yet."

After taking a deep breath, he sprinted toward the serpent. Once again it began spitting acid bombs, missing him by inches each time. He stopped under the mouth and looked up. "Boy, you're a lot bigger close up."

It snapped down at him and he flipped backward to dodge it.

"Get in the middle of it!" Sarah called.

"That's easy for you to say! Okay, here goes nothing."

Mark ran to the middle of the coiled tail. When reached his destination, the snake was glaring at him with eyes burning and fangs shining. Every muscle in Mark's body was braced and ready to move. He knew that with one quick motion their plan was going to work or he was going to be a midnight snake snack.

Finally it made its move, but even quicker than the snake, Mark jumped away and rolled. Standing up, he wasn't sure if it had bit itself or not. Then it was all too obvious as it stuck both heads straight into the air.

The free head let out an ear-shattering shriek into the night. Then every inch of scaly skin began to melt off the bones until all that remained was a shell.

"Umm, I think it worked, Jacob," Mark said looking in awe at the display.

"Yes, we managed to overcome yet another obstacle unscathed."

"How many more of these challenges are we going to have to face?" Jonathan asked.

"It won't be long before this is all over. The four of us have been brought together to bring him down and he knows it. He can't run from us forever."

"So do we find him or does he find us?" Sarah asked.

"I don't know, but I want to get back to the castle as soon as possible. This whole thing was strange."

"You're just now finding this stuff strange?" Mark asked.

"No. I mean did you notice that he didn't even put up a fight for the children? He didn't even sick his minions on us. It was as if all this was just a… distraction to get us away."

"I see what you mean," Jonathan said. "If he had really wanted to sacrifice the children, then he would have went to a lot more trouble."

"Exactly."

"So, do you think he has a plan for the castle?"

"I don't know, but I would feel a lot better if we left right now. Andrew is a good fighter, but I don't know if he and the other guards can handle another onslaught by themselves."

As they approached the castle gates, Jacob feared his assumption was right.

"Smoke," Sarah said pointing.

"It looks like you were right," Jonathan said.

"Yes. That little scene back at the graveyard was just to lure us away from here. Well, let's hurry, but be on guard. There is no telling what we are liable to run into in there."

"That three-headed dog, Cerberus, is the only thing he hasn't thrown at us yet," Mark said.

Being as careful as possible they busted through the front gates to see something they never suspected.

"What the…?" Mark asked scratching his head.

What they saw were all of the townspeople and many soldiers laughing and dancing all around. The smoke was coming from two separate bonfires blazing in the middle of town.

"What is going on here?" Jonathan asked.

"They're drunk off their tails is what's going on," Sarah answered.

"I'm as confused as you are, Jonathan," Jacob said.

"Why weren't we invited to the party?" Mark asked.

"My God," Jacob said looking around. "I know these people were all confused until my sermon, but we come back and its Sodom and Gomorrah."

Two men were fist fighting near an alley with a crowd cheering them on. People were turning up bottles of wine and devouring them, missing their mouths with half of it. Sarah looked to see something that shocked even her.

"Whoa! There's something even I never did," she said turning away.

The other three gasped as they also saw a couple publicly having sex. This actually left Mark speechless. All three were wide-eyed, but Jonathan took particular offence.

"Get up, you two!! Make yourself decent. Is this how you celebrate the memory of your king?"

The man looked up and sneered. "Shut up, you dimwitted walking tin can!"

"Why, you insolent…"

Jacob stopped him as he began taking out his sword.

"Wait, Jonathan."

He turned his attention to the couple.

"Tell me, what changed while we were gone? Why are you doing this?"

"We learned that we can do whatever we want," the woman said.

"Where did you learn that?"

"From the truth tellers."

"The truth tellers? Who are they?"

"I'm a truth teller," a voice said behind them.

They turned to see a young girl, maybe fourteen years old, wearing a black hood that looked all too familiar.

"Who are you?" Sarah asked.

"As I said, I am a truth teller."

"What exactly is this truth you tell?" Jacob asked.

"Hmph! Foolish preacher. We tell the truth of how they don't have to be held prisoner by you and people like you."

"Prisoner?"

"What do you call it? You force people to believe every word you say. You tell them not to drink or commit adultery. You tell them to hold all people equal. You have even poisoned the minds of your friends here."

"I don't force people to do anything. That is why god gave us free will. As far as drunkenness, adultery and holding all people equal, that is God's law and the only truth I know."

"How blind are you? Look around."

"I have unfortunately, but I'm not impressed."

"You wouldn't be, but this is true paradise. These people are free to do as they wish. They are truly free."

"I'm afraid not. True freedom can't exist. A life without rules or laws would be chaos. No, this isn't paradise. This is a mockery of god's word. True paradise is a land flowing with milk and honey. These people will still shed tears and blood. In true paradise, no blood or tears will ever be shed. This isn't heaven; this is hell."

The girl snarled and hissed at him. He grabbed her by the throat and began to lift her. They all gasped.

"Whoa, Jacob!" Mark said. "She's just a kid!"

As he lifted her, she turned into horrifying and demented creature, hissing and trying to kick away. Shoving it forward he shot it with an arrow and it turned to ashes.

"All tempting things are beautiful on the outside, but you will always find they are rotting on the inside."

Suddenly, they heard a voice laughing behind them that they knew all too well.

"Tell me, preacher, don't you just love what I have done with this place? They have gone from spouting the mercies of Jesus and the Father to a den of sinners my master could be proud of. Do you finally understand? Murder, fornication, adultery, stealing, drunkenness, and pride. They are all the source of this

world. Your God may have planned for it to be kindness, mercy, and peace, but that plan went horribly wrong thanks to my master. Tell me, do you fear me now?"

"No," Jacob said bluntly.

"What?!"

"Do you really think you have given me any more reason to fear you? All you have done is taken lost sheep and led them the wrong way? Would I fear a man who convinced a child to steal a piece of fruit that didn't know any better? I think not. Your time has come, demon. This all ends now."

"Yeah!" Mark said stepping forward. "Stop running your mouth, running away, and fight us like a man, demon, or whatever the hell you are."

Sarah stepped forward. "Since we joined forces, there hasn't been anything you've thrown at us that we haven't slaughtered. There's only one thing left and it is standing right in front of us."

Jonathan joined her. "Yes, demon, united there isn't any way in hell that you can stop us. With the four of us together, your destiny is a hole six feet under."

The demon was silent a moment before bursting into laughter once again. ***"Oh, your over confident ramblings never cease to amuse me. Very well. If all of you are so eager to die, then I will fight you."***

They all took a fighting stance.

"Not here."

"What? You want to fight us behind the school at lunch tomorrow?" Mark asked sarcastically.

"I'll give you a few minutes to say good-bye to this world you love so much. Think of it this way. You good Christian people would never want to live in a world like this so I'll be doing you a favor. Meet me on Death Hill. Your noble friend knows where it is. Death Hill will be an appropriate place for you to meet yours."

At that, there was a cloud of fog and he disappeared. Nobody said anything at first.

Jacob broke the silence. "The time has finally come."

"Lord Jonathan! Lord Jacob!"

It was Andrew running from the castle.

"Thank goodness you're back."

"What happened, Andrew?" Jonathan asked.

"Everything was normal except for everyone grieving the King. Then the guards and I noticed many townspeople acting strangely. They were dancing and singing the praises of the truth tellers. We thought they meant you and your friends, Jacob, but when they began drinking and stripping their clothes we knew something was up."

"Where are the other guards?"

"Some are scattered around trying to get things under control. Many have joined in with this madness."

"Uhhhhhgh," Jonathan sighed in disgust.

"To be honest, sir, none of us has a clue what to do."

"There is only one thing to do," Jacob said. "The four of us have to fight. Tell me, Jonathan, what is this place Death Hill?"

"It was the site of the last battle between the villagers and the King's Grandfather. Many from both sides died that day and Death Hill is a memorial to them all."

"Basically he wants us surrounded by dead people?" Sarah asked.

"If that's the way he wants it, it's the way he'll have it," Jacob said. "At least he won't have to go far to be buried. Can you take us there Jonathan?"

"Yes, of course. Andrew, you and the other soldiers do what you can to bring things under control."

"Yes, sir. Be careful, all of you."

"We will, Andrew. We will."

They all took a deep breath.

"Well," Jacob said. "This is it."

As they arrived, surrounded by gravestones, all was quiet. The sky was solid black with no stars and a cold wind blew through the dead trees.

"Boy, this place is as quiet as a graveyard," Mark joked.

"Where is he?" Sarah asked looking in every direction.

"I have a feeling he'll be making his entrance very soon," Jacob assured her.

There was a thick patch of fog to one side. It slowly began to fade and their hooded nemeses came into view. He was pointing at four empty graves with four tombstones.

"Greetings! I've been busy making preparations for your arrival. I hope you like it. It was the best I could do on such short notice."

They walked closer to the graves to read the words on the stones. Each one had a name on it. Jonathan Lancaster, Mark Raven, Sarah Mist, and Jacob Cross. Under each name were the words "Died in agony."

"Enough of your mind games!" Jacob snapped. "There is no place to run. All that is left to do is face us and be sent back to where you came from."

"You might be able to beat one of us," Sarah added. "But you can't beat the four of us."

"Well then, I guess we find out now!"

At what seemed like the speed of light the demon streaked forward and lifted Sarah by the throat and thrust her forward. Knowing there was no time to be shocked by anything, Jacob slashed him in the side.

Without flinching, the demon turned and backhanded Jacob ten feet away. Mark, not even bothering to use his sword, began fist fighting him. After a few uppercuts and straight punches, the demon lifted him by the shoulders and head-butted him nearly unconscious.

Jonathan came from behind and slit its throat like an assassin. He was disturbed to see him turn and the wound heal. The creature hissed and kicked him into a tree.

Jacob was already back up and slashing at the demon's back. He held out his hand and a ball of fire exploded from it sending Jacob flying once again.

Sarah came from the side and began beating in his ribs and stomach. He caught her last swing and fire-balled her to join Jacob.

Mark, finally using his sword, rammed it through the back of his knee. As Jonathan had seen, the wound merely healed up. The demon lifted his hand and Mark began floating in the air before he was tossed into Sarah and Jacob.

Jonathan, not giving up, charged in and stabbed through his gut ten times before he stopped him. Lightning flew from his fingertips, lifted him, and tossed him to join his three comrades.

As they all laid there in pain and confusion, he continued the lightning storm on all of them until all three cried out in pain.

"ARRRRGH! Why do I get the feeling this isn't going the way we planned?!" Mark yelled.

"Hold... on!" Jacob said.

The lightning stopped and smoke was lifting. The demon picked Jacob up by the throat.

"Now do you finally understand, preacher? I am a god. This world belongs to hell now. Your precious teachings of Jesus mean nothing! Now you truly know that I can at any time end your life with ease. Now, stare into the eyes of your master!"

Dropping Jacob, he disappeared into the fog. They were all numb and barely able to move, but nothing hurt worse than the pain of defeat.

THE FINAL CHAPTER

Their heads hung low and their spirits even lower as they headed back to the castle. All of them were confused, but none of them more than Jacob. All he could wonder was why God had allowed them to suffer such a miserable defeat at the hands of the demon. Suddenly he stopped in his tracks. Jonathan, Mark, and Sarah all looked back at him.

"I don't understand this," he said.

"You aren't the only one pal!" Mark said disgusted.

"Yeah," Sarah said. "We go in there as God's errand boys, expecting to kick the thing's butt, and he wipes the floor with us without even breaking a sweat."

"I thought the four of us together was what would defeat the demon," Jonathan said.

"Yeah, what happened to that?" Sarah asked.

As they all turned to go again it came to Jacob.

"Wait! That's it. We've been putting all of our faith in ourselves. All we have been depending on is the fact that the four of us fighting together would defeat the demon. We've been forgetting the most important thing, our faith in God. We haven't trusted him. That's why we lost."

Sarah looked insulted. "Are you telling me we're down here doing all of the work while he sits up there and watches and he makes us lose just because we didn't mention his name?"

"It isn't like that, Sarah."

"Then how is it? Explain it to me!"

"God is the reason we are alive. The bible teaches us that if we don't put our total faith in God that we can't accomplish anything. This was a lesson."

"Us getting our butts kicked was a lesson?!" Mark shouted.

"All the hooded demon can say is that he can destroy us at any time, but do you notice that we're still alive? It's because he can't kill us."

"There are some things worse than death," Jonathan said.

"He has a point," Mark agreed. "He may not be able to kill us, but he can beat us to a pulp time after time. I don't know about you, but that doesn't sound too appealing to me."

"But..."

"Enough, Jacob!" Sarah yelled. "It's over."

"So, this is it?" Jacob said as they turned to walk away. "After all we have been through. After all the demons we have slain, we suffer one defeat and you're ready to quit?"

"What else can we do?!" Mark asked.

"Keep fighting. It doesn't look like you would just stand around and allow the world to be turned into the abomination that the demon has created."

"Why Jacob?" Sarah asked. "We've lived life like this most of ours. Why should it be any different now? I guess if we're supposed to be willing to get our tails handed to us on a silver platter, just to say we're fighting, then I guess we're not the chosen ones after all."

Just when Jacob thought he couldn't get any lower, all he could do was hang his head down and say, "What now God?"

Andrew met them as they walked back into town.

"Lord Jonathan! Is the demon dead?"

"No, Andrew. He is very much alive, but soon this world will be dead."

He never even turned his head to Andrew and walked away. Mark and Sarah didn't bother to reply and followed Jonathan into the inn. Andrew was shocked and confused. He didn't know what to say.

"What happened, Lord Jacob?"

"We lost, Andrew."

"But I thought you were the chosen ones."

"We are, Andrew. The others just haven't realized it yet. Will you do something for me?"

"If I can be of any help, anything, Jacob. What can I do?"

"Get your horse and go to every town you can. Then find as many Christian people you can that are willing and bring them here. Maybe all of their combined faith will at least weaken the demon."

"But, what about the others?"

"I don't know, Andrew. We can only hope they come around."

"Yes, sir. I'll leave immediately."

As Andrew walked away, Jacob didn't have the slightest idea what he was going to do. In all honesty even he was beginning to believe that God had abandoned them. He walked into the inn to see his friends back to their old habits.

Sarah was flirting with a blonde-haired, blue-eyed pretty boy. Mark was taking a shot of God-knows-what at the bar. Jonathan was in the corner looking down on everyone as if they were the scum of the earth.

"As a dog returns to his vomit, so does a sinner return to his sin," he said under his breath. Not wanting to see this a moment longer he proceeded upstairs where all he wanted to do was sleep and hope everything would solve itself.

As Jacob slept, it seemed that the world disappeared. There was nothing in sight and only silence until the images came. He saw himself walking through the graveyard where they had just lost to the hooded demon. Mark, Sarah, and Jonathan were nowhere to be found. It was only him and he could sense someone else. Suddenly different scenes began skipping before his eyes with no sound.

In one scene he was being slammed against a tree. In another he was slicing the demon with everything he had. There were many images, but the last one was the most disturbing. In this one the demon had him lifted by the throat.

It only held him there, letting him dangle like a worm on a hook. He had no grip on his sword or crossbow. All he could do was attempt to struggle free and stare into the eyes of his destroyer.

It was then that the demon sent him flying through the air until he was stopped by something.

He felt a sharp pain go through his back and he soon realized that he wasn't falling. He looked down to see where he was, but all he noticed was the sharp piece of metal protruding from his stomach. At the end of the dream the only image was of him impaled on the tree dying

Jacob gasped as he woke in a cold sweat. Out of reflex, the first thing he did was grab his stomach. No gaping hole. He had come to the point where he couldn't even sleep in peace. Now that he was awake and would probably be for the next month, he decided to go downstairs and see if there had been some miracle and the other three were waiting to go for one last fight. When he reached the bottom of the stairs, they were there though they looked no more enthused than they were before. They were, however, giving him a strange look.

"What?"

"Nothing," Mark said. "We just thought you would never wake up."

"Huh?"

"You've been asleep nearly twenty-four hours Jacob," Jonathan said.

"I came and knocked on your door three different times, but you never answered," Sarah said.

Twenty-four hours? I don't feel like I've been asleep twenty-four minutes

"We were wondering what you're going to do now," Mark said.

"I'm fighting," Jacob said walking toward the door.

"What?!"

"I'm going to Death Hill and I'm having one last showdown with the demon."

"You're going by yourself?" Jonathan asked.

"Since you three have decided to do nothing, I guess so."

"Jacob! That thing will kill you!" Sarah pleaded.

"Well, Sarah, I would rather die fighting and go on to meet my master than to live in a world like this and do nothing. You are still the chosen ones to me. If you want to come you know where I'll be." At that he walked out the door.

"Damn fool!" Sarah yelled shattering a glass into the wall.

"Basically our friend just told us he's committing suicide," Mark said. "This liquor isn't good enough for this situation. If you need me I'll be at the bar."

"I too will be going for a walk, Miss Sarah. If you need anything call for me."

Sarah buried her face into her hands and sighed deeply. Then she felt a hand on her shoulder. It was an athletic and handsome curly haired man.

"A sad look on a sexy woman doesn't look too good," he said.

"Ha, nice line, but I'm not in the mood for sex right now pal."

"Why not? Your friends are gone and we may not be alive to enjoy the pleasures of life much longer. I have a room. Now all I need is a beautiful woman."

She looked down thinking then looked back at him. "Let's go."

Arriving on Death Hill, sword in hand, all was silent until the voice of Jacob's nightmares came from the night.

"Oh, this is too much! I know you want to entertain me, but this is much too easy. I annihilated four of you and you come to face me one on one with me? Don't make me laugh."

"Enough, demon! You may kill me and feed on my dead body, but I will not stand by and watch you destroy the world my God has created."

"All you talk about is your God when it is your God that is about to let you die. If you renounce him now I just might let you live."

"That isn't going to happen demon."

"My, I must say that you are truly faithful to your God. You are in luck seeing as you are about to meet him!"

⟩⟨⟩⟨

The bartender had a friendly and inviting smile on his face.
"What do you have?" Mark asked.
"Any drink you could possibly want," The bartender replied.
"Sounds good. Give me a bottle of whiskey."
"Very good. First bottle is on the house."
"Huh? Is it my birthday? What's the occasion?"
"Heh. Let's just say I'm a kind fellow."

⟩⟨⟩⟨

As Jonathan was walking he heard someone screaming. He ran to help if someone needed it. As he turned the corner he saw a teenage boy on the ground, being stomped by a clean-shaven man dressed remarkably like Jonathan.

"What are you doing to that boy?!" he shouted.

The man looked at him scowling. "This peasant boy had the audacity to address me without kneeling or even calling me sir. I see that you too are a noble. Perhaps you would like to teach this lowlife scum a lesson."

These were words Jonathan knew all too well.

⟩⟨⟩⟨

Sarah backed through the stranger's door, wrapped her arms around him and kissed him. As he laid her on the bed and began kissing her neck, Jacob came to mind. She dismissed the thought as quick as it came. Jacob was the last thing she wanted to think about.

⟩⟨⟩⟨

"Ghaaaaah!" Jacob cried in pain as he was slammed into a tree.

"Ready to give up?"

"Not a chance!" he yelled leaping forward and putting his blade through the demon's gut and twisting."

"Arrrgh! Grrr! You are a persistent little maggot!"

"I told you. To make me go away you will have to kill me."

"I'll grant your wish, but first let me show you something that might interest you."

"What?" The demon grabbed his head and everything went dark. All he could hear was the demon's voice.

"Even if you manage to defeat me and save this pathetic world, it will still belong to my master in time."

Suddenly Jacob began seeing the countless sins of the future.

"There will come a time when sin lies at every corner as it did in the old world. Marriage vows and being a virgin at sixteen years of age will be a joke. Mothers who don't want to bear the burden of a child can simply have a procedure in which the child is ripped from her womb and destroyed like a disease! People will wipe the name of God and his son from every corner of the earth. His name will be as a swear word to people. There will be substances that people willingly put into their own body that is worse than any drink there is. When they don't have it they will long for it. They will be willing to give up their spouses, their children, their bodies, and even their very souls just for a taste of it. Religion and Christian people will be non-existent. There will be no hope".

Jacob began weeping. All of this was too much for him to see and hear at one time. Now it was time for God to step in.

"Don't listen to him Jacob," Another voice said.

"What?!"

"There is always hope."

It was the voice of the angel who first appeared to him. Suddenly it was new and hopeful images Jacob was seeing. He saw a young girl saying no to a hormone-crazed boy. He saw a young boy rejecting drugs from a street punk. He then saw a preacher like himself preaching a fire-filled message to his church. Jacob then felt a sudden burst of energy run through him. He jumped forward and shoved his blade through the demon's throat. The demon froze, gurgling and gasping for air. He released Jacob's head and slowly pulled the blade out. Jacob watched as before, the wound slowly healed itself. But he also noticed that it didn't heal quite as fast this time.

"Now this ends!"

"I won't go down without a fight demon!"

)<)<

As Mark sat enjoying shot after shot of whiskey, he couldn't help but to think of Jacob. He thought of the first time they had met and the first fight they had together. Jacob was the best friend he ever had, but he just couldn't handle the whole Christian thing. Still he couldn't stop thinking that Jacob was out there being ripped to shreds, fighting for what he believed in. All of these thoughts were numbed by alcohol, but an image supernaturally entered his mind. It was the image of Jacob impaled on a tree.

"Ahhhh! My God! What am I doing? I can't let Jacob die by himself fighting."

As he turned to leave, the bartender grabbed him by the shoulder.

"Where are you going?!"

"To save a friend."

"Not today you're not."

He punched the bartender and he fell backward against the wall. The man then turned into a howling minion and melted away.

"Please, God, don't let me be too late."

)<)<

Meanwhile on Death Hill, a shooting pain went through the demon and he went to his knees. Jacob took advantage of this and slashed him in the face.

)<)<

Jonathan was so tempted by this sight. He began to remember his upbringing, his pride, and all of those old feelings of superiority came flowing back. Then Jacob came to mind. He thought of all his words, but the temptation was becoming too much for him. Then the image of Jacob impaled on a tree went through his mind and brought him back to his senses.

"What?"

He looked at the noble and backhanded him to the ground.

"This boy or anyone for that matter has any reason to bow

down to you!" The noble looked up at Jonathan and transformed into a hideous creature before melting away.

"I have to help Jacob."

><><

Meanwhile, another sharp pain shot through the demon allowing Jacob to ram his blade through its eye.

"Ghaaaaaaaaaa!"

Mark and Jonathan literally ran into each other as they ran toward Death Hill.

"Jonathan! Did you get the extremely strong feeling that we should be helping our buddy, too?"

"We owe Jacob our lives for trying to help us live better. I'm going to fight with everything I have to help defend him!"

"I'm right behind you."

><><

The demon slammed a tombstone into Jacob and it shattered, knocking him to the ground. He looked around to see the iron fence and thought of the perfect way to get rid of the thorn in his side. Waving his hands he made two spears of the fence break off. Bringing them to him, fire flew from his fingertips, welding them together to make a sharp metal cross.

Taking it in his hand he hurled it like a javelin into a distant tree. Looking down at Jacob crawling around only half conscious he laughed out loud.

"Now to get rid of you, Jacob Cross!"

><><

Sarah was in her own personal heaven as the man was doing everything she thought she wanted. As he began to take off her shirt, Jacob stubbornly came back to her mind.

"No, not now," she whispered.

Suddenly the same image that had come to Mark and Jonathan entered her mind and brought her urges under control

"Ahhhh!"

"What's wrong?"

"I… I can't do this."

"Yes you can," he said pinning her wrists down.

"Get off me!"

"No."

She kneed him in the groin, head-butted his nose and threw him to the floor. He looked up and turned into a hissing creature before melting away.

"I have to help, Jacob."

)<)<

Meanwhile, one last pain shot through the demon, but he toughed it out and took Jacob by the throat. Lifting Jacob with one arm, he looked him right in the eyes. Jacob felt his hot breath as all he could do was struggle free. The demon laughed out loud, then became dead serious.

"Now you die, preacher!" He tossed Jacob forward toward the spear in the tree.

As Jacob flew through the air, he closed his eyes and waited for the agonizing pain through his back and the end of his life. Something changed from the dream though. He stopped in mid-air, but with no pain. He felt arms wrapped around him. The first thing he thought was angels. He opened his eyes to see the next best thing.

"That would have hurt buddy," Mark said smiling.

"Yes, Jacob. What say we cut this beast to pieces?" Jonathan asked.

"I knew you guys wouldn't let me down."

"Ha, Ha. Well, now I get to have three times the fun."

"Shut your ugly mouth and get ready to die!" Mark shouted.

The demon began to raise his hand and fire some form of destruction. Mark didn't wait for the surprise and cut in between the demon's middle and fourth fingers, slicing it's hand almost in half.

"Gahhhh!"

It stared at its hand momentarily before it healed back up. Once again Jacob noticed that it took a little longer than before.

"I grow tired of these annoyances. Now to finish you all!" He reached down and used his favorite defense, grabbing Mark by the throat.

"Hold on, Mark!" Jonathan yelled coming to his aid.

As he got there the demon made it a double choke hold and lifted them into the air. Jacob was still weak, but he brought out his crossbow and took aim. Before he could pull the trigger an object came flying past his head. It soared straight at the demon and hit dead center at where the nose should have been and blood spewed. It was Sarah's Bo. Jacob looked behind him to see her standing there grinning.

"Miss me, boys?"

"Very much," Jacob replied.

Mark grabbed her Bo and he and Jonathan jumped back to join them.

"Well, the gang is all here," Mark said. "Do we have a plan?"

"Of course we do," Sarah answered. "We beat the ugly creep within an inch of his life, then we take the inch away."

"Does that sound good to you, Jacob?" Jonathan asked laughing.

Their huddle was interrupted by strange sounds coming from the demon, still clutching his nose area.

"Gaaah! RRR! Grrr… Grahhhhhhhhhh!!!" It then let out a hellish howl that made the ground rumble.

"I think he's mad!" Mark said holding his ears.

The demon's voice began to deepen and echo. ***"I have had enough of the four of you!! Now you will see my true power!! Now, may all of the powers of hell and all of its inhabitants enter me!!"***

They watched on as the hooded demon became the hoodless demon. Ripping off his cloak, he was nothing more than a giant blade arm without any blades. Its eyes glowed redder than they ever had, blinding them and making red daylight. Its claws on its hands and feet grew another three inches, gleaming at the points. Black bat wings began to sprout from behind its shoulders, giving it a ten foot wingspan.

Finally right above it, a strange dimensional portal opened. A huge sickle with a glimmering blade floated down and he latched on to it.

"HA HA HA HA HA! DO YOU NOW SEE WHAT TRUE POWER REALLY IS?! NOW TREMBLE AT MY FEET AS I DEMONSTRATE THE TRUE POWERS OF HELL!!!"

Mark stared at him.

"Wow," he said. "That was some trick. You actually managed to get even uglier."

"DIE!"

The demon tried the light speed move again, but seeing it all before they jumped out of the way. One was in each direction of him. He didn't know which to go after first. He chose the one he hated most, Jacob. As he turned to him, Sarah waylaid him in the back of the head with a baseball swing. He went to one knee, turned and hissed at Sarah. This time when he turned he caught an arrow in the small of the back. He howled and turned back to Jacob. This time Sarah jabbed him in the back hard enough to break any man's spinal cord. He went to one knee again, growled, then raised both hands and sent them flying with hyped up electric bolts.

Now it was Mark and Jonathan's turn to go on the attack. The demon swung his weapon down at Mark, who blocked. As Mark held his attention, Jonathan cut through his chest and sliced down. He attempted to slash down at Jonathan, but as he block, Mark cut through his stomach and sliced up.

"Gaaaaah!"

The gaping hole healed, but not quickly. He took Jonathan and Mark, head-butted them together and tossed them to the side. Mark got back up instantly and gave him a bring it on motion. He sent the sickle hurling at Mark who ducked as it flew past him.

"You missed me, tall dark and gruesome!"

"Mark!" Jacob shouted. "Get down!" As he hit the ground the weapon came flying back like a boomerang.

"YOU WERE SAYING, FOOL?!"

Sarah charged in and began beating him in the ribs. They should have been dust and the demon should have been coughing up his lungs, but he was still healing too quickly. Even though they weren't killing him they were still causing him a massive amount of pain.

He slashed down at her and she blocked with her Bo. It was cut in half, but she didn't care. It was just one more club to beat the demon with. Twirling both pieces, she laid them across his jaw.

Blood poured from his mouth, but he still found enough strength to kick her away.

Jacob shot three arrows into him. One in the heart, one in the left eye, and the last in the throat. While it was stunned he slashed away at its chest and stomach.

All of the wounds healed themselves. This might have been a curse to the demon. All of the pains with no chance of dying. He managed to slice Jacob's leg. Not too deep, but not a scratch either. He picked Jacob up over his head and threw him into one of the empty graves. Jacob looked up to see the demon staring down at him smiling and kicking dirt over him. Mark cut its fun short by chopping his left wing off.

"Ahhhhg!" He turned to Mark and the wing began to slowly grow back.

"Let's see if your head grows back when I cut it off," Mark said.

He began slashing away at Mark, but he blocked each blow. Jonathan joined the fight, taking up more of his attention. Mark dodged a swing and the sickle's blade stuck itself into a tree. This left the demon a sitting duck. Mark began hacking away at the upper body while Jonathan took the lower part. Mark was stabbing at its neck and chest while Jonathan cut away at the legs and ankles. One big swing from Jonathan took it's left leg off.

"AAAAAARGH!" It pulled its blade loose and fell to the ground. The leg grew itself back.

"Grrrr! How do we get this thing to stop growing everything back?!" Mark asked.

"Just keep fighting," Jonathan said.

The demon reached up and slashed Jonathan's chest with it's massive claws and punched Mark into a tree. Before it could mount an attack, Sarah clubbed it in the back of the neck, knocking its weapon away. It was now infuriated as it turned and began choking her with both hands. While its attention was on her, a gravestone came busting over its head.

"I won't be needing this," Jacob said.

He took Jacob's head in both hands and tried to squeeze it until it collapsed. That plan ended as his own blade came through his chest with Sarah holding it. As he got madder he got stronger. Taking the blade in his hands he pulled it from Sarah and pulled it through his own body. He turned and slashed Sarah in the shoulder and rammed the butt of the weapon into Jacob's face.

Mark jumped on the demon's back and stabbed away at his heart before slitting its throat. The healing process was getting slower and slower, but still it slung him over its shoulders. As it turned around Jonathan kicked it with everything he had and it backed into the iron cross impaling itself.

"Graaaagh! Graaaah! AHHHHH!"

It now squirmed like a worm on a hook. It wrenched in pain and pulled itself loose. Even though it was Jonathan who kicked him, he looked straight at Jacob scowling.

"YOU!!"

It slung the blade at him as it had Mark earlier, but this gave Jacob an idea. After ducking the blade he ran straight to the demon. As he swung his sword it caught it in both hands. Listening for the deadly boomerang Jacob timed it perfectly and ducked again, letting the weapon bury itself in the demon's throat.

It froze and wobbled backward. Blood pooled on the ground. They though that this just might be the end. They were wrong. Eyes burning red once again it pulled the blade free and healed once again.

"NOW DIIIIIIIIIIIIIIIE!!!!"

It began floating in the air, its cries booming louder than ever. A strange fusion of fire and lightning flew from its fingertips and into them. They floated in the air and jerked while being tossed in different directions.

Jacob hit a tree full force. Sarah crashed into the steel fence. Jonathan hit his head on a tree root as he hit the ground. Mark went through his tombstone and rolled into his grave.

The demon breathed in fury before bursting into laughter. He turned and walked away, knowing with assurance that his enemies laid dead. A voice shattered that assurance.

"Where… do you… think you're going?" Mark asked crawling out of the grave with a stream of blood running down his forehead.

"We're not done yet," Jacob said limping toward it.

"You'll have to kill us to be rid of us," Jonathan said.

"Guess what? We're still breathing," Sarah said fighting forward.

The demon turned around and there was a look on his face they had never seen before. It was the look of pure terror.

"No… It can't be. What are you?!"

"We are servants of God," Jacob said proudly. "That means either we leave here dead, or you do."

"Lets finish this!" Mark said.

"No……..NOOOOOO!"

Jacob saw someone joining them from the corner of his eye. It was Andrew. He had forgotten all about him. He had at least twenty people with him.

"Lord Jacob! All of these people are here ready and willing to fight beside you."

Jacob looked at everyone. They included Johnny the bartender, Mark's informant Kain, the Doctor from the castle, the leader of the church village, and others he had never met.

Jacob looked at them, then at the demon. He noticed a small hole in the demon's throat.

Johnny stepped forward. "I'm closing my bar, Jacob. All I do is give people a place to come get loaded, then wreak havoc. I'm going to start a nice restaurant where families can come for a good time and good food."

The demon went to all fours and the hole in its throat opened and bled out.

Kain stepped up. "All I do is get dirt for people and help them get booze, hookers, and stolen stuff. I'm going to become an honest man."

Parts of the demon were becoming disfigured and sinking in where bones had been broken.

Ben the leader of the church village stepped up. "I try my best to be a good Christian, but I can always make an effort to be better."

The Doctor joined him. "I too have led a fairly good life, but I have forgotten many times to thank God for my gifts and once I thought I could heal people without him. I promise I will do my best to live for God and do his will."

The wing that Mark had cut, fell off.

A young couple stepped up. "We've been having sex since we were fourteen," the girl said.

"We've had many partners," the man said. "But we want to have a second virginity."

"We're waiting until we're married," the girl added.

The demon's leg fell off.

One by one, they all began to confess and vow to become better Christians. By the time they were done, the demon was a pitiful sight. Every wound was open and every broken bone showed. It wasn't much more than a pile of flesh. Jacob walked up to it.

"It's over demon," he said. "You fought God and you lost."

Pulling out an arrow, he armed his crossbow.

"Do me a favor. When you get back to hell, give your master a message for me. Tell him to read Revelations. In the end, he loses too."

At that he shot the creature in the head. It let out one last howl and went to dust. Jacob turned to everyone, then looked at Mark, Sarah, and Jonathan and smiled.

"It's over," he said.

As Jacob packed his supplies onto his horse, he winced from his injuries. He couldn't be more relieved that the demon was dead, but he was still somewhat saddened that the adventure was over. He was especially saddened to say good-bye to all of his friends. They were the best friends he had ever had. He hoped desperately that he would see them again someday.

As if being drawn by his thoughts, his friends walked up bandaged as he was and all smiles. Jacob returned the gesture and looked to the ground.

"I guess this is good-bye," he said sadly.

The three of them looked at each other confused.

"Good-bye?" Mark asked.

"Jacob Cross, do you think for one second that after all we've been through saving the world, that we're letting you get away from us?" Sarah asked.

"I… I thought that you would want to get back to your lives."

"Jacob, you are a part of our lives now," she replied.

"Yes, Jacob," Jonathan said. "Didn't God say that as long as we're together nothing can stop us? He didn't say it would end when the demon was dead."

"Yeah buddy!" Mark said putting him in a headlock. "In other words, you aren't getting rid of us until you're dead."

"I wouldn't have it any other way."

"Now where ever you go there is going to be three houses right beside you," Mark said. "Wait, should I make that two houses? Huh, Sarah?"

"Oh, quiet, Mark. I'm not ready to be a preacher's wife… not yet anyway."

"So?" Jonathan said. "Friends for life?"

He held out his hand and they all put theirs on his.

"Friends for life," Mark and Sarah said in unison.

They looked at Jacob.

"Friends for life," he said at last.

THE END

25658573R00127

Made in the USA
San Bernardino, CA
06 November 2015